Gab

Bear Stalker

A Gabriel Hawke Novel
Book 10

Paty Jager

Windtree Press
Hillsboro, OR

BEAR STALKER

Contact Information: info@windtreepress.com

Windtree Press
Hillsboro, Oregon
http://windtreepress.com

Cover Art by Covers by Karen

PUBLISHING HISTORY
Published in the United States of America

ISBN 978-1-957638-63-8

Author Comments

While this book is set in Wallowa County, Oregon, I have changed the town names to old forgotten towns that were in the county at one time. I also took the liberty of changing the towns up and populating the county with my own characters, none of which are in any way a representation of anyone who is or has ever lived in Wallowa County. Other than the towns, I have tried to use the real names of all the geographical locations.

Special Thanks to Nickie Norman for joining me on my research trip to Montana to get a lay of the land for this book.

Prologue

Her mind whirled and her heart thudded with excitement. She stared into Adrian's smiling face and knew her answer. "Yes, I'll marry you."

Adrian pulled her into his arms and kissed her. Her heart nearly burst thinking she had finally found the right man to take home to her mom and brother. They made love on the small island not far from the resort where their company was holding a week-long corporate retreat.

They lay in one another's arms enjoying the warmth of the sunshine, the birds calling to one another, and the rustling of leaves in the trees. "We need to get back before they realize we both snuck away and didn't attend the Opening Dinner." She grabbed her shorts and shirt and stood. "I'm going for a dip in the water. I'll be right back."

"Don't be gone long. I want to spend as much time as we can alone together. Even if it's just planning our future." Adrian's smile faded. "Or how to figure out what to do about the discrepancy I told you about the other night."

She stared down at the man she'd just promised to marry. "Don't worry about it. Once we get back, I'll look into things."

He stood. "I think they know I found out." He reached out and grasped her hand. "We have to be careful. I don't want anything to happen to you."

She smiled. "I know how to be discreet in my inquiries." She wrapped her arms around his neck and kissed him. When he started to pull her tighter, she eased out of the hold. "I'm going to clean up, and we'll get back before anyone realizes we're gone."

Adrian nodded and she hurried through the brush toward the west shore of the small island. She dropped her clothes on the sandy beach and walked into the cold water. Goose bumps popped out on her arms and her legs stung from the cold, but she continued until the water was up to her waist, and then she swam around before exiting the water and walking back to her clothes.

Her mind sifted through all the ways she and Adrian could get a vacation at the same time to visit her family and his to tell them about their engagement. She strolled back to Adrian, humming.

She stopped. Something was wrong. The world felt cold and off. As if someone had thrown dark netting over the small island. She listened beyond the silence.

A man's gruff voice asked, "Where is she?"

Creeping toward the spot where she'd left Adrian, she didn't hear a reply. Cautiously, she peered through the bushes. A man had her bra wrapped around Adrian's neck. She pushed the bushes apart to go to Adrian's aid.

The man with her bra fisted in his hands, spun her

way. The coldness in his eyes sent a chill through her.

He threw the bra still wrapped around Adrian's neck away from him. Her fiancé fell hard to the ground; his eyes open and his lips purplish-blue.

The man with cold eyes started in her direction.

Asking her lean legs to run, she sprinted back the way she'd come, running into the water and swimming for the far shore. She thanked the Creator for the mornings she spent swimming at the local YMCA. It had been her favorite sport growing up and she'd continued it as an adult to keep in shape.

As she pumped her legs and kept a fast steady pace with her arms, all she could think was to get as far from the man who'd killed Adrian and find help. Because it wasn't just the man, but the police, and ultimately the company she worked for that would be looking for her. They had to know she and Adrian had been dating and he told her about their illegal actions. That had to be why the man had strangled Adrian with her bra. She swallowed the wail that clawed its way up her throat. She wanted to mourn the man who had asked to marry her, but first, she had to stay alive.

Chapter One

The sound of his phone ringing woke Gabriel Hawke. He didn't have to worry about the sound waking his girlfriend, Dani Singer, she was up in the Wallowa Mountains running her lodge.

He glanced at his watch. Two a.m. He didn't recognize the number.

"Hello?"

"*Pyáp*, I need help." A woman's voice sounded out of breath.

Only one person ever called him *Pyáp*, older brother. "Marion?"

"They killed Adrian." She choked back a sob. "They're after me." She sucked in air. "Hurry!"

The line went silent.

"Marion?" He tried to call the number back but no one picked up. "Damn!"

Dog had appeared at the bed when Hawke answered the phone. He ruffled the hair on the animal's neck.

Two a.m. wasn't a good time to call his mother and ask questions about Marion. However, he'd heard the desperation in his sister's voice. It had been nearly two decades since he'd actually set eyes on her. Once she became a corporate lawyer, she'd disappeared back East and rarely came home. Her calling him *Pyáp,* the name she called him until she started school, told him she was asking as a sister for his help. She needed him to shelter her as he had when her father, his stepfather, drank and raged through the house throwing punches at anyone in his way. His protective instincts kicked in. He would find *Kskís Yáka,* Small Bear, and bring her home.

Sliding his legs over the edge of the bed, he sat up, rubbed a hand over his face, and tried to remember where he'd put that box of personal papers and things when he and Dani moved into this house six months ago.

Hawke was pretty sure that somewhere there was a business card Marion had sent to him when she'd landed her job. If he couldn't find that, he'd call their mother. Hopefully, he wouldn't have to wake her.

Hawke walked through the house in his boxer shorts. It was early June. The nights still held a nip in the air, but the last few years Wallowa County, Oregon had started heating up by the end of June and staying hotter than usual through July.

He opened the door to the bedroom they'd made into an office and walked over to the closet. Pulling the doors open, he stared at Dani's side of the closet. All the boxes were neatly labeled. His side of the closet…he wasn't sure what was in any of the boxes.

Dog whined.

"Yeah, you and me both. I'll let you out and make a pot of coffee. This could take a while." Even as he walked to the back door and let Dog out, his head told him there wasn't time to mess around digging through boxes. He needed to call his mom and find out all she knew about Marion. Their mom would forgive him when he brought Marion home.

The coffeemaker was gurgling and emitting the strong aroma of the coffee he and Dani preferred as he dialed his mom's phone number.

"H-hello?" Mimi Shumack answered in a sleepy voice.

"I'm sorry to wake you, Mom, but I think Marion is in trouble. I need to know everything you know." He walked over to pour a cup of coffee. The notepad and pen by the fridge caught his attention. He tossed it onto the table before pouring the coffee.

"Marion? What kind of trouble?" Mom's voice warbled. She wasn't completely awake.

"I don't know. She said something about Adrian. Do you know who Adrian is?" Hawke settled at the table, giving his mom time to wake up and think.

"I believe it is a man she's been seeing for a while. Why?" He heard her shuffling down the hallway. Most likely to make herself a cup of coffee.

"I need to know who she works for and her phone number and address."

"I have her business card on the side of the fridge. Hold on." There was a pause and Mom said, "Pannell Financial Services in Dallas, Texas." She read off the phone number and address.

He heard the flipping of pages and she read off Marion's address and phone number. "Don't you have your sister's phone number?" Mom asked in an accusing tone.

"I had one some years ago but she must have gotten a new phone number because the last time I tried calling, it said the number had been disconnected."

"That would have been five years ago. Why didn't you ask me for her new number?"

Hawke shrugged. His sister never called him. Not even for his birthday. He'd stopped trying to call her on hers after getting the disconnected notification. He figured she didn't want him to know her number.

"Thank you. I'm sorry I had to wake you. I'll try this number and see if I can find out where she is and what has happened."

"When you learn something let me know," Mom insisted.

"I will. Try to go back to sleep." Hawke ended the call and glanced at the clock. Dallas was two hours ahead of the Pacific Standard Time in Oregon. It was 4:30 AM in Dallas. A financial service would have people working around the clock, wouldn't they?

He dialed the number his mom had read off the business card. Two rings and a woman answered. "Pannell Financial Services. How may I direct your call?"

"I'd like to find out if Marion Shumack is in the office," Hawke said.

"She works eight to five, Monday through Friday," the woman replied.

"And she will be in at eight, then?"

The woman clicked some keys. "No, she and a group from the offices are at a corporate retreat."

"Can you tell me where the retreat is located?" Hawke wasn't sure what kind of trouble she was in but he didn't want to use his State Trooper badge to discover information until he knew what he was up against.

"We don't divulge that information."

"I hate to ask you to go against any kind of protocol but I'm her brother and our mother is deathly ill. Mom asked me to contact Marion. She's not answering her cell phone. That's why I called her work number." His mom wouldn't like knowing he'd said she was in poor health. But to help her daughter, he was pretty sure Mimi Shumack would do anything, short of killing someone, to find the truth.

"Oh, I'm sorry to hear that. They do make the members at the retreat turn off their cell phones. I'll call the person in charge of the retreat and have them give the message to your sister."

"I don't think it would be a good idea for someone else to tell Marion that our mom isn't doing well. She and my mom are very close. Could you just tell me where she's at and I can go through the proper channels to contact her there?" Hawke needed to know where the retreat was. He wanted to be headed in that direction as soon as he'd contacted his ex-landlords, Herb and Darlene Trembley, to take care of his horses while he and Dog searched for Marion.

The woman sighed. "I'm not supposed to give out the information…"

"This is a matter of a dying woman's desire to see her daughter one last time. My mom has been asking for Marion. I can't tell her Marion can't be contacted." He put as much whining as he could stomach into his statement.

"You didn't hear this from me," the woman whispered. "They are staying at the Island Resort on Salmon Lake in Montana." She ended the call.

Hawke smiled at the small victory. He was one step closer to finding his sister.

Chapter Two

Driving along the interstate with Dog in the passenger seat, Hawke went over the phone calls he'd made. First, his ex-landlords to watch his animals, then his boss, Sergeant Spruel, of the Oregon State Police, and last his mom.

Herb and Darlene said they would take care of things while he looked for his sister. Spruel had offered to gather information on the corporation Marion worked for, the person Adrian she'd mentioned, and the Island Resort on Salmon Lake. Also, he offered to find out about the phone number Marion had called from. Hawke was grateful nearly every day for the people in his life that believed in him.

Mom had been ready to jump in her car and join him. He'd told her to stay home by her phone in case Marion tried to call her. He also gave her Sergeant Spruel's phone number in case she couldn't get a hold of him. He'd check in with his boss every day.

They were halfway to Salmon Lake, nearing Lolo Pass when his phone rang.

"Hawke," he answered without looking at who was

calling.

"It's Dani. Where are you and Dog?" She wasn't upset but sounded concerned.

"Are you at the house?"

"Yeah, I flew in to pick up clients tomorrow morning and thought I'd surprise you." She chuckled. "The surprise was on me."

"Marion called in the middle of the night."

"Marion? Your sister? I thought you and she—"

"She's in trouble. She didn't have time to tell me more than she was in trouble, someone was killed, and she needs help. I'm headed to Salmon Lake, Montana. That's where she is on a corporate retreat."

"Damn! If I'd known this sooner, I could have flown you there."

"It's okay. I need a vehicle. I'm going to lose you, I'm about to head over Lolo Pass. Can you call mom and talk to her this evening? I had to call her to get information." Guilt had been gnawing at his gut over having to drag their mom into this. He wouldn't have had to if he'd kept in contact with his sister. But damn, she should be the one who kept in contact with family. She was the one who ran away as soon as she could.

"I'll call her. Be careful."

The bars for his phone service disappeared.

Marion rubbed her hands up and down her arms. She'd taken a long-sleeved shirt, pants, and a pair of athletic shoes from the house she'd broken into to call Gabriel. She'd pulled them on over her shorts and tank top since her underwear were back on the island leaving evidence that she had been with Adrian when... Her chest burned from the sobs she'd held in all night as she first swam, then ran barefoot over the ridge and down the other side. She'd been thankful to focus on remembering Gabriel's phone number as she searched for an empty house with a phone. She'd passed up nearly a dozen that either had people in them or she didn't see any electricity or phone lines. Knowing the man who had killed Adrian would be looking for her, she hadn't wanted anyone to see her. She couldn't have lived with herself if someone innocent was killed because they had helped her.

She hadn't seen phone lines at the cabin she'd broken into but had been lucky to find a working landline. And even luckier Gabriel had answered the call and knew it was her. Before she could calm herself and fill Gabriel in, she'd had to flee. Lights had illuminated the house and she didn't want to be caught. She'd run out the backdoor and through the trees until she couldn't breathe. Her stomach rumbled. She wished she'd thought to fill the pockets of the clothing with food.

She'd been a child the last time she'd gone hungry for more than an hour. And almost as long since she'd spent time in a forest. If she weren't running for her life, she could enjoy the sights, sounds, and smells. But fear kept her chest tight and stalled her brain from thinking of anything other than survival.

Marion sat on a downed log to rest. The minute her muscles relaxed, they began to burn. And her heart ached, as her last sight of Adrian flashed through her mind.

She had to find Gabriel. They would make sure Drew Pannell and the man with the cold eyes went to jail for Adrian's murder.

Hawke's stomach was growling as he drove up 83N

and spotted law enforcement vehicles clogging the small parking lot alongside the ferry shuttle building on the lake shore. He spotted a dirt road leading up the ridge on the opposite side of the highway from the lake. He drove up the road even though it had a sign: PRIVATE KEEP OUT. He parked, rolled down the window, and used his binoculars to watch the small motorboats hauling law enforcement personnel to the island with the resort and to a smaller island beyond the resort island.

He spotted State and County police. Someone in a fancy jogging outfit stood on the dock at the resort, greeting the law enforcement who arrived. Hawke wondered if it was the manager of the resort or someone from Pannell Financial.

His phone rang. A glance at the name and he slid his finger across the screen.

"What have you found out? This resort is crawling with law enforcement," he said, by way of answering the phone.

"Then you made it to Salmon Lake," Spruel said.

"Yeah. Any chance I can flash my badge and get in there?" he asked.

"Word is they found Adrian Ulrick strangled with a bra. He was naked. They believe it was an erotic role play that went wrong." Spruel sounded embarrassed. He'd talked about such matters before in cases and never seemed to bat an eye.

"They think Marion did it, don't they?" That would be the only explanation for his boss being embarrassed to say it.

"Yeah."

"Well, she didn't. She said 'they killed Adrian.'" Hawke continued to watch the happenings. "I think I'll rent a boat and make my way out to the small island. Do you have any contacts in this area I could work with to learn what they are finding?"

"I'll see if an old friend is willing to help you. And that number your sister called from? It's from a landline." He rattled off the address. "From what I can see on Google Earth, it's a house south of Placid Lake and west of Salmon Lake."

"Thanks. I'll head there before I rent a boat. I'll let you know what I find out." Hawke ended the call, studying the goings on. He spotted a boat carrying a gurney with a body bag. That would be the victim. The man his mom said Marion was involved with.

Hawke put the address Spruel gave him into his phone's GPS and backed down the dirt road onto the highway. He followed the directions to the end of Salmon Lake, turned left, and followed the gravel road past vacation homes along the end of the lake.

He spotted some trees that had been painted with scary faces and continued to a sign that said Placid Lake. He made a left following a dirt road around the end of the lake and along the south side weaving through trees until he came to a small cabin. This must have been the end of the line for power and phone lines.

Two large dogs ran out of the trees beyond the cabin, barking and baring their teeth.

A man stepped out onto the porch with his arms crossed. The dogs ran over and sat down on either side of the man.

Staring at the dogs and man with a face that said, 'Get off my land,' Hawke wondered how Marion had managed to get past the dogs and use the phone.

Dog's hair rose along his spine.

"Put that down. You aren't getting out and they

19

aren't getting in." Hawke ran his hand down his friend's back, settling the hair in place.

Hawke eased his door open and stepped out.

The dogs and man remained on the porch. "This is private property. Unless you're the police, you need to get back in your truck and leave," the man said.

It appeared the man was either looking for the police or had a good rapport with them. If the man had called the police, Hawke hoped it had to do with Marion. "I'm Hawke with the State Police." He pulled his badge out from under his shirt with the chain around his neck but didn't get close enough for the man to see he wasn't a Montana trooper.

The man scowled. "Since when do Staters walk around out of uniform?"

"On a day when I was called away from R & R to call on you." He flipped open a notepad he'd pulled along with a pen from his breast pocket. "Sorry, I didn't hear your name when they called it in. Barely caught the address."

"Will Rule. What did they tell you about the call?" The man was still skeptical.

Hawke figured someone who lived clear out here with two bristly dogs didn't want the police poking around. "You had a break-in?" He made that up, hoping that was how Marion had used the phone. If he'd said, 'you found a woman,' that might be more than the man knew.

"Yeah, I came home last night and found my back door open, a pair of fishing pants, shirt, and shoes missing." Rule looked down at the dogs. "Me and the boys went to Seeley Lake for dinner."

"What time did you leave and what time did you get

back?" Hawke scribbled everything the man said in the notebook.

"And you didn't see anyone when you returned?" Hawke asked.

"Nope. Just the back door standing open and the clothes missing." The man ran a hand over the back of his neck. "You don't think this has anything to do with the woman that strangled her boyfriend and took off, do you?"

"Over at Salmon Lake?" Hawke asked, hoping the man would say more since he knew very little about the event.

"Yeah. I heard the couple didn't want anyone to know where they were going or what they were doing." He sneered. "I bet one of them was married. Anyway, they took separate paddleboards and met up at the small island northwest of Sourdough Island. I guess the sex got rough and she strangled him with her undergarments." The man's eyes were nearly bulging out of his head as he told the story.

"Where did you hear all of this?" Hawke asked.

"Bud Abbot. He called to tell me. He lives on Christmas Stocking Island and has been watching everything through his telescope, and his daughter works at the resort on Sourdough Island. She called and told him what she'd heard. That corporate group that's staying there is going about things as if one of their own hadn't been killed by another one." Rule nodded as if he expected that kind of behavior from the likes of the people who stayed at the resort.

"And you think the break-in has something to do with that?" Hawke asked, while his head was thinking, the man had surely messed up any prints Marion might have left on his phone if he spent time gossiping with his neighbors.

"I can't think of any other reason someone would take a set of clothes and shoes. She must have been trying to hide and needed dry clothes." The man uncrossed his arms and touched one finger to his temple. "It makes sense if they were playing around and she pulled too tight. She'd have killed him and then didn't know what to do and took off. I bet she swam to this side of Salmon Lake and came all the way over that ridge. That would have been one hell of a climb in no clothes. I bet she's got scratches all over her." Rule stared over Hawke's shoulder.

"If you think of something or find anything else missing," Hawke wrote his cell phone on a piece of paper, "give me a call."

As he walked back to his vehicle, Hawke was torn between, looking for Marion's trail and getting a look at the scene of the crime. He decided finding Marion was more important than seeing the island. Spruel would do his best to get him as much information as he could.

Hawke drove down the road a mile, parked his pickup off to the side of the road, and pulled out his backpack. "Come on, Dog. We need to find Marion."

Dog leaped out and Hawke locked the doors. He walked through the woods, keeping in mind to stay far enough away from the cabin that Rule's dogs wouldn't detect them. Keeping his gaze on the ground and underbrush, he scanned back and forth as he walked. At some point, he should intersect with Marion's trail as she headed west. At least, he figured she was headed west. It would make sense for her to head toward home and away from anyone who might know her.

Chapter Three

Tired, hungry, and limping from blisters caused by the too-large shoes, Marion sat down on a rock alongside a lake. She took off the shoes and eased her feet into the cold water. She'd slowed her pace to not get too far away from where Gabriel would start looking—the cabin where she'd called from. But her twisting hungry stomach wanted her to keep moving. To find nourishment. She'd studied a map of Montana before she'd left on the retreat. She liked to know where she was at all times. There was a road that came down the west side of Flathead Lake. On that highway was the Flathead Reservation. She'd left the Umatilla Reservation over twenty years ago to better herself and forget where she'd grown up. Now her best chance of hiding from the people hoping to pin Adrian's murder on her and give Hawke a chance to find her was to go to the reservation. She knew from experience that Indigenous people were leery of Feds and white people who asked too many questions.

A six-inch fish swam to within three feet of her toes. Her stomach did a happy dance as she reached inside the large pocket on the leg of the cargo pants she wore. She'd discovered a roll of fishing line and a small plastic box of hooks, lures, and sinkers in the side Velcro pocket of the pants when she'd wanted to find out what kept banging against her leg.

Marion fitted the end of the line with a small fly hook and sinker just like Gabriel had taught her. She hoped she could catch a fish by tossing the nylon cord as far out as she could and skipping it along the bottom of the lake. Standing with her feet still in the cold water, she unraveled a length of the cord and twirled about three feet of the line like a lasso. When the weight on the end pulled harder, she released the nylon line, allowing the weight of the sinker to carry the fly out about twenty feet into the water.

A smile tipped her lips for the first time since she'd found the man strangling Adrian. That thought wiped the smile away. She'd been thinking about how Gabriel had taken her fishing when she was small. He'd been patient with her queasiness at putting a worm on a hook and had praised her when she'd caught a fish.

Over the years, she'd realized he had been her protector when she hadn't known she'd needed protecting. It wasn't until Gabriel joined the Marines that she discovered he had been shielding her from the monster that was her own flesh and blood. Gabriel had taught her to leave the house and hide when her father came home weaving all over the road. She'd thought it was a game, until one night a month after Gabriel left. She'd been eight. Hawke was ten years older than her.

Her father came home, his old beat-up car weaving back and forth on their long driveway. She'd giggled and said something to her mom about how funny Daddy drove. Her mother had told her to go to her room and lock the door. "Don't come out until I tell you."

Marion had heard the fear and the command in her mom's voice. She'd dragged her feet and just got the door to her room closed when her father's voice blared through the small old farmhouse.

"Why hasn't that boy of yours sent us any money?" her father had shouted.

"He's only been gone a month. He probably hasn't been paid," her mom said.

But Marion had seen a letter from her brother just the day before. Mom had read it, put something from the letter into her purse, and threw the letter away. Why was her mom lying to her father?

He must have known she was lying. "You lying bitch!" he'd screamed and slapped Mom so hard she'd hit the wall five feet behind her.

Marion had screamed. Her father turned his gaze on her and wobbled over to the bedroom door. She tried to slam the door and lock it, but he was surprisingly quick.

"Do you know if your brother sent money?" He raised a hand. "Don't lie to me. You saw what I did to your mom for lying."

"I-I don't know. I never saw any money." She cowered in a corner of her room, seeing her true father for the first time. Now she knew why she'd seen bruises on her mom and Gabriel after her father fell asleep and Gabriel would bring her back to the house.

After that night, she always ran when she saw her father coming and then would creep back into the house after he'd left or passed out and help her mom doctor her injuries. Tears trickled down her face. That was why she'd picked a school as far from the rez as she could get and only applied for jobs that were half a continent away. As an adult and having pieced together her life before her father died in a car crash, she couldn't face her mom. The woman who gave her birth and then took all the blows her father dealt to keep her daughter safe. While that same daughter hid like a coward.

The line tugged and she pulled, hooking a fish. Her stomach growled as if it realized there would be food coming soon.

Hawke and Dog had found Marion's trail. The footprints indicated the shoes were too big. They made scuff marks from falling off the heels and her weight was distributed differently with each step. He also discovered she was marking the way.

A grin spread across his face. He may have only spent eight years with Marion but what he'd taught her had stuck. She was breaking the low limbs at the height of several wild animals, clearly pointing in the direction she was moving. Hawke added three or four more broken limbs when he'd find her markings. He didn't want someone else to pick up her trail from what she had left for him. He also walked on her prints, covering them up.

When he found a spot where she'd stopped and peed, he had Dog sniff and they were soon covering the ground faster as the animal followed her scent.

Hawke had to admit that Marion had to be in good shape to have swum from the island to the west side of the lake, hiked over the ridge, and now continued at a good pace. But then she had their mother's genes, ones that had endured and continued to thrive. Their mother had given them the will to survive.

Hawke continued until after dark. Even with a flashlight, he was having trouble finding all of the trail, and Dog was getting tired. Hawke rolled out his bedroll and leaned against a tree, sitting on the canvas and eating an energy bar. He poured a pile of dog food on the oilcloth encasing his sleeping bag and wondered how Marion would survive the cold night with only the clothes on her back.

The fire Marion made to cook the fish was all she had to keep her warm through the night. She'd piled dried limbs next to the fire and every time she woke up feeling cold, she'd throw wood on the fire, warm up, and drop back into a fitful sleep.

Sunlight lit her eyelids as she wiggled her cold toes and fingers, slowly moving blood to all of her extremities. Her muscles were tight and ached. She'd worked them hard since Adrian's murder and sleeping on the cold ground, curled in a ball, hadn't helped the tightness and soreness.

What she wouldn't give for a cup of strong black coffee with a dollop of cream. Her stomach growled. She'd only caught the one fish and cooked it after dark. Studying the gray clouds gathering overhead she wondered if she should look for shelter or catch more fish to cook later.

Shelter wouldn't be necessary if she fell over from starvation. Though clearly, as long as she stayed hydrated, her body would continue to work with little food. She had read something about a person could survive for eight to ten days as long as they had water. If they didn't have water, they would only survive three days.

Staring at the stream she'd followed away from the lake, she didn't have to worry about not having enough water to drink. However, she did worry about the safety of drinking the stream water. It was early in June, she hoped the fresh snow melt water held less bad bacteria than later in the summer.

Feeling as if she were out of sight of anyone coming along, Marion decided to make a shelter and wait for Gabriel to come to her. He should find her in the next few days and she wouldn't die in that length of time.

Using the job of finding fallen branches to build a lean-to, she shoved the thoughts of Adrian out of her mind and focused on staying alive. That had been his last words to her. He wanted to keep her safe. He couldn't, but she could by staying alive and helping Gabriel catch the person who killed the man she'd loved.

Hawke boiled water for coffee and ate a protein bar while Dog ate dog food. They had been up with the sun and started out, only stopping now because Dog had found where it looked like Marion had caught a fish. He wondered what she had used. Had she a knife with her, or used a sharp stone to put a point on a stick and stab a fish? He only knew she had caught one because her tracks led to the water at the edge of a lake and there were fish scales on a rock as if she had tried to use the rock as a knife.

He couldn't stop the smile. His little sister had run away from her heritage and here she was foraging in the forest like their ancestors. There had to be a deep meaning to this, but he wasn't sure what it could be.

"She must be close. Those scales are still shimmering. They haven't dried out much." Hawke tossed the last of his coffee and stored the tin cup in his backpack.

The sound of a helicopter flying low caught his attention. No one would think twice of a man hiking in the wilderness, but he made sure he could see the aircraft. Standing at the edge of the lake, he waited for the copter to fly by and studied the logo. Scrutinizing the cockpit, he spotted two people inside. The pilot and another man. They were scanning the terrain.

Knowing it wasn't law enforcement, Hawke wondered if they could be the people behind the victim's murder, looking for the eye-witness.

"Come. We need to find Small Bear." He wasn't going to speak his sister's name out loud just in case there were also people on the ground looking for her.

He mucked about in the mud at the edge of the lake, covering her tracks, before following her prints along the stream that fed the lake. A hundred yards upstream, he found where she'd built a small fire and eaten the fish. A few of the bones lay at the edge of the cold charred pine limbs in the circle of stones.

Dog had his nose to the ground, he ran into the trees a bit, then to the side, and back into the trees.

Hawke studied the ground and discovered Marion had been walking in all different directions. From the drag marks, she was gathering long limbs. What was she doing? He followed each set of footprints and drag marks until he discovered where she had piled several limbs.

That's when he also discovered hoof prints. From the marks he could discern that she was now on a horse with someone.

Chapter Four

Marion was startled by the sound of something large cracking the limbs on the brush and trees. She ducked behind a tree, expecting to see an elk walk by. To her surprise, it was a woman on a horse. And even though Marion tried to stay hidden, it was as if the woman sensed her.

"You, behind the tree. Come out," the woman said.

Marion stepped out from behind the tree and stared up into the face of a woman she guessed to be in her sixties. Definitely older than Gabriel but not as old as their mother. The woman had on a denim jacket, jeans, and scarred cowboy boots. A bright-colored scarf was tied around her neck.

"Are you lost?" the woman asked, peering down at her from the back of a long-legged paint horse.

"Yes and no." Marion was trying to decide if she could trust this woman.

The woman nodded. "Man trouble?"

"You could say something like that." Marion took another step toward the horse and rider.

The woman studied her. "Those aren't your clothes."

"They aren't. I had to borrow them." She continued to hold the woman's gaze.

"I have a place between here and Arlee. You're welcome to ride there with me and call someone." The woman pulled her foot out of the stirrup and put a hand down to help Marion up.

"Thank you. I appreciate this." Marion grabbed the woman's hand, put her foot in the stirrup, and hoped she could contact Gabriel.

Once she was situated behind the woman's saddle, the horse set out deeper into the forest.

"Why are you going where it's harder to navigate?" Marion asked.

"Because there's a copter out there. I don't like being watched from the air."

"How do you know?" Marion wondered if she'd just put herself in the hands of someone unstable.

"Listen." She stopped the horse.

It felt as if everything went quiet and then she heard the thump of helicopter blades beating the air. There was someone in the air flying around. Could it be someone looking for her?

Hawke stared at the hoofprints. Did he continue following the horse or go back and get his vehicle and see what was to the west of here?

He didn't have cell service and couldn't be contacted by Spruel to learn more about the victim. Hoping the person who picked Marion up wasn't deranged or the killer, Hawke and Dog turned around. With the helicopter flying around, he'd lead them right to Marion if he could walk as fast as a horse. But he couldn't and the animal would outdistance him quickly, even with two riders.

He and Dog hiked straight back to his pickup, getting there at dark. He wasn't surprised to find a note from Rule asking him to park elsewhere. At least the man hadn't called the cops. If he had, they'd have tagged his vehicle and been waiting for him since he was related to their missing suspect.

Hawke decided to drive to the ferry landing for the resort and see what info he could pick up. It took thirty minutes to drive around Salmon Lake and end up at the ferry dock. There was one state patrol car in the parking lot. The lot wasn't very big. He tucked his vehicle as far off to the side, practically in some bushes, to keep it out of the way and to make it harder to see. If he couldn't rent a boat to get to the island, he'd find another way.

He walked toward the dark building. The door was locked and the sign said no one would be around until the next group was to arrive. Hawke wandered to the dock. There was one canoe, sitting upside down to the left of the dock. He found out why it hadn't been stored, it had a crack in the front where someone must have hit or dropped it on a rock. These newer composite canoes could take a pretty good beating. From the look of the crack, he wouldn't sink before he made it to the smaller island, where he could dump out any water he took on, and then he could go to the island with the resort on it to walk around and talk to people.

He went back to his vehicle, let Dog out, and grabbed his small pack and foldable shovel to use as an oar. Back at the dock, he shoved the canoe into the water.

"Get in," he said to Dog, who leaped in and took a seat at the front.

Hawke stepped in, pushed off from the dock, and started paddling with the shovel. He maneuvered the vessel to the right to go around the resort where he was less likely to be seen by anyone in the log and rock structure.

Paddling this route took him between Sourdough Island, as Rule had called the island with the resort, and a smaller island with one building on it. Using the moonlight, he headed toward the next island about 300 yards from Sourdough Island. This island was where Marion and the victim were when the murder occurred. Hawke hoped he could find a clue as to what really happened.

He knew from what his mom had said that the victim was Marion's boyfriend. But he couldn't believe the two of them, he'd guess the man would be in his forties as well, would have been out here using unorthodox methods of having sex. It didn't fit with the girl he knew growing up or the woman who spoke only of her career when they did have brief conversations.

He paddled around the south end of the small island and noticed a light glowing in the center of the brush and trees. It appeared there was someone watching over the crime scene. He ran the front of the canoe aground on the south end of the island. Dog leaped out, and Hawke balanced his way to the front and stepped out. He pulled the vessel all the way up on land and tipped it over. There was minimal water that had seeped in but it was better to be safe than sorry.

Dog had his nose on the ground.

"What do you smell? Is it Small Bear?" Hawke asked quietly. He knew it was only his paranoia that had him talking about Marion as Small Bear. However, he didn't know if the light came from a police officer or the killer waiting to see if Marion returned.

Dog took off through the brush before Hawke could call him back. Hawke followed at a more leisurely pace. He had most of the night to— He stopped and listened. A male voice was talking to Dog.

Continuing slow and quiet he caught the conversation. "What are you doing out here? You couldn't have swam, you're dry."

Dog had a low soft growl rumbling.

Hawke peered out from behind a bush and spotted a Montana State Trooper sitting on a folding stool next to crime scene tape. He relaxed knowing the trooper was just doing his job, guarding a crime scene.

"I see you found my dog," Hawke said, stepping out from behind the bush. "I ran my canoe to ground, and he took off like his tail was on fire."

"You're not supposed to be on this island." The trooper stood. He was equal to Hawke in size but a good twenty-five years younger.

"Sorry. I arrived this evening at the park and didn't want to wait until tomorrow to get a good paddle in. I figured this island looked uninhabited and would be a good place to get out and stretch my legs before I head back to camp." Hawke didn't move any closer even though he was curious. Best to let this trooper think he didn't give a rip about whatever had happened here.

Dog had walked over to Hawke and now sat at his feet.

"You need to go back to your canoe and back to

camp. We had a homicide here this morning and I'm to keep people away." The trooper continued to stand with his hands on his duty belt.

"Wow! I came to Montana to get away from the crazies." Hawke turned to leave and spun back around and asked, "Am I safe camping at the Salmon Lake Campground?"

"The person of interest is at large, but we don't think she is in the area."

"She?" Hawke feigned surprise.

The trooper looked around, pulled up on his belt, and said, "They say it was a lover's quarrel, so I think you're safe."

"A woman killed her lover?" Hawke shook his head. "That's why I just live with my dog. It's safer that way."

The trooper laughed. "My wife can get pretty mad at me sometimes, but the making up is fun."

Hawke stared up at the stars and smiled. "Yes, there is that." He pointed up at the sky. "At least you have these beautiful stars to keep you company all night."

"It is peaceful out here. I can see why the two lovers came here to be alone. Though they think the man was lured out here because he wasn't the outdoors type." The trooper remained standing, but he shifted from foot to foot as if he wanted to sit or needed to take a pee.

"Well, good night." Hawke headed back the way he'd come, then turned to the right, keeping Dog at heel, and made his way down to the shore of the island. He glanced at the silhouette of the tall pine tree. The crime scene had been at the base of that tree. When he'd stared up at the stars, Hawke had been memorizing the tree tops.

"Quiet," he whispered to Dog and they began a

cautious approach to the crime scene area. He stopped when he spotted the yellow and black tape. Beyond the circle of plastic sat the trooper, his back to what he was guarding.

Hawke wished he'd had a chance to talk to Marion and discover what had happened. As he crouched, the little bits of information he did know flashed through his mind. The victim was strangled with Marion's bra. She must not have had it on. And she must not have been with the victim when the killer approached or she would be dead as well. She'd stolen clothing from Rule's house. The two lovers would have approached the island from different directions. Leaving their paddleboards in different spots. Had Marion used her paddleboard to leave the island?

That scenario didn't work if she was trying to get away unseen. She must have swam. Was she naked or did she have on her outer clothing?

Which direction did the man looking for them come from? Since he'd used Marion's bra as the murder weapon, he had improvised. Had he come out here to kill them or to learn what they knew? But what did they know?

He eased back away. They wouldn't find any answers here with the crime scene being guarded. He'd have to wait and see what Spruel could get out of the investigating law enforcement.

Quietly, he and Dog returned to the canoe and paddled toward the glow of lights illuminating the side of the resort that faced the lake. He spotted a sandy shore on the northwest side of the island a little out of sight of the resort and ran the canoe aground.

"Stay," he told Dog and stepped out onto the island.

Hawke studied the building. On this side there were balconies off of rooms, many of which had the curtains drawn. He continued along this side and turned the corner. Couples and small groups sat at picnic tables on the long deck in front of the bank of glowing windows. He wondered if anyone had noticed his arrival by canoe.

Walking along until he found stairs up to the deck, he took those and stopped in front of a table of four people.

"Can you tell me who is in charge?" he asked.

One man looked him up and down. "You're not with Pannell, who are you?"

"I'm looking for my sister. I was told she was here on a corporate retreat." Hawke decided to see what these Pannell employees thought of Marion.

"No one is to have contact with family or friends while they are here," a woman said.

"Our mother is ill and I need to speak with my sister," Hawke glanced around. They'd caught the attention of the next table.

"Who is your sister?" the woman asked.

"Marion Shumack."

Some faces reddened, others glanced down at the table.

The woman stood. "You'll want to talk to Mr. Pannell." She led the way into the building.

Hawke stopped her just inside the door. "Do you know my sister?"

The woman nodded. "I'm surprised you haven't heard. She-she killed Adrian, her boyfriend, two nights ago. She's not here. The police are looking for her."

He studied the woman. "Were you a friend of my sister's?"

The woman shook her head. "Not really. She didn't socialize much. Not like the other lawyers." The woman glanced around. "Everyone knew she and Adrian were friendly, but I can't see her, well them, having kinky sex."

"I know Marion and Adrian were seeing one another. Was he a lawyer, too?" Hawke decided to see how much he could get out of this woman. She seemed to want to talk.

"No. Adrian was in accounting. But he and Marion spent lots of hours together working on strategies for corporate takeovers." She continued walking toward the registration desk.

Hawke put a hand on her arm, stopping her. "I don't want to talk to Pannell. I want to learn all I can about Marion and Adrian." Hawke pulled on the chain around his neck, revealing his badge from under his shirt.

The woman stared at it. "Oregon State Police? You're not here about your ill mother, are you?"

"No. Marion called me and asked for my help." He studied the woman. "What's your name?"

"Adele Barnes. Why?"

"What is your job with this company?" Hawke asked.

"I'm the executive secretary to Mr. Pannell."

Did he dare see if she'd help him collect information about Marion and Adrian?

She watched him studying her. "You are trying to decide if you can trust me to tell you the truth, aren't you?"

He nodded. "Is there somewhere we can go that no one will hear us talking?" Hawke had noticed the two tables out front watching their discussion.

"Follow me." She headed up the stairway to the right of the registration desk. They turned and entered what appeared to be a small conference room.

Ms. Barnes sat in one of the chairs.

Hawke closed the door and sat at a spot across from her. He didn't want to give away anything other than Marion called him. There was the possibility this woman was loyal to the head of the company, in which case, Hawke didn't want her to know too much.

"What exactly did my sister do for this company?" Hawke asked.

The woman studied him. "She never told you?"

He shook his head. "She never talked about her work other than who she worked for and that she worked on contracts."

Ms. Barnes leaned back in her chair. "Marion is one of our best contract lawyers. She finds all the loopholes in incoming contracts and makes sure the contracts we send out are in the favor of Pannell Financial."

"How was it that she and Adrian came to work together?" he asked, also leaning back in his chair and wondering how much this woman knew about his sister.

"Mr. Pannell had Adrian looking at the books of a potential client and wanted Marion to talk to Adrian about some of the outside interests of the company to see if they were something that could be bound to the contract."

Hawke only partially understood what the woman said, but refused to ask for more clarification.

"It was after that several of us noticed the two talking in out-of-the-way hallways and they stopped coming to company parties. We pretty much all knew they were a couple without them telling anyone." She shrugged.

"Is there anyone here who was close with either my sister or Adrian?" Hawke wanted to find someone who would talk to him about their relationship.

"One of the other accountants, Caleb, is here. I think he and Adrian hung out together outside of work." She picked up the phone sitting on the conference table and pushed a button. "Hello, this is Ms. Barnes. Could you have someone find Caleb DeLan and ask him to come to the conference room at the top of the stairs?" She listened for thirty seconds and replaced the phone. "He should be here soon."

Hawke studied the woman. "Are you helping me because you like Marion or so you can report to your boss?"

She sighed. "If I am asked if I talked to you, I will tell him what has been said. Will I go running to him to tell him about our talk? No. One thing I've learned being Mr. Pannell's executive secretary, while my boss pretends he doesn't want to know anything about his employees' personal lives, he knows everything. Anything I or Caleb tell you is probably something Mr. Pannell already knows."

"And does your boss run a squeaky-clean business?"

The woman's eyes widened slightly before her facial expression returned to all business. "That is something I would rather you found out from him."

That sentence told him the man wasn't above killing an employee or two who might know some dirt on him.

The door opened. A lanky, red-haired man with black-rimmed glasses, slacks, and a button-up shirt walked in. He stopped, his gaze darting between Ms. Barnes and Hawke.

"Who were you expecting to meet up here, Mr. DeLan?" Hawke asked.

The man glanced at him and back at Ms. Barnes. "I thought it might be Mr. Pannell."

"What did you think he wanted to talk to you about?" Hawke asked.

The man barely flicked a glance at Hawke. "Why was I called up here to talk to this man?" He directed the question to Ms. Barnes.

"This is Marion's brother. He's a state trooper. He would like to know how much you know about Marion and Adrian." The woman stated the fact and nothing more.

Hawke admired the woman's business attitude.

Caleb dropped into the chair beside Ms. Barnes. "I didn't see her killing him. And like they said, with…" He shook his head. "Adrian was excited about this trip. He planned to propose." Caleb glanced at Ms. Barnes. "I told him it was a solid plan. They were both moving up in the company."

She nodded.

"You don't think the two of them would go in for kinky sex?" Hawke asked. His blunt question took both the man and the woman by surprise.

"She wouldn't have killed him because he proposed." Caleb blurted out.

"Would someone else have a reason to kill Adrian?" Hawke asked, watching them both.

Caleb shook his head. Ms. Barnes didn't move a muscle. She knew something.

Hawke settled his gaze on Ms. Barnes. "Is there a chance you can get me into Marion and Adrian's rooms?"

"I was sharing with Adrian. I can take you up, but the police have already been through everything," Caleb said.

"Thank you." Hawke returned his gaze to Ms. Barnes. "And Marion's room?"

"She never roomed with anyone. But we were told her room was off limits to anyone but the police."

Hawke grinned and drew his badge out from under his shirt. "I'm police."

Chapter Five

The woman, Dolly, no last name, handed Marion a towel, underclothes, jeans, a long-sleeved shirt, and antibiotic ointment. "Take a shower, but don't take too long. The tank doesn't hold very much water."

Marion grasped the clothes and walked over to the small building Dolly said was the shower house. It had a metal tank on the top of the building. She was grateful for the shower, the clothing, and that the woman hadn't asked her any questions.

She undressed, assessed all the scratches on her legs and arms, and stepped under the showerhead. It took her a minute to figure out she needed to pull the chain hanging down beside the pipe coming out of the ceiling. Barely warm water rained down. Once she was wet, Marion soaped up her body and shampooed her hair, then pulled the chain and rinsed.

Walking over to the towel, she heard voices outside the building. Marion peeked out the crack in the old boards. It appeared to be a man and a woman younger than Dolly. She hadn't heard a vehicle arrive.

Keeping an eye on them, she dried and dressed. She was too far away to hear what they were talking about. Dolly never once glanced toward the shower.

Marion knew there was a back door to Dolly's house. It led into the kitchen where they'd had a meal before Marion's shower. However, she didn't believe she could get there without the guests seeing her.

She wondered what Gabriel was doing and when he'd catch up to her. It had been a lot of years since she'd laid eyes on her brother. Would she even know him? Tired from fleeing the killer and staying hidden, Marion sat on the stool under the wooden pegs where she'd hung the towel and leaned her head back against the wall. She was safe here for a while. Her eyelids grew heavy and closed.

Hawke searched Marion's room first. He rifled through her clothing in the closet and the dresser drawer. He even checked through the luggage sitting in the closet. He didn't find anything that would give him a clue to anything. Which was good. It would mean the police didn't find anything either. Though he wondered if the police had taken her phone and possibly a computer as there was an empty computer bag on the shelf in the closet. They would be looking for her connection to the victim. He wondered if from the sounds of how the two had kept their relationship hidden if she would even have anything on her work computer to connect them.

His phone rang. "Hawke."

"It's Spruel. I found a contact in the Montana State Police who is willing to give you information. But you have to be upfront with her and let her know what you find out, including turning your sister in when you find her."

Hawke shook his head. "Marion's running for her life. She said 'they' killed Adrian when she called. I'm not turning her over to anyone until I know who 'they' are."

"I understand how you feel. But if you want to get help from Montana, you'll need to compromise." Spruel's tone wasn't that of his superior but of his friend.

Sighing, Hawke said, "What's the name and number of the contact?"

Spruel rattled off a phone number and said, "Lieutenant Brandy Gernot will be waiting for your call."

Hawke glanced at his watch. It was nine p.m. "I'm going through Marion's room right now and am heading to Adrian's room when I finish."

"How did you get access to the rooms?"

"I happened to ask the right person about Marion." He went on to tell Spruel about the trooper sitting on the crime scene and the executive secretary willing to help to a point.

"Lt. Gernot will be expecting a call from you tonight. I suggest you either call her while you're looking around or soon after. I'm sure she'd like to go to sleep sometime." Spruel ended the call.

Hawke grinned, walked out of Marion's room, and down the hallway. Caleb was in a discussion with a woman wearing high heel boots up to her knees, tight pants, and a long flowing top. She spun on her heels and strode down the hall to the room at the end. She stopped with her hand on the door handle, peered at Caleb, and entered the room.

"Who was that?' Hawke asked, causing the man to jump and spin toward him.

"What? Her? Just a guest with a different group." The man seemed still preoccupied by the woman.

That explained to Hawke why the woman was dressed as if she were headed out on a date while all the women employed by Pannell were dressed in athletic clothing.

"Did you find anything in Marion's room?" Caleb asked, opening the door.

"Nope." One foot inside the room and Hawke knew this would be a harder room to investigate. There were clothes and shoes everywhere. "What is yours and what is Adrian's?" He had expected with the two men being accountants that the room would be as clean and put in order as Marion's had been.

"Most of this is mine. You'll find Adrian's stuff in the closet and drawers."

Hawke nodded and walked to the dresser. He began a thorough search through all the clothing and then the closet and luggage in there. Again, there was an empty computer case.

"Did the police take his computer and phone?" Hawke asked.

Caleb shook his head. "I didn't see them take anything out of the room."

Hawke made a mental note to ask Lt. Gernot about the computers and phones. If the police didn't take them, it had to have been someone from Pannell Financial and that was why Ms. Barnes was so accommodating about letting him look in the rooms.

Shoved in a pocket of one of the luggage pieces,

Hawke found a receipt for a jewelry store. From the numbers and description of the ring, it had to be an engagement ring. "Did the police find a ring?"

"I'm pretty sure he had it with him when he left here to meet Marion." Caleb's face reddened. "He spent a lot of money on that ring. He also spent a lot of time with a jeweler to have it special made."

Hawke's chest squeezed. It appeared Marion had finally met the right man and their life together had been taken from her.

"Thank you for allowing me to have a look around." Hawke walked to the door. "Do you happen to know if the police took Marion's phone and laptop?"

"I can't answer that. I was in here when they went through her room." Caleb shrugged.

"If you think of anything else that could help me find Marion or help prove she didn't kill Adrian, contact me." Hawke handed him one of his State Trooper cards. "My cell phone number is on the back. If you can't contact me, call the number on the front and ask for Sergeant Spruel. He'll get your message to me."

Hawke walked out of the room and down the hallway. A thought struck him. He backtracked and caught Caleb before he headed back outside. "Other than you, did Adrian have any other friends? Ones that didn't work for Pannell?"

Caleb shrugged. "You could ask his sister. She lives outside of Dallas. Adrian was always over at her house playing with her kids and helping her husband."

"What's her name?" Hawke felt more confident he would learn more about the man his sister had planned to marry.

"Alice Mendoza. That's all I know."

"Thank you. Adrian wouldn't have happened to have mentioned any of Marion's friends outside of work, did he?"

"He said something about a book club she went to once a month and she went to the Y to swim every day." Another thin-shouldered shrug.

That was why Marion had made the choice to swim away rather than take the paddleboard. She was a gifted swimmer in school and it appeared she had kept up the sport.

Hawke pivoted on his heel and headed to the top of the stairs and descended. More people milled about in the lobby. He looked each person in the eye. Many looked away, others returned the gaze. There was one man sitting in a chair pretending he didn't care about Hawke, but his gaze followed Hawke to the door and when he looked back, the man was watching him from inside the lodge.

Keeping his pace steady, Hawke walked to the canoe. Dog sat in the front, waiting and watching.

"Good dog." Hawke patted the animal's head and shoved the canoe into the water. He climbed in and picked up the shovel, paddling the canoe away from the island. This time he didn't care who saw him. He paddled along in front of the glowing windows, around the end of the island where the docks were, and across the short expanse to the boat house and dock where he'd borrowed the canoe.

Inside his pickup, Hawke pulled out a map and found the most direct route heading west was an undeveloped road, Jocko Road. He'd cross through there tonight. But first, he needed to call Lt. Gernot.

He dialed the number and listened to the ringing on

the other end. He was waiting for a voicemail message when an out-of-breath female voice answered.

"Lt. Gernot."

"Lieutenant, this is Oregon State Trooper Hawke. My superior, Sergeant Spruel contacted you."

"Yes. I had about given up on you calling me."

"I was doing some digging of my own. I discovered you have someone watching the crime scene."

"I thought given it was in an isolated area it would be a good idea to keep someone there for a few days until forensics is certain they have all they need."

He liked that she was thorough. "I also went through the victim's and my sister's rooms. Did the police take their computers and phones?"

He heard a keyboard clicking.

"No. There is no mention of laptops or phones being taken as evidence. Why?"

"There were computer cases in both their rooms but nothing in them." Hawke wasn't going to add that they may contain the reason behind Adrian's death. That was something that would have to come out later. After he'd found Marion.

"Why would someone take them?" Lt. Gernot asked in a soft voice as if mulling it over in her mind.

"Did Spruel tell you about my call from my sister?"

"Yes. He said she mentioned someone else had killed the victim. However, there hasn't been any evidence to prove anyone other than the victim and your sister were on the island."

"They'd make it look that way wouldn't they, if they had killed someone? Why would my sister leave her bra around her lover's neck if she were guilty? She's not stupid. She's a corporate lawyer who makes sure all points are covered in a contract and that nothing slips by. There is no way she would run off and leave her undergarments behind if she'd accidentally killed someone. And she damn sure wouldn't if it was premeditated." He knew his sister. She would have confessed if she had accidentally killed her lover, and she wouldn't have killed him on purpose and left behind damning evidence.

"You know families can't believe when their daughter, son, mother, father kills someone. You need to keep an open mind about this." Lt. Gernot sounded like a teacher reprimanding a student.

"I was hoping we could have a working relationship, Lieutenant. But if you are closed to the idea my sister was set up and I'm closed to the idea that she did it, I have a feeling we will be of no use to one another." He ended the call and wished the woman had been more open to the fact someone else could have killed the victim.

He put the vehicle in drive and headed north to the end of Salmon Lake and turned left. Jocko Road ran parallel to the area where he had tracked Marion. If he was lucky, he'd find her before the killer did.

Chapter Six

"Thump!" Something under Marion's head bounced. She forced her eyes open and they slowly focused on the woman standing inside the small wooden structure. About a dozen blinks later, Marion remembered where she was and that this woman was Dolly.

"I wondered what was taking you so long," Dolly said, reaching out a hand to help Marion to her feet.

"There were people out there talking to you. I sat down to wait and fell asleep." Marion ran a hand over her face. When she removed her hand, Dolly was staring at her.

"Are you a fugitive? My neighbors were telling me some woman killed her lover over at Salmon Lake." Dolly peered at her with light blue non-judgmental eyes.

Marion held out her left hand. "The man that was killed gave me this and asked me to marry him. I accepted, then we made love on the island. I went to wash off and when I came back there was a man…" She swallowed down the bile rising in her throat. "He was strangling Adrian and asking him where I was. I rushed forward to help and the man threw Adrian to the side and ran after me. I ran into the lake and kept swimming to the other side. Then I ran over the ridge and when I found a house with a phone, I borrowed clothing and called my brother. He should be looking for me. He's with the Oregon State Police." Marion stared into the woman's eyes. "I didn't kill Adrian. We had talked about a future that night and I had accepted his ring." Tears burned her eyes and slid down her cheeks. She swiped at them. "I did not kill him, but my brother and I will make the person who did kill him pay."

Dolly nodded her head once. "Then we need to get you to a phone so you can call your brother. Come on. We can either use my sister's phone or I can take you to Arlee and you can call him from the Senior Center. I'll vouch for you."

Marion hugged the woman. "Thank you! Where do you want the wet towel?" She pulled the towel off her head. Damp hair tumbled down her back. She had kept the tradition of not cutting her hair mainly because she received so many compliments about her long, thick hair.

"Hang it over the line stretched out behind the house. I'll get you some shoes that fit better than what you were wearing."

"Do you have a sack I can put these clothes in? I want to return them." Marion felt as if things were looking up. This woman believed in her and she'd be able to tell Gabriel where she was.

<>><<>><<>>

Marion sat in a bright yellow kitchen. Dolly's sister,

Lynn, lived in a small house tucked back in the trees just as the road turned from gravel to pavement.

Lynn had insisted they eat a piece of her chocolate caramel cake as soon as they arrived. While they ate, Dolly explained that Marion needed to use the telephone.

"Go right ahead. It's in the living room on the table next to my chair." Lynn started collecting the empty dessert dishes.

"Thank you." Marion stood and walked into the dimly lit living room. She found the square phone with square, numbered buttons you pushed to dial. Saying Gabriel's number to herself, she pushed the correlating numbers and waited while the phone on the other end rang. His voicemail picked up.

"*Pyáp*, it's me. I'm safe. I can't give you this number as I won't be here. But you can call and Lynn will tell you where to find me." She ended the call and stared out into the darkening night. She knew her brother would find her, but how long would it take? The longer they were apart the more time the killer had to incriminate her and cover his tracks.

Hawke traveled the gravel road faster in the dark than he would have in the daylight. Poor Dog bounced on the seat beside him but he didn't complain.

Even though it would be a long shot to see Marion out through the trees, he'd scoured the trees and underbrush that his lights illuminated. He was on pavement now and drove by small farms. At Highway 93 he turned right and looked for the first motel he could find in the town of Arlee.

As soon as he had a room, he and Dog collapsed, but not before he plugged in his phone to charge. It was the only way Marion had to contact him. He placed it on the bedside table and flopped back on the bed. A good night's sleep and he'd be ready to go. Dog curled up on the bed beside him.

A buzz barely registered, but it brought Hawke back awake. He reached for his phone and saw there was a message from a number he didn't know. Pressing the voicemail icon, he listened to the message. "*Pyáp*, it's me. I'm safe. I can't give you this number as I won't be here. But you can call and Lynn will tell you where to find me."

Marion had to have called when he was on the gravel road and out of service. Damn! A glance at the clock and he knew it was too late to call the number. Whoever it was would be deep asleep.

Hawke lay back on the bed, closed his eyes, and fell deep asleep knowing Marion was safe. He'd catch up to her tomorrow.

Hawke woke, made a cup of coffee in the room, and hit redial for the number that Marion had called from.

"Hello?" a mature female voice answered.

"My sister called from your phone last night. I wondered if you could tell me where she is this morning?" Hawke kept his tone casual.

"Oh, yes. Marion was here with my sister, Dolly. They drove back to Dolly's place last night after we had dessert. Dolly doesn't have a phone is why they came here." The woman's friendly voice revealed she didn't know anything about Marion's predicament.

"Could you give me directions to Dolly's?" Hawke asked, his notepad and pencil ready to write.

"She lives off Jocko Road. Eleven miles after you

leave the pavement, look for a dirt track to your left. Follow it to her house. Mind you, it's not a very good track but her truck makes it in and out just fine."

"Thank you. I appreciate your information. If anyone else asks about Marion, you don't know where she is." He didn't add the urgency he wanted for fear the woman would ask questions. But if someone was checking on the calls to him and from him to find Marion, this woman could be questioned.

"Oh, don't worry. Dolly told me all about her fearing for her life. I don't remember this call." The line went silent.

Hawke grinned. As long as the woman could persuade anyone who contacted her that she knew nothing, she'd be fine. "Come on, Dog. Let's grab some breakfast to go and pick up Marion."

Driving the opposite direction on Jocko Road in the daylight, Hawke drove slower and took in the scenery. The vibrant greens of early summer were a bright backdrop to the brown trunks of pine and fir trees and the grays and pinks of the rocks. They crossed a creek and followed it for a good distance.

Dog's hair bristled and he growled.

"What do you see?" Hawke stopped the pickup and stared in the direction Dog had his nose pointed. Something brown was moving in the brush. Another minute and a young brown bear moved out from behind a bush. He was pulling over rocks and eating insects, oblivious to being watched.

"He's just getting his breakfast." Hawke patted Dog on the head before putting the vehicle in drive and heading up the gravel road. It started to rain. His wipers kept a constant tempo as they continued along the road.

They had met only one other vehicle. There were homes scattered here and there out among the trees, away from the road. A road veering off and a glimpse of a roof or glint of a window was the only hint someone lived out here.

At mile eleven, he studied the ground on his side of the road and spotted a track that veered off into the trees. He turned the pickup and followed the narrow path between trees and brush for half a mile before he spotted a small log cabin and a shower set-up like Dani had at Charlie's Lodge.

No dog greeted him. Half a dozen chickens flew off the porch as he parked next to a 1963 Ford pickup.

A woman older than him with gray hair pulled back in a braid, wearing jeans, a long-sleeved shirt, and cowboy boots appeared at the door. "I think you're lost," she said, not a bit of sarcasm or joking in her tone.

"I'm Gabriel Hawke. Marion's brother." He stood beside the driver's door, his heart thrumming in his chest hoping that this hadn't been some kind of set-up.

A woman appeared in the doorway. She said something and stepped around the older woman.

"*Pyáp?*" she asked hesitantly.

"*Kskís Yáka,*" he replied.

Marion ran out to him and hugged him tight. "I'm so glad you found me. I didn't know what to do."

"I've always protected you when I could. I'm here. There are things I need to know." He released her and peered into her eyes. "I know you didn't kill Adrian."

Tears tumbled down her cheeks and she hiccupped before saying, "I didn't. But I saw who did. He came after me and I fled."

Hawke glanced at the woman still standing in the

doorway. "We need to go."

"Dolly knows the whole thing. She picked me up with her horse. When we returned, she learned from a neighbor about what had happened. Or rather, what Pannell is telling the newspapers." The scorn in her words told him what he had guessed. Her own company had turned on her. "I told her what really happened. That's when she drove me to her sister's so I could call. I had to leave a voicemail."

"Yeah, I was coming across Jocko Road when you called. No service. I called back first thing this morning and was given directions. Even if this woman knows the story, she isn't safe if Pannell is looking for you." He glanced at the woman watching them. "It's safer for her to not know what we are going to do next. We need to just leave."

"I need to get the clothing I borrowed. I want to return it."

This was the sister he remembered. Always doing the right thing, unless to not do the right thing would annoy their mother. "Get the clothes and say goodbye."

She nodded and walked back to the woman. They said a few words, Marion disappeared into the cabin, then returned with a brown bag. She hugged the woman and walked out to the passenger side of the pickup.

Opening the door, Marion asked, "Who is this?"

"Dog meet Marion. Marion, Dog." Hawke said, sliding in behind the steering wheel.

"Dog?" she said and chuckled. "Couldn't you come up with a better name for this animal?"

He backed up, turned around, and traveled out the dirt path. "Kitree, a young friend of mine, calls him Prince. But he prefers plain ole Dog. Don't you boy?"

Hawke said, ruffling the hair on Dog's head. The animal smiled. At least that's what it looked like to Hawke.

"I agree with Kitree, Prince is a much better name." Her happiness dimmed. "I'm in huge trouble, aren't I? But I didn't have any other choice. If I hadn't run, I'd have been dead right alongside Adrian."

Chapter Seven

Marion's throat constricted as her mind flashed through the last seconds of Adrian's life. "It was horrible." She held up her left hand, showing Gabriel her engagement ring. "Adrian and I went out to the island for some alone time. He proposed and I accepted." She felt the tears coming, burning behind her eyeballs and growing a lump in her throat. Swallowing, she played the afternoon back in her mind. "We made love and I had gone to the water carrying just my shorts and top. When I came back, this man had Adrian on his knees and was choking him with my bra. I rushed forward to stop him, but he tossed Adrian to the side. I saw…" she choked down the wail that she'd yet to let free. "I could see Adrian's lips were blue, his eyes unseeing." She drew in a sharp intake of breath and continued. "The man was coming after me so I ran into the lake and swam to the shore. Then I ran over the ridge and found the clothing and a phone. When I was talking to you, headlights flashed in the front window. I hurried out the backdoor without closing it. Did he call the police?" Marion hoped the police hadn't figured out she'd been the one there. That poor man might be visited by the man who killed Adrian.

"I talked to the guy. His name is Will Rule. I'm glad he and his two dogs weren't there when you entered and that you got away before they spotted you. The man seems okay, but the dogs are mean. They would have chewed you up before he could stop them."

Gabriel's tone was one she remembered as a child. When he was telling her to stay or hide when her father came home drunk. She knew by the tone that he wasn't kidding. She'd learned that bad things would happen if she didn't listen to him. However, she wasn't a child anymore. She did need his help and would follow his rules. He was, after all, law enforcement. She was a lawyer, but she knew nothing of policing laws, only the laws of corporate transactions and contracts.

"Why would someone from Pannell take yours and Adrian's computers and phones?" Gabriel asked.

The question took her by surprise. "Our work laptops?"

"Both of your rooms had empty computer bags and I couldn't find a cell phone." He glanced over at her.

Marion peered into his eyes until he had to return his attention to the road. "All they will find on our work computers is work. Now our phones would show calls we made to each other and texts." She thought about that for a moment. "Do you think they will try to make something out of those texts to prove I had a reason to kill him?"

Her brother shrugged. Noncommittal. That was

something new. She remembered him as having an opinion and giving it to her whether she wanted it or not. Had he mellowed over the years?

"Why would someone from Pannell want Adrian dead?"

The straightforward question sounded like the Gabriel she grew up knowing. "Because Adrian discovered two accounts that someone had been filtering money into over the last five years. He told me about it a week ago. We were going to start an investigation into it when we returned from the retreat."

"Did he tell anyone else about these accounts?" Gabriel asked.

"No. He wanted to wait until we had more information before he took it to his supervisor or Mr. Pannell." An ache centered in the middle of her chest. She rubbed it. "They must have found out he knew something."

She sat sideways on the bench seat as they left the gravel road. The cab was quieter as they continued on the pavement. "I heard the man ask Adrian where I was before I came upon them. It's obvious they think I know more than I do."

Gabriel glanced over at her. "You're sure you don't know any more than you just told me?"

"Nothing." She caught a glimpse of Lynn's house as they drove by. "Where are we going?"

"I thought I'd look up an old friend in St. Ignatius. He can help us find a place to stay and connect us to the internet. He's a retired Montana State Trooper I met about eight years ago at a conference." Gabriel drove into Arlee and continued north.

"But that's far away from Salmon Lake. Don't we

need to be there? Or close by?" Marion knew, according to their mother, that Gabriel had solved a large number of murders, considering he was more a game warden than a state trooper.

"We can learn a good deal of what we need to know from the internet and contacting people by phone. You'd be surprised how much Dani and I learned while we were both physically laid up after we found a body in her barn at Charlie's Lodge." The smile on his face said he liked this Dani person and that they had worked well together.

"Is Dani the woman mother said you are living with?" She only learned about her brother through their mom. He hadn't called her in years. Which made her sad and angry. "Why haven't you called me?"

He stared at her, then turned his attention back to the road. "The last time I tried, the number was no longer in use. You seem to know my number, why haven't you called?"

Touché. She could have called him instead of having her work consume her. Look what that had gotten her. A dead fiancé and her company was out to prove she had killed him.

Hawke glanced over at his sister. Sadness made her pretty face sag and her eyes weep. He placed a hand on hers. "Don't worry. We'll find the man who killed Adrian and we'll prove someone in your company is corrupt."

She gave him a weak smile. "Thank you for coming since I've done a poor job of keeping in contact with you."

He squeezed her hand. "When you called me *Pyáp*, I knew you were in trouble. I would never let my little sister down." He released her hand and followed the signs directing travelers to St. Ignatius. Hawke hoped the Montana Trooper who lived on the Flathead Reservation was willing to help him.

<<>><<<>><<<>>

Hawke pulled into the parking lot of the St. Ignatius mission church. "Why don't you go in and enjoy the church while I make a few phone calls."

Marion studied him. "Why do I need to leave for you to make phone calls?"

He shifted in his seat and returned her stare. "Because, I need to bring my superior up to date on what I've done, contact Lt. Gernot of the Montana State Police to see what they've discovered, I need to call my neighbors to see how my horses are doing, and Dani to let her know I've found you." He stopped. There was one call that needed to be done first.

He held his phone out to Marion. "You need to call mom and let her know you are okay. I had to call her after you called to find out the name of your company and their phone number."

"Mother knows I've been missing and I'm involved in a murder investigation?"

"Only that you were missing. Call her." He made to leave the vehicle.

"Stay. I'm sure she'll want to talk to you too." Marion scrolled through his contacts and poked at the screen.

"Hello, Mother." Tears streamed down his sister's face as she listened to their mom. "I'm fine. Yes. I'm with Gabriel. No, I can't come see you. Not yet. But I will when…" Marion's sad gaze landed on him. She seemed helpless in knowing what to say to their mom.

Hawke took the phone from her. "Hi, Mom."

"Is she really okay? She didn't sound like herself," his mom said. He could hear worry in her voice.

"She'll be fine. We have some things to do here before she can come to see you. But I promise I will bring her home to visit." He meant that. It had been far too long since his mom had held her youngest and visited.

"I would love to see both of you and your Dani. We could have a special dinner." Her voice shook.

"That sounds nice. We would all like to do that when Marion and I are done here." He hesitated then decided he should say something. It would be easy for Pannell to learn where Marion grew up and anticipate she would go there to hide. One of the reasons he'd decided to stay at the Flathead Reservation. Not her home and he could count on the tribal members to not give anything away to outsiders.

"Mom, if anyone comes around there asking about me or Marion, you don't know where we are. You heard from us but we didn't tell you anything." He hated to say this but it was imperative that she not give away where they were.

"You are both still in danger?" she asked.

"I'm not, but the people looking for Marion by now know I am also looking for her and might try to get to her by asking you where I am." He glanced over at Marion. Her hands were twisting in her lap.

"I don't know where you are. You never told me anything. You just asked me for Marion's employer."

Hawke smiled. "That's right. And that's all you need to tell anyone. See you soon." He ended the call. "Go on. Go in and enjoy the beauty of this church. I'll make the other calls I need to do."

Marion slipped out and stood at the open door. "Can

Dog go with me?"

Hawke dug in the front pocket of the seat cover and pulled out a choker leash. It wasn't that Dog needed it but he didn't wear a collar and it was easy to slip over his head. "Use this. I'm pretty sure dogs need to be on a leash. It might be a good idea to take him over there along that fence and let him do his business before you go in there. That way you don't have to clean up after him."

Marion nodded and she and Dog walked over to the green grass coming up alongside a pasture to the south of the church.

Hawke kept his gaze on them as he dialed Herb Trembley to inform him, that he had found his sister but he would be gone a while longer.

"Hawke, did you find her?" Herb answered the phone.

"I did, but I won't be back for a few more days. How are the boys doing?" Hawke knew his two horses and mule would be fine with him gone. They now had a pasture to roam in instead of stalls as they had occupied for over ten years at the Trembleys'.

"They are happy as can be. I check on them a couple times a day just to make sure. Doesn't take much to ride my four-wheeler over and take a peek."

"Thank you. I'm grateful that the property next to you came up for sale when it did." He and Dani had barely been looking for a place when they looked at the property next to Herb and Darlene and then Dani's apartment was burnt by a biker gang. That made her ready to purchase the place.

"We enjoy having you and Dani for neighbors. Where are you at?" Herb asked.

"Can't tell you in case someone comes around looking for us." Hawke was glad he hadn't told anyone other than Spruel where he was headed. Made it easier for them to tell the truth if asked.

"But your sister is okay? You know Darlene is going to ask and she's going to want to meet her."

"She is with me. But there are some extenuating circumstances we have to work on. And I don't know if Marion will want to come to Wallowa County. I will make her go see our mother though." This was the big brother talking. He would insist she visit their mother for at least a week when this was over.

"Well, maybe the two of them could come for a visit. I bet your mom would like to see your new place."

Hawke smiled. That would be a way to get his mother and sister to their place. "I have several other calls to make. Good talking with you, Herb."

"You, too. Keep us posted."

"I will." Hawke ended the call and dialed Sergeant Spruel.

"Sergeant Spruel," the man answered.

"It's Hawke. I have my sister and she is innocent. She saw the man who killed her fiancé and that is why she ran. In fear." He wanted to make sure his superior knew she was innocent.

"You believe her?" Spruel asked.

"Yes. I may not have seen my sister much over the last twenty-some years but I know her heart and what she is telling me is the truth." He smiled watching his sister talk to Dog as they walked to the church. "She said her fiancé, an accountant for the company she works for, had mentioned to her he'd found two accounts money from the company were filtering into. They, she and her fiancé, were going to look into it when they returned from this retreat."

"You need to take her to Lt. Gernot and have her make a statement."

Hawke shook his head. "I won't take her anywhere that the Pannell company can find her. They are a large company with lots of money. There is no telling who they might pay to make sure she doesn't say anything."

"You have to at least get a description of the man she saw to Gernot and tell her what you know." Spruel pressed.

"I was going to call her next." Hawke would ask his friend about someone to make a drawing of the man Marion saw.

"Where are you staying?" his boss asked.

"Not sure yet." Which was partially true. Best to not let anyone know where they were just in case Spruel let it slip to Gernot or someone else that would have ulterior motives to find out.

"Let me know when you land somewhere."

"Have you found out anything about the Pannell company and its owner, executive assistant, and partners?"

"I sent your email a folder on them."

Hawke silently cursed. He didn't bring his work laptop. Knowing he was going to a different state, he hadn't even thought it would be helpful. "Can you send it to Lt. Gernot so she can give me a hard copy? I don't have a way to access the folder."

"I'll do that. Be careful." Spruel ended the call.

Now Hawke would have to meet with the lieutenant. He stared at the church door where Marion and Dog had disappeared.

Chapter Eight

Marion stood in awe looking at the turquoise walls and vividly colored murals. The church made her heart sing. It was beautiful and full of life. She especially loved the murals on the walls where she entered. They were paintings of a Native American Mary and Jesus and God. So fitting for a church on a reservation. It appeared the Indigenous people were being embraced by the church. Up front to the right of the altar was a small teepee. There were several touches to bring to life the Native heritage.

Having mostly forsaken her heritage for over twenty years, she wondered at how seeing this made her happy. She sat in a pew in the middle of the chapel and slowly took in every mural and piece of stained glass. Staring at the beautiful detail in the scenes, she remembered a gallery she and Adrian had visited during a Native American art show. She'd been drawn to many of the pieces, yet when Adrian offered to purchase one for her, she'd declined.

Adrian had been surprised she'd turned down his offer since she obviously enjoyed the artwork. She'd explained how she'd left that behind to make a new life for herself. He'd countered but it is in your blood. It is who you are, how can you ignore it?

She'd told him how she had loved to dance at powwows. But at one when she was eighteen, non-Indians had said such horrible things to her and threatened her that she'd decided she didn't want to be different. She wanted to fit in.

Adrian had looked at her with sad eyes. "You didn't run from your heritage, you allowed someone else to take it away from you." She'd stared into his eyes and tears had fallen. She had allowed someone to take her happiness at being Indian away. She'd hugged him and promised they would go to a powwow and she would dance for him.

A tear trickled down her cheek. That would never happen. Someone had taken Adrian from her. Dog nudged her arm. She put her hand on his head and pet him. When they found out who killed Adrian, she would go home and she would immerse herself in the things she had allowed those men all those years ago to take from her.

The door to the church opened. She swiped at the tears but continued to sit faced forward. Dog looked back and his tail started thumping. She knew it must be Gabriel.

The pew behind her creaked.

"It's a beautiful church," he said in a soft voice.

"Yes. It is on so many levels." She turned and peered into his eyes. "What did you learn?"

"Horse, Jack, and Dot are doing fine."

She studied his face. "They are?"

"My mule and two geldings."

"I see. Horse? Really? That's as bad as naming this regal creature, Dog."

Gabriel shrugged. "If you knew Horse you would know he needs to be reminded to act better than the contrary mule he is."

She laughed despite the sad memories she'd been having. "Okay. But what about me, the man we need to catch?"

"I talked to my superior. He is sending a file on Pannell to Lt. Gernot—"

She interrupted. "I know everything there is to know about Pannell and the company. I have been writing contracts and meeting people he deals with for twenty years."

"This is information you might not know. Legal—" he held up a hand. "Not business, personal. If he's been arrested, if he's been a subject of any investigations. That sort of thing. Things he might not want his business lawyer to know."

Marion nodded. She did know he had a different lawyer to take care of personal matters. "You might want to see if anyone can talk to Perry Mathers, that's his personal lawyer."

Gabriel pulled a notebook out of his breast pocket and wrote in it. "I have contacted Lt. Gernot of the Montana State Police. She isn't happy I refused to bring you in for questioning. I feel it is not in your best interest to have anyone at Pannell know where you are, even a police station. If we go there, they can follow us to where we are staying."

"Which is?" she asked.

"My friend, Bo Laraby, has a cabin at Poulson on the south end of Flathead Lake. He said we could stay there and no one would question what we are doing. He uses it for friends and relatives to stay." Gabriel glanced at her. "We need to go to a thrift store and get you more clothes."

Marion stood. "Is there one here or from here to Poulson?"

"Poulson is a good-sized town. We'll find one there."

As they walked out of the church, Marion stopped and took one more sweeping gaze. "I'm going to follow my heritage once we find your killer," she whispered as visions of Adrian filled her mind.

"What did you say?" Gabriel asked.

"I made a vow to Adrian. Once we find his killer, I'll re-immerse myself in our heritage. I've been running from it. He made me see, I can't and shouldn't't." She studied her big brother. "You would have liked him."

"If you picked him, I'm sure I would have." He put an arm around her shoulders and they exited the church.

Hawke would have never guessed how easy it was to pick back up with his sister. They were both older, but he still felt protective of her and he could still read her emotions. Right now, she was heartbroken and determined to find justice for Adrian.

She had also proven helpful in knowing Pannell's personal lawyer. Once he received the folder from Lt. Gernot, he'd have Marion take a look at it.

When they were settled in the pickup and headed north, Marion asked, "How do you plan to get the folder from the lieutenant and not have someone follow you back to me?"

"I am obstructing justice. They can legally pull me in. While Lt. Gernot doesn't sound like she will do that, we don't know what kind of strings Pannell might be able to pull in Montana and have that happen. We'll be leaving this pickup at a garage in Ronan since the Oregon plate makes it easy to spot, and picking up a vehicle down the street from someone else." He grinned. Once he'd told Bo what he was dealing with, the now-former Montana State Trooper was more than happy to help him.

"Okay, that keeps the police from finding us as easily but what about the folder?" Marion persisted.

"It's being mailed to a PO Box in St. Ignatius, where Bo will have his cousin bring it to him. His cousin runs the mailing facility and will put something that looks similar in the PO Box to make anyone who is waiting for a pickup think it hasn't been picked up." He grinned and glanced over at his sister. "The *šuyápu* have always underestimated us."

She returned his smile and relaxed into the seat.

In Poulson, they found a thrift store where Marion purchased four changes of clothing and underwear. Also two pairs of shoes. Then they went to a grocery store and purchased supplies.

He found the cozy cabin on the end of Flathead Lake without trouble. There were two bedrooms, one bath, and a beautiful deck overlooking the lake.

Hawke's gaze landed on the laptop sitting on the kitchen table. He put down the bags of groceries and grinned. Bo had come through.

"Which bedroom do you want?" Marion asked.

"Pick which one you want. Dog and I aren't particular when it comes to sleeping. Bed, floor, ground, we're used to all of them."

Marion stood in the opening of the small hallway leading to the bedrooms and bath. "Now that we are stuck with each other, you're going to have to tell me all about what you do and Dani."

Hawke nodded. "And I want to know all about what you've been doing the last twenty-five years."

She shrugged. "My life has been boring. I worked, went home to eat and do more work at my apartment, and fall into bed. Get up, swim, go to work and do it all again."

"What about weekends?" Hawke began unloading the grocery bags and putting the food away. The few times he'd called her, she'd gushed about how fascinating her work was, how much money she was making, and that she had the life she'd dreamed of. But he could tell she was putting too much energy into trying to persuade him.

"Until I met Adrian, there'd be a date here and there, and a party for someone at work. After meeting Adrian, we'd go on hikes, drives, see movies, and go out to dinner." She sighed. "He was showing me what I'd been missing all those years of all work and no play."

"The best way to pay tribute to his life is to live your life as he would want you to." Hawke finished putting the food away and studied his sister.

She nodded. "I would like to stay with Mother for a month when this is over. I'd like to reconnect with her and my roots."

"That's a good idea. I know she would love to have you stay." He picked up his duffle bag she'd dropped by the front door. "Which room is mine?"

Marion peered at the floor. "If you don't mind, I'd

like you to take the one nearest the living room and outside doors. I'd feel safer that way."

"Done." Hawke smiled and walked into the first bedroom. He dropped his duffle bag on the bed and walked back out. "What shall we make for dinner?"

Marion shrugged. "Shouldn't we see what we can find on the computer?"

"Not until our stomachs are full so we don't get distracted." Hawke walked into the kitchen area that was in the main cabin along with the small dining and living areas.

"I don't care what you make. I'm going to take a shower and get out of these clothes." She waved a hand down the front of her. She still wore the clothes Dolly had given her.

"Then I'll come up with something on my own. Enjoy the shower." Hawke opened the fridge door to inspect the food he'd just placed on the shelves.

Looked like he was making a taco salad. Before he and Dani bought the house next to the Trembleys, he would order food from a restaurant to take home or nuke something in the microwave. Since having an actual kitchen, Hawke had found he enjoyed cooking. Even if it was mainly for him and Dog most of the time.

He put the ground beef in a frying pan and turned on the laptop his friend had left, along with a note that gave him the password to get into the computer and a reassurance that this computer was hard to trace should he find himself exploring files off limits to him.

Hawke smiled. He and Bo had hit it off from the minute they'd bumped into one another, literally, at a SAR conference in Montana. Being part of Search and Rescue had given him trips he wouldn't have taken otherwise and he'd met some good people. Like the SAR conference he'd attended in Iceland a couple years before. He hated that the person helping him had ended up dead, and Hawke had spent most of his time in the country finding his killer, but he had met some very nice people and hoped he and Dani could go back there again one day.

He booted up the laptop and walked over to the stove to stir the browning meat. Opening a cupboard, he found taco seasoning and set it on the counter next to the stove. When he'd purchased the ground beef, he'd planned to make hamburgers on the grill, but seeing as how Marion was scared, he doubted she'd be spending much time sitting out on the small deck.

Hawke liked the idea of Marion staying with their mom for a while after this murder was cleared up. His mom missed Marion and it was easy to see Marion needed to get back to her roots. Damn, he wished he could have met the man who had shown Marion there was more to life than working.

The sound of Marion walking down the hall, had him stirring the contents in the pan. He didn't want to let her know how badly he wanted to find the man who killed Adrian and was after her.

"Smells like tacos," Marion said, crossing to the stove and standing next to him.

"It's my specialty," he said. "Want to put some plates and silverware on the table and I'll get out the toppings."

Marion smiled. "I know you made me food when I was little before you joined the Marines, but I never thought you'd cook for yourself."

"I don't. I cook for me and Dog. And sometimes

Dani when she's home." He studied his sister. "I think you and Dani will get along fine. She was a career pilot in the Air Force. She knows something about hard work and making it up the ladder."

Marion's head tipped sideways and she peered at him. "I can't see you with a bossy woman."

Hawke laughed. When he got himself under control, he said, "I won't tell Dani you called her bossy without meeting her."

Chapter Nine

After they ate, Hawke and Marion sat at the table with the computer in front of them. Hawke pulled up the website for Pannell Financial. He wanted to see the faces of the people who worked there.

"The man you saw kill Adrian. Had you ever seen him before?" Hawke asked while studying the photos he scrolled through.

"No. I would have remembered the coldness in his eyes." Marion shivered.

"Then he must have been someone that was hired to do the job." Hawke studied his sister. "Do you know if Mr. Pannell kept anyone on retainer to 'clean' things up?"

She stared at him. "Until Adrian found out someone was stealing, I would have told you everyone at Pannell was the epitome of a business professional. Now…I'm not sure who I can trust from there."

Hawke nodded. He understood. There had been

times when he wasn't sure whom to trust and who not to trust in the legal system.

"Who would be the most likely to have had access to skimming the money?" Hawke asked.

"Anyone in Adrian's department could have hidden what was happening. But the brokers could have also shuffled things around. Or Drew, Mr. Pannell, could have ordered someone to manipulate numbers." She stared at the computer screen.

Marion pointed at the woman who had answered his questions. "Adele might know something. She is Drew's personal secretary. She'd know everyone he talks to and what his plans are at all times."

Hawke leaned back in his chair. "Would she have told him about my visit and looking in the rooms?"

Marion's shoulders slumped. "She is very loyal to him. I'm sure she told him everything you did or said."

"Is there anyone at Pannell who would be willing to check out things for us?" Hawke wanted someone on the inside of the business who could keep an eye on people.

Marion shook her head, then her face brightened. "Louise. She was demoted because she complained about her boss sexually harassing her."

"What is her last name?" Hawke asked, having pulled up the search bar in Pannell Financials' website.

She hesitated. "What if they find out she is helping me? I don't want anyone to get in trouble, or worse, because of me."

Hawke shoved the laptop to the side. "Marion, if Pannell is trying to pin Adrian's murder on you, it would be stupid to hurt anyone else."

"Unless they make it look like I hurt them to cover my tracks." She peered into his eyes.

He could see she believed her actions could hurt others. His sister had always had a soft heart. Because of that, he'd always found it hard to think of her as a lawyer. Someone who had to be tough to do right by their clients.

"We have to reach out to someone at Pannell. We need to at least know what is being said." Hawke studied Marion. Her eyes were focused on the computer. Her hands worried the edge of the T-shirt she wore.

"If all we do is ask her to keep an ear out for what is said about me and Adrian, I'm okay with that. I don't want them thinking she's getting nosey and fire her, or worse." Marion glanced up at him. "But I can't guarantee she will even help if she thinks I killed Adrian."

"It's worth a shot to reach out to her. According to Bo, this computer can't be traced. Do you want to contact her via email or call? I can have Spruel find her phone number." Hawke reached for his phone.

"I should probably talk to her. I would be able to tell right away if she believes I killed Adrian or if she will help."

Hawke nodded. He'd hoped she'd say that. He agreed, they could learn more about her attitude toward helping by talking to the woman than by a text.

It was getting late. "I'll text my boss and he can get me the phone number when he gets to work in the morning. Let's get some sleep, and maybe we'll come up with some more ideas on how to approach all of this."

Marion nodded and stood. When Hawke stood, she gave him a hug. "Thank you for coming and helping me. I have no one else to turn to."

Warmth built in his chest and he felt dampness soak through his shirt. Hawke held her away from him, wiped the tears on her cheeks, and smiled. "Family will always have your back."

The next morning Hawke and Dog were up early. He'd sent out several emails and texts the night before and many of them had responded. The one he was most interested in was the information he'd received from his friend, Special Agent Quinn Pierce of the FBI. He'd discovered that Drew Pannell was under investigation for fraud. Which made it clear why Adrian was killed if he had somehow uncovered the fraud. It also meant the FBI wanted to talk to Marion, even though she was suspected of murder.

Hawke sat on the deck, watching the lake, and drinking coffee. He trusted Pierce not to arrest his sister but, then again, the special agent was by-the-book and when on an investigation had a one-track mind. Mostly. He was pondering whether or not to disclose their location or meet with Quinn someplace where he couldn't show up with a bunch of his agents.

"Why are you glaring at this beautiful lake?" Marion asked, taking the chair beside him, holding a cup of steaming coffee.

"I found out that Pannell is being investigated by the FBI for fraud. I'm trying to decide if my contact in the FBI would be willing to work with us without giving you up."

"I see."

He glanced over at Marion. She was staring at the lake. From the side, she looked a lot like their mother. As his sister grew, he was happy to see she resembled their mother and not her mean, angry father. "This is your life. What do you want to do?"

She shook her head. "It might be my life but you

know the person and you work in law enforcement. By all rights, you should have hauled me in as soon as you found me." She glanced over. "But I'm glad your sense of fairness doesn't always go by the law you swore to uphold."

He nodded. His sense of fairness had helped him over the years, but it had also bit him in the ass. This time it was his sister's life on the line, and he didn't give a damn what the law said, he was keeping her alive.

His phone rang. Spruel.

"Morning," Hawke said, answering the call.

"How are things going there today?" Spruel asked.

"We're still trying to come up with a plan." Hawke went on to tell his sergeant what he'd learned from Pierce.

"It sounds like there is ample reason to believe your sister didn't kill the victim. And her boss would want to keep whatever the victim found hidden," Spruel said.

"Yes, sir. That's what it's sounding like. Did you get the phone number I asked about?"

"Yes. Why do you need this woman's cell phone number?"

"Marion thinks she would be willing to keep an ear out at Pannell Financial to see what is being said and what Pannell is doing." Hawke knew Spruel hated to bring civilians into anything law enforcement was working on.

"Do you think it's wise? I agree it would be quicker and easier than trying to get someone from law enforcement in there right now. And we need to know what is being said." Spruel was quiet for several minutes.

Hawke knew his boss was running everything around in his mind.

"What if she runs straight to Pannell?" Spruel always liked to play devil's advocate.

"Marion doesn't think she will. Ms. Beltane has a grudge against the company and is friends with my sister." At least Hawke hoped she liked Marion.

"It would be good to have someone on the inside to know what Pannell is doing," Spruel said as if to make himself feel giving them the woman's number was a good thing.

Sergeant Spruel recited the number. "Keep me updated," was his last comment and the line went silent.

Hawke spun his notebook toward Marion and handed her the pre-paid phone he'd purchased the day before. "Was Ms. Beltane's number in your phone?" Hawke asked. He'd thought of that as he talked to Spruel. Pannell could be keeping tabs on all the incoming calls to the people on Marion's contacts.

"No. We only talked at work or work-related events." Marion picked up the phone. Her hands shook as she dialed the number and pressed speaker. Her poking around to save her life was one thing, but bringing another person in, one that could get hurt as well… made her stomach clench. What if Louise wasn't willing to help her? She was pretty sure the woman would help if it was something that would get Drew Pannell in trouble. She'd been treated dreadfully over her complaint. Louise wasn't the only woman who had asked to be moved. But she had been the only one to take matters higher when her move was a demotion.

"Hello? If this is a telemarketer I'm not interested—"

"Louise, it's me, Marion," she said before the woman hung up and blocked the number. She received a good job nod from her brother.

"Marion?" She said in a quieter voice, "Marion Shumack?"

Marion hoped the surprise in the woman's voice was a good sign. "Yes. It's Marion Shumack. I have a favor to ask."

There was a long moment of silence. Marion glanced up at Gabriel. He held up a hand as if saying just wait.

Louise would still be in Montana as she had attended the retreat. Unless Mr. Pannell had hauled everyone back to Dallas.

"Okay, I can talk now. Where are you? Were you really with Adrian when—" she didn't finish.

"I can't tell you where I am. Yes, I was with Adrian but I didn't kill him. He'd just proposed to me when a man…" Marion put a hand to her mouth, stifling the sorrow and swallowing the lump that clogged her throat. She sipped the cold coffee from the cup Gabriel handed her. "Louise, I'm hiding from the man who killed Adrian. He saw me. I swam away and am safe with my brother. But we need your help." She controlled her voice, holding back the desperation she felt. Louise had to help them.

"Oh my God! You saw…" Louise dropped her voice, "the killer?"

Marion closed her eyes but that didn't stop the scene from playing in her mind again. "Yes. Louise, I know you don't have a lot of loyalty to Mr. Pannell or the company, and I hoped you could listen to conversations and see what people are saying about me, Adrian, and the company."

"You want me to spy on people?" Louise asked with

too much enthusiasm.

"Not spy. Just listen to the gossip and keep tabs on what Mr. Pannell is doing with the company. Don't ask questions. Just listen."

Gabriel shoved a note in front of her. ASK HER WHAT SHE'S HEARD SO FAR

"Louise, are you all still in Montana?" Marion asked.

"Yes. Because we had several days interrupted by police, Mr. Pannell paid the resort to allow us to stay for another week."

Gabriel made a sound of disgust. Marion studied him. It was clear he suspected her boss had another reason for hanging around. To be close when his hired killer found her.

"What have people been saying? About me and Adrian." Marion watched Gabriel pull out his little notebook and pen. He sat down, ready to take notes.

The woman on the other end of the conversation blew into the phone. "Well, are you sure you want to hear?"

Gabriel nodded.

"Yes. We need to hear it all."

"We?" Louise sounded surprised.

"My brother and I. I have you on speakerphone. He is taking notes. He is with the Oregon State Police."

"He's a policeman and he is helping you?" Again, the woman didn't hide her surprise.

"Yes. Because he knows I would never kill someone I love and he believes I am hiding from the real killer."

Gabriel spoke for the first time. "You are not to tell anyone you have talked with us."

"Oh! Hello. Okay. Yes."

"Now tell us everything, even if it is against Marion," Gabriel added.

"Mr. Pannell is telling everyone that Marion killed Adrian while they were having kinky sex."

Marion rolled her eyes and started to say, 'Only to cover up his implication in the murder,' but Gabriel put a hand on her arm and shook his head. She understood what he meant.

"What are other people saying?" Marion asked.

"Adele Burns says she always knew you weren't so quiet and innocent."

Marion believed that. Just because she was quiet and listened rather than butted in like that woman. And the woman would mimic whatever Drew said.

"Caleb said he knew that Adrian was proposing to you on this trip. That he knew you two were more than colleagues." She stopped, then said, "You surprised a lot of us. Most of the people here had no idea you and Adrian had even been dating."

"We wanted to keep our relationship quiet. We would have told people about the engagement and pending wedding." A sorrow squeezed her chest. It had been a short engagement and there would never be a wedding.

"What about Mr. Pannell? Did he seem surprised about them dating?" Gabriel asked.

Marion wondered why that mattered.

"Mr. Pannell? I'm not sure. But since he wasn't surprised by the kinky sex, I would think he might have known." Louise sighed. "I've heard several people say they can't believe you did it and ran. That you wouldn't have run. Others say, no one really knew you that well and you could be a black widow."

Marion could visualize Louise shrugging. That was the one thing she knew about the other woman. She would stand up for her rights, but she wouldn't begrudge anyone else how they wanted to live.

"I'm not. My heart is aching for Adrian. I didn't kill him, but I'm damn well going to find the person who did."

Chapter Ten

Hawke ended the phone call, thanking Ms. Beltane for the information and asking her to continue listening and that they would call her for updates. He studied Marion. "You did well. I know it's hard to keep your emotions in check when you're digging for information. You can rant, throw punches, or whatever you need to do and I'll take it. I know it is just your way of grieving and trying to understand."

Marion stared at him. "How did my bossy, know-it-all brother become so sensitive?"

He laughed, dried his eyes, and said, "I'm not sensitive. I just know what it's like to lose someone and the feelings that go with it."

"Who did you lose?"

"In the Gulf War I lost one of my best friends." Hawke swallowed the knot in his throat. He hadn't talked about Miguel for decades. And now he'd thought of the man twice in the last two years. He and Dani had shared a few military stories and Miguel had been in all of the stories he'd told her. And now, he'd brought up Miguel, again.

"I'm sorry. I knew your first wife left you and you'd never had children. I hadn't thought about a best friend. The only best friend I've ever had was Adrian." Tears glistened in Marion's eyes. "It looks like we have more in common." She sniffed, wiped at her eyes, and tried to smile.

"Yeah. But most of it is bad." He thought about how he'd hidden Marion to keep her safe when her drunken father came home and now having both lost a good friend.

"Come on. Let's get to work." He opened up the computer and found the file he'd asked Spruel to send to his private email. He could get into that account from this computer but not his work email.

"What do you have?" Marion refilled their cups with coffee and sat.

"My boss sent me all the information he's received on Pannell Financial Company. And I had my FBI friend send me what he had. Though he did leave out some of the crucial evidence they can't have bouncing around and getting into Pannell's hands."

Marion nodded. "Are we reading it together?"

"Get a large pad of paper and pens, while I read through here. Then I want you to read through and tell me what you did know and what you didn't."

While she was gone, Hawke skimmed the beginning of what appeared to be a very long document from Pierce. He figured the FBI Agent would have more information important to the death of Adrian. He also wondered if the man, Caleb, who had been rooming with

Adrian and seemed to know a lot about the relationship between Marion and his roommate, would be helpful to the investigation.

"All I could find was printer paper, but it wasn't with a printer?" Marion said it as a question.

Hawke shrugged. His friend might have a printer hidden somewhere. It sounded like this cabin was used for clandestine meetings and hideouts. For who or what groups, he didn't know and wasn't going to ask.

"I read through these. Tell me what you read and if you knew about it." Hawke slid the computer in front of Marion and pulled the paper and pen over in front of him.

After about five minutes of her reciting and Hawke taking notes, Marion pointed to the screen. "I've never heard of this person. Not that I know the names of all of the clients we do business with but with the amount and how it is being dispersed, there would have been a contract drawn up and I would have been the one to do it."

Hawke wrote down the name of the business. "Would this have been something Adrian would have worked on?"

"Possibly. He, being the senior in accounting, normally dealt with the larger investors." She sighed. "But we can't ask him." She sat up. "But if we could get his computer or his phone, I might be able to find it. A year after we started dating, we gave each other our passwords to get into our work computers and our phones. In case something happened to one of us…"

Hawke put a hand on her arm. "That was a smart thing to do. But I'm sure you were thinking more along the lines of sickness or accident, not death."

She nodded. "Yeah."

"I'll text the name of this company to Pierce and have him look them up. Keep reading." Hawke pulled his phone out of his pocket and sent the text. His phone buzzed. Bo.

"Hey, thanks for the use of your cabin," Hawke answered.

"No problem. I've got your files and some information. I'll be there in about thirty minutes. Just wanted to give you a head's up so you didn't jump me."

"Thanks for the warning." Hawke ended the call. "Bo's on his way over with the Montana State Police report and some information."

Marion nodded but didn't look up. She was finding something interesting in the files on his computer.

"What are you reading?" Hawke asked, refilling their cups with coffee.

"Adele went to college for Business Finance." Marion glanced up at him. "Why is she only an executive secretary when she could be making twice as much money as a financial consultant?"

"Good question to ask her." Hawke wrote down the woman's name and the question. While he liked digging up information and following a paper trail, he was getting antsy staying in one place when the murder had happened a couple of hours away. "After Bo gets here, I think I'll go for a drive over to Salmon Lake and see if I can learn anything new."

Marion's attention jerked away from the computer. "What if someone sees you and follows you back here?"

"They won't. I know how to cover my tracks." He smiled, but he hoped he didn't get seen and he could keep her whereabouts a secret until they caught the killer.

"What else do we need to write down?" he asked,

changing the subject.

"The only things I saw in this information, you already have written down." Marion shoved the computer forward to the middle of the table. "I'd like to call Alice, Adrian's sister."

Hawke studied her. "How well do you know her?"

"We've met once, and I've talked to her a couple of times when she's called Adrian."

"Will she believe you killed her brother in a fit of passion?" Hawke peered into his sister's eyes. "Because that will be the story she'll get from the police and Pannell."

Marion inhaled deep, and slowly let the air hiss out between her teeth. She'd never felt so humiliated and gutted. "I think she would know better, but...I'm not sure."

"Then it would be best to not contact her. She could get the police to track the call, not to mention your boss could already have her phone tapped since he suspected Adrian of catching on to his embezzlement."

Rubbing her face with her hands didn't scrub away the feeling she would never feel unsoiled again. How one moment of exaltation could be suddenly wrenched from her, and this? Running to stay alive and prove she didn't kill the man she loved.

Dog started growling.

Marion stood as Gabriel walked to the front window.

"It's Bo," Gabriel said, opening the front door. He didn't step out, he waited for the man, half a foot shorter and twice as wiry to step into the house. Then they clasped hands.

"Good to see you, Hawke. Wish it was for a fishing

trip but, I'm here to help with whatever you need." The man's dark eyes, crinkled at the edges as he greeted her brother.

Marion immediately liked him.

"I don't know how I can ever repay you," Gabriel turned, nodding toward Marion. "My sister, Marion Shumack."

She stepped forward and clasped hands with the man.

"We have to keep our sisters safe," Bo said, smiling. Again, his eyes crinkled, and she felt like they had been friends forever. Now she understood why Gabriel trusted the man.

Bo handed the packet in his left hand to Gabriel. "I don't know what that says, but what I've been hearing from sources, they are still saying it was passion gone too far that killed the victim." Bo looked her up and down. "I don't need the details, but I have someone out in my pickup who can draw what the man looks like while you describe him."

Marion glanced at Gabriel. He nodded. She was relieved he wanted this detail. "I'm more than willing to have someone come up with a rendering of the man who killed my fiancé."

"I hoped you'd say that." Bo pulled out his phone and sent a text. "Let's take a look at the forensics."

The two men sat at the table as someone knocked on the door.

"Come in!" shouted Bo.

The door opened only far enough for a slender young woman to slip through. She smiled timidly.

"This is my niece, Sunny. She's been proving very good at doing renderings from descriptions people tell her," Bo said by way of an introduction.

"Hello, Sunny. I'm Marion. Where would you like to do this?" Marion motioned to the living room.

"I'd prefer outside, but Uncle said it was best to stay inside." Sunny gave her an apologetic smile. The young woman's hair was pulled back in a long braid. She had a straight slender nose with large round glasses perched on it.

"Then let's sit on the couch, unless you prefer me to be facing you?" Marion didn't know how this worked but she wouldn't want someone looking on while she wrote up a contract.

"I need you beside me to make sure I get things right. The couch will work." Sunny sat and pulled a pad and pencil out of the bag she'd had slung over her shoulder.

Hawke closed his ears to the two women as he pulled the forensic report out of the envelope. He said in a low voice, "A friend in the FBI says Pannell is under investigation."

Bo nodded. "That's what I heard, too. Seems to me he might have more reason to quiet the victim than your sister."

Hawke nodded. His eyes landed on the report of what was found at the scene. This time he whispered. "Marion said her bra and panties were left behind. Nowhere in this report does it say there were any panties found." He peered into Bo's eyes. "The guy who killed Adrian must have taken them."

"Yeah, only champagne, two plastic cups, and the victim's clothing." Bo tapped the list of items found at the scene of the crime. "And the bra around the victim's neck."

"And the police didn't take their computers or phones. They did note, as I also saw, that there were empty computer bags in both their rooms." Hawke leaned back. "That means Pannell had their laptops and cells retrieved before the police arrived. What was he afraid the police would find on those devices?"

"Did Marion and the vic talk about what he'd found in emails or texts?" Bo asked.

"I don't think so." Hawke drew his gaze from the report and asked, "Marion, did you and Adrian talk about what he'd found in any emails or text messages?"

She glanced up. "No. We only talked about that in person. Why?"

"We're just trying to figure out why Pannell would take away your phones and laptops before the police arrived." Hawke returned his attention to the reports. He studied the photos of the crime scene. Marion had said the man had flung Adrian's body to the side when he spotted her. The photos gave the appearance as if he had been laid out to look in the throes of sex. Flat on his back in the middle of a blanket. There was a green canvas backpack next to the blanket. The neck of the bottle of champagne sticking out.

He didn't want Marion to see the body but he wanted to know how much of the scene was staged. They might be able to shed some light on how long the person may have watched them before committing the homicide.

"Do you have some painter's or masking tape here?" Hawke asked.

"Yeah." Bo stood and walked over to a drawer. He brought back a roll of blue painter's tape.

Hawke ripped off pieces, covering the body in the middle of the blanket. When he was done, he took a deep breath and said, "Marion, can you come over here for a moment? I'd like you to tell me how much of this photo is set up as you remember it."

Marion rose from the couch and slowly crossed to the table. Her worried eyes and sallow complexion told him she expected to see Adrian's body. She glanced at the photo then away, before her gaze traveled back to the image. Tears glistened in her eyes as she said, "Thank you for covering him up."

"Is this how things looked when Adrian proposed to you?" He wanted to keep the attention on the good that happened that night, not the bad.

"Yes. The backpack was there with the champagne and the glasses. But…" She put her hand on a tree. "We weren't this close to the shore. We didn't want to be seen. Adrian had burrowed out a space in some bushes that was just large enough for the blanket. That's where we were before…" Her fingers drifted over the painter's tape.

"The killer must have followed one of you out to the island, waited until Adrian was alone, and after killing him went after you. When you got away, he moved the body out where it would be easily found so the police would be after you quicker." Hawke looked at his friend. "I think we need to go fishing on Salmon Lake."

Chapter Eleven

Hawke was happy with the rendering Bo's niece had made of the man Marion said killed Adrian. He'd taken a photo of it and sent it to both Pierce and Lt. Gernot. With the subject line- This is the killer.

With one of Bo's relatives and Dog at the cabin with Marion, Hawke and his friend were headed to Salmon Lake with Bo's boat. He wanted to have a look at the island in the daylight. They needed to find the real crime scene and see what forensics missed.

On the drive to the lake, he and Bo caught up on life since they'd last gone fishing.

"So, you now have a woman in your life. It's about time. My Ava said you would make a good husband."

Hawke put up his hand. "I'm not marrying Dani. We both don't want to go that far. We are just enjoying the other's company and seeing where it goes. Since we're both too old to have children, it seems pointless to be legally bound."

Bo nodded. "That makes sense. That way if you do want to leave there are few things tying you together."

Hawke thought of the house they'd recently purchased together. That would have to be decided over, but that was the only thing. He liked the idea he could walk away without any hassles should he choose. Dani felt the same. They were both independent people and liked the idea of not being tied to someone.

Bo pulled into the Salmon Lake Campground and backed his boat down the landing. In fifteen minutes, they had their gear loaded and the boat in the water.

"Let's not be obvious we're headed to the island," Hawke said, noticing a man on the jut of land Will Rule had called Christmas Stocking Island, watching them through binoculars. They found a good spot to try to fish and put their poles in. After about forty-five minutes, they pulled up their lines and headed to the west side of the island where the body was found. Once they were out of sight of the resort and Christmas Stocking Island, Hawke motioned for Bo to pull up to the small island.

They disembarked.

"Lead the way," Bo said.

"According to Marion, she and Adrian were more on this side of the island than where I found the deputy watching the crime scene. Let's spread out and look for a hiding spot in some bushes." Hawke stayed within thirty feet of the shoreline and Bo was about twenty feet.

He walked no more than forty feet and he found the spot. One quick scan of the area and he knew this was it. He gave a sharp whistle.

Bo arrived with the backpack they'd put together to do a full grid search of the crime scene. After stretching string in foot increments to make a grid, Hawke began searching each square while Bo photographed and put the evidence Hawke found in bags.

"You do know without an official law enforcement person here, this isn't really evidence," Bo said, marking an evidence bag holding a piece of cloth, Hawke was sure came from the blanket.

"I'll hand it over to Lt. Gernot and explain what we learned."

"She'll tell you, you should have let forensics handle it," Bo countered.

"You and I both know they wouldn't have sent anyone back out here. If she's not interested, I'll see if the FBI will run the evidence." Hawke wasn't going to hand this over to anyone until he had their full attention and they took it seriously.

"I found the missing panties." Hawke pointed to a pair of black, bikini-style panties made from fabric that was slick and shiny.

"That should get their attention. There would be no other reason for the underwear to end up over here if they hadn't even been in this area." Bo took a photo of the underwear where it lay shoved under a small bush.

Hawke picked it up and dropped the clothing into the large evidence bag Bo held. It took them three hours to collect everything in their grid. Some of what they picked up probably had nothing to do with the crime, but he was being thorough. It was his sister's life he was saving.

They dropped their lines in the water and slowly trawled back to the boat landing. They managed to catch enough fish for a nice barbecue when they returned to the cabin.

Hawke called Lt. Gernot from the burner phone as

Bo drove them back.

"Lieutenant Gernot," she answered.

"It's Hawke. I found the real crime scene on that island today."

"What do you mean the real crime scene?" she asked, her voice going up an octave.

"When I showed the crime scene photos to my sister, she said that wasn't where they were when the man strangled the victim. A friend and I went out to the island today and I found the real spot. The scene that forensics photographed and worked was staged."

"How do I know you aren't just saying this to get us off your sister?" Gernot asked.

"We took photos of our evidence collecting and I have all the items dated, tagged, and sealed. I can drop them off at the nearest State Police station if you like. But I won't do it unless I have your word you will take the evidence seriously." He waited.

"Send me the photos. I want to make sure you aren't just trying to draw suspicion elsewhere."

"Did you get the photo of the drawing of the man Marion saw kill the victim?" Hawke asked.

"Yes. Again, how do I know you both aren't just trying to mess with evidence?" She said it as if she wasn't on their side.

"Fine. I'll send it to the FBI." He hung up on the lieutenant and called Pierce.

"Special Agent Pierce," he answered.

"Pierce, it's Hawke. Did you get a hit on the photo I sent you?"

"We did. He's a mercenary for hire. Name of Philip Longo. He was last seen in Texas."

Hawke smiled. "Texas. The same state where

Pannell Financial resides."

"Yes. The agency has had someone following his movements for the last couple of months. I won't have anything for you for a few days." Pierce sounded disappointed.

"At least you believe Marion." He went on to tell the Special Agent about what Marion had said about the crime scene and evidence he and Bo retrieved.

"Can you drop it off at the Missoula Field Office? I'll have someone there take it to the nearest forensic lab."

"Thanks. Lt. Gernot didn't believe me when I said we had evidence from the real crime scene." Hawke was glad the agent was willing to help.

"She doesn't know you. I do. I also know that this wasn't a passion killing. We received a letter in the mail today from the victim. It seems he knew he was being watched by Pannell. He sent us a letter stating Drew Pannell was embezzling and that he had proof. We just have to find the proof. Ask your sister if she has any ideas where Ulrick would have hidden it."

"She said she didn't know, but I'll ask again. And thanks." Hawke ended the call.

"Will the Feds take the evidence?" Bo asked.

"Yes. He said to drop it off at the Missoula Field Office and they'd get it to a lab." Hawke scratched his head.

"Missoula is on our way back," Bo said, glancing over. "What's bothering you?"

"I could tell by the questions Pierce asked that he thinks Marion knows more." He shook his head. "I know I haven't been around her for several decades but I could always tell when my sister was lying. She hasn't got a clue about hidden evidence." He went on to tell Bo everything that Pierce had said.

"She may not think she knows, but I bet if you give her time to think about it, she might figure out where her friend would hide something important."

Hawke hoped that was true. They would need that evidence to clear Marion.

Marion and Dog paced across the small open area of the cabin. She stopped and stared out the window, while patting the animal's head. She knew Gabriel had left Dog with her to help her feel safe. And she did. But she also felt confined. She hadn't killed Adrian but she was the prisoner until they proved otherwise. Fresh air would make her feel less caged. She wanted to sit out on the deck or go for a walk, but the woman Bo had left to sit with her, would have nothing of it. The middle-aged woman had sat on the couch, knitting, ever since she'd arrived. They said little. Marion had asked if the woman wanted to play cards. Tilly only shook her head and continued knitting.

Giving up on the idea of getting out in the fresh air, Marion and Dog went to her bedroom. She opened the window and sat on the bed. Dog lay down at her feet. Her mind drifted to the memories she had of Adrian. If only he'd told her more about what he'd found or even taken it to the police as soon as he'd discovered it, he might still be alive. And they could have planned their wedding and long marriage.

She sighed and swiped at the tear trickling down her cheek. Men! They always have to try and fix things. He should have let someone else fix it once he'd found the discrepancy.

While she had told Gabriel she wanted to go stay with their mom when this was over, she also wanted her belongings from her apartment. There were mementos there she didn't want anyone else to get their hands on.

Dog sat up. His ears flicked back and forth moments before she heard the sound of an engine. Peeking out the window she recognized Bo's pickup and boat. Checking the mirror to make sure there weren't any traces of her tears, she exited the bedroom followed by Dog. They walked into the living room as Gabriel and Bo entered.

Tilly shoved her needles and yarn in the bag she'd brought with her and stood. Without a word, she marched to the open door and left.

"She is a woman of few words," Marion said.

Gabriel studied her while Bo grinned and closed the door.

"Did you find anything?" she asked, not letting her hopes get too elated.

"We found the spot where you and Adrian met," Gabriel said. "The State Police didn't want anything to do with the evidence since it hadn't been collected by their forensic team, but the Feds were interested. We dropped it off in Missoula."

For the first time in nearly a week, Marion felt a bit of the doom that had filled her lift. "Do you think there will be anything they can use against the man who killed Adrian?"

Gabriel shrugged. "Won't know until they look at it." He continued into the kitchen. "Want something to drink?" His head disappeared into the fridge.

Bo took a seat at the table. "Anything cold."

Marion glanced from one man to the other. They weren't telling her something. "What's up? What else did you discover out there?" She sat at the table, watching her brother.

He turned from the fridge with three cans of soda pop in his hands. He nudged the refrigerator door closed with his shoulder and placed the drinks on the table.

Bo grabbed one and Gabriel waited for her to choose a drink before he took the last one.

They all grasped the rings and pulled. Three separate clicks pierced the quiet followed by the fizzing as the carbonation escaped the cans.

"We didn't discover anything else at the island. But I talked to Special Agent Pierce on the way back and he said they'd received a letter from Adrian telling them about Drew Pannell."

Her heart beat rapidly as elation bubbled in her like the carbonation in the pop. "Then they have the proof Drew killed Adrian!"

He shook his head, and she deflated against the chair back.

"He sent a letter saying he had evidence. But he didn't send it with the letter." Gabriel set his drink down and leaned toward her. "Can you think of anywhere he might have hidden it?"

Marion searched her brother's face. He'd grown into an old man in the time between their last meeting. But it was a face of strong character, earnestness, and empathy. All traits that had drawn her to Adrian.

"At the moment, I can't think of a single place, but let me think about it."

Gabriel nodded.

Chapter Twelve

Saturday morning, Hawke felt they needed to do something more than sit around
waiting for replies from emails and texts. If Adrian had the evidence against Pannell, it would be at his home or possibly at Marion's. That was where they needed to be. And he doubted the person looking for Marion would think she would go back to Dallas.

The quickest way was by airplane. Hawke pondered the idea while sitting out by the lake. He wondered if Dani could fly them from Missoula to Dallas. They'd only be gone for a day and no one would know where they went.

He couldn't call Dani, he'd have to contact her with a radio. He texted Bo. *Where can I find a radio to use to call someone in the Wallowa Mountains?*

I can bring one over in an hour.

Hawke glanced at his watch. That would be eight. If they could make contact with Dani before nine there was a good chance they could fly to Dallas today. *Roger.*

Marion walked out of the cabin as Hawke rose. He shooed her back into the building and set to work making breakfast.

"What has you moving like a man on a mission?" she asked. "Did you learn something new?"

"Nothing new. If all goes well, we'll be in Dallas later today and check out your apartment, as well as Adrian's."

Marion stopped pouring coffee and stared at him. "We're going to Dallas? Isn't that risky? I'm sure with Pannell's money he has someone at the airport letting him know if I buy a ticket."

Hawke grinned. "We're going by private plane."

"I don't want you spending money on me. I'll pay for half of the cost. I've been saving my money." She finished filling her cup and faced him.

"All we have to do is pay for the fuel."

"Another one of your friends?" she asked.

"Yeah. A good friend. If she can do it. I'm waiting for Bo to bring over a radio so I can contact her."

He watched his sister as she spun things around in her head. He wasn't going to help her. Mom should have told her that Dani was a pilot. And he'd mentioned she was at Charlie's Lodge. Or he thought he had.

"Is this the mysterious Dani?" Marion asked.

"Yes. If I can contact her, and if she isn't already flying clients, I'm pretty sure she'll help us." He finished mixing the pancakes and started pouring the batter onto the hot griddle.

"It will be nice to have some of my own clothes." She was quiet for several minutes. "Do you think I'll have time to box some things up and have them sent to

Mom?"

"Best to box up only what we can carry in the plane. Dani can store them at the lodge until no one is looking for you."

Marion nodded.

He spotted a glint of a tear in her eye. "I'm sure we can manage to bring back a large suitcase of your clothes or belongings you can have here."

She gave him a weak smile. "Would it be against the law for me to snag Adrian's favorite sweater?"

"I don't think his sweater will have anything to do with the case."

As he'd hoped, Dani said she could be at Missoula airport by eleven and after fueling and scheduling a flight plan, they could be out of there by eleven-thirty and into Dallas by four.

"Pack an overnight bag in case we end up spending the night," Hawke told Marion.

Bo offered to take them to the airport and pick them up when they came back. "It's better to not leave your vehicle there. Someone might get wind you flew somewhere and check it out."

Hawke agreed with him.

The three of them, plus Dog, loaded up into Bo's truck and he drove them to the Missoula airport. He knew where to let them off to get into the small aircraft hangars. Hawke told Dog to stay with Bo. Then he and Marion grabbed their bags and walked toward the tarmac.

Hawke spotted Dani's plane as he and Marion stepped out from between two hangars. They walked over to the plane and he heard Dani talking to someone.

"So, you think the best place to land is Arlington Municipal Airport?" she asked.

"Yes, ma'am. That would keep you out of the air traffic around the international airport and they could keep your plane overnight if you ended up staying."

Hawke rounded the tip of the plane as a man removed the fuel nozzle from the plane's wing and tightened the cap.

"Where do I hand in my flight plan?" Dani asked, her gaze landing on Hawke.

"When you get it written up, I'll be over there in hangar one." The man dragged the fuel hose back to the tank. Dani unclipped the ground wire allowing it to retract into the compartment by the fuel tank.

"Thank you. I'll be in with the flight plan and payment for the fuel in five minutes."

Hawke held out his credit card as Dani walked back toward the Cessna. "Use this to pay for the fuel," he said, by way of saying hello.

She smiled and took the card. "I'm glad you're footing the bill for this. My card is only for flights in and out of the lodge."

Hawke knew she was a stickler for keeping her records straight when it came to the lodge expenses.

"I'll pay for the fill-up when we come back," Marion said.

Hawke shifted to let the two women meet. "Dani Singer, this is my sister, Marion Shumack. Marion, Dani."

The two shook hands.

"Pleased to meet you. I didn't think Hawke would ever settle down after his first marriage didn't last," Marion said.

Hawke didn't think it was a slight, but Dani must have. He saw her cheeks deepen in color and her eyes narrow.

"He wasn't at fault for what happened. He's lucky to be out of a marriage with a woman who couldn't see his duty came first." Dani stared at Marion.

Marion put up her hands. "Sorry! I just meant once burned and all that."

"Why don't you go write up your flight plan and pay for the fuel? We'll get settled in the plane," Hawke said, spinning Dani toward Hangar 1.

When Dani was out of earshot, Marion turned to Hawke. "I didn't mean anything against you."

"I know. Dani has high regard for duty. She was a career pilot with the Air Force. She'd still be there if she could have gone farther up the ladder and still be in a plane all the time." He opened the door and pulled the seat forward. "Get in. Take the seat behind the pilot. We'll put our backpacks in the other seat."

There were two more seats lower to the floor behind the middle row. This was an older Cessna but Dani kept it in excellent shape. Hawke enjoyed flying in smaller planes with people he liked over the large commercial planes where you couldn't wipe your nose without poking the stranger next to you with an elbow.

They were settled in when Dani returned. She did a check of the aircraft, then climbed in, put her headphones on, and began the ritual of turning the engines on and talking to the air traffic control.

Once they were in the air and cruising, she pulled one headphone off her ear and turned her head, peering behind her at Marion. "Do you know where the Arlington Municipal Airport is from Dallas?"

"Yes. I've flown out of there a few times when I had to meet clients at their offices." Marion shouted over the sound of the airplane engine.

"Good. That's where we're landing. I learned it is easier to get in and out of because there is less commercial traffic than Dallas/Fort Worth International." She put her headphone back on after giving Hawke a smile.

He glanced back at his sister. Her gaze was on the clouds outside the airplane. But he could tell her mind was elsewhere. Marion didn't have any of her belongings. How would she get into her apartment? Would there be someone there waiting for her? He'd wrestled with all of these questions since deciding they needed to go to Dallas. And how would she get them into Adrian's apartment? These were questions he'd have to ask when they were back on the ground.

At the airport, Hawke rented a car, but he let Marion drive. She knew the area and wouldn't have to ask for directions. He had wanted Dani to stay with her plane but she'd insisted on tagging along.

"Where are we going first?" Marion asked.

"Do you have a way to get into Adrian's place?" Hawke asked, studying his sister. She was a competent driver on the busy highway.

"I can see if his neighbor is home. He has an extra key for emergencies. I have one, but it's wherever my purse and keys have ended up." Her voice trailed off.

"Let's go to Adrian's first." Hawke settled back in the passenger seat. He was glad Dani hadn't asked any questions so far. She sat in the backseat peering out the window.

She piped up. "How will you be able to get into your apartment if you don't have the keys?"

Marion glanced in the rearview mirror at her brother's significant other. The only words out of Dani's mouth had been derogatory. It made her wonder what Gabriel saw in the woman. "I have an extra key hidden outside. Only Adrian knew about it. I've never had to use it, but wanted to make sure if my purse was lost or stolen I could still get in my place."

"Do you live in a bad neighborhood?" Dani asked.

"No. I live in an apartment not far from downtown. But there have been some incidents in the areas where I like to commune with nature that has had purse snatchings."

Once she entered Dallas proper, she went into offensive driving mode. It felt like every year there were twice as many cars on the road as the year before. And half of them didn't know how to drive. An hour after landing at the airport, Marion drove through the gates of the golf course community where Adrian lived. She'd loved the three-bedroom townhouse she was going to move into when they married. She swallowed the lump clawing its way up her throat. Now wasn't the time to let her grief overcome her. She'd wait until the person who killed Adrian was caught.

"Nice place," Gabriel said.

"He bought it five years ago after saving up." She sighed, pulling up to the garage door and parking. "I love this house. The deck overlooks one of the greens and a water feature." She stared at the house across the street. "I'll go see if his neighbor is home."

"We'll have a look around," Gabriel said, exiting the car and opening the back car door for Dani.

"Just don't try the doors or the windows. There is an alarm system." Marion walked across the street and rang the doorbell. Adrian had told her this neighbor, Leo, worked from home.

Just as she decided no one was home, the door opened. A short, stocky man with thick-lensed glasses wearing sweats and flip-flops answered the door.

"I don't buy anything from door-to-door salespeople and I don't go to any church." He moved to close the door.

"Leo, I'm Adrian's girlfriend, Marion. He might have mentioned me?" she said before the door shut her out.

The motion of the door closing stopped.

"You're Adrian's girlfriend? I thought the two of you were away this week. Adrian told me to keep a lookout on his place." The man stood on his toes to look over her shoulder.

"Yes, we were away together. And he was called to his sister's and asked me to stop by and check on the plants inside and grab him some clothes. But he forgot to give me a key before he left. I wondered if I could borrow his emergency key to get in and get the things he needs?" She hated making things up but she didn't want this man to know Adrian was dead. He would have lots of questions and she'd only have to tell more lies.

"Okay, sure. Let me get it." He disappeared through the entryway and into a room.

Marion glanced over her shoulder. She didn't see Hawke or Dani anywhere. She had the odd thought they were somewhere making out. They'd barely said anything to one another since they met Dani at the plane. It was an odd relationship if all they did was grunt and exchange a few words. But who was she to deny her brother a chance at happiness even if it was with a woman, she had yet to make a decision one way or the other whether she liked.

"Here you go. Just drop it back by when you leave." Leo held out a key.

"Thank you. I will." Marion grasped the key and spun around.

"What's wrong with Alice?"

Chapter Thirteen

Marion stopped. She searched her memory before she turned around. What could Adrian have said about his sister that would make sense to the neighbor who seemed to know a lot about Adrian's life? Slowly, she faced the man. "I'm not sure what was happening. Adrian said he needed to help his sister and asked me to come here and get his things. I'll find out the circumstances when I meet him later tonight."

She spun back around and hoofed it up to Adrian's front door. After using the key to gain entry, she quickly pressed the numbers to shut off the alarm. Then she walked through to the main area of the house and spotted Dani and Gabriel sitting at a table on Adrian's patio. They were deep in conversation.

Marion walked over to the patio door, unlocked it, and opened it to the 90° weather. She'd enjoyed the mid-seventies in Montana. She had never liked the heat here. One of several reasons she would be looking for work elsewhere.

"Are you enjoying the patio?" she asked, as the two stood and walked to the door.

"It is pleasant in the shade but you'd never catch me playing golf in this weather," Dani said, entering the house first.

Gabriel stepped in right behind her. "Ditto. What did the neighbor say?"

"He was a bit skeptical. I told him Adrian was called away to help his sister. I hope he believed me." She had never been a good liar. That was why she'd decided to do corporate law rather than criminal. She could have never worked for a guilty person.

"Where do you think Adrian would hide something he knew was valuable?" Hawke decided he needed to keep Marion focused on why they were here. Not give her time to conjure up the memories she had made with Adrian in this house. Well, he'd thought that but Dani had voiced it as they sat talking on the patio.

"He has a lockbox in the back of his closet. You know, one of those that is supposed to survive a fire." Marion headed out of the main room and across a tile floor to a small hallway.

"Is there a home office?" Dani asked.

"This door," Marion opened a door on the right of the hallway.

"I'll look in here," Dani stepped inside.

Marion didn't take a step. "Does she know what she's doing?"

Hawke grinned. "Yes. She's helped on a few cases with me. And we know anything that he has hidden could be what we're looking for." He motioned for her to continue to the bedroom.

Stepping into the room, his first impression was neat and tidy. But then a man who made his living adding up numbers would probably have a mind that needed order.

Marion walked across to a door and opened a large walk-in closet. She moved shelving that was on some sort of rollers and revealed a two-foot by two-foot black safe.

Hawke knelt in front of the safe. Before he even touched it, he knew they weren't the first to take a look. "It's not latched shut."

"He always has it locked. It has the deed to this house, his birth certificate, car title, and some cash. Also a pair of his mom's diamond earrings. Before she died, she gave him the earrings and Alice the necklace. He was going to give the earrings to me on our wedding day." Marion started moving about the closet.

"What are you doing?" Hawke pulled on a latex glove and opened the safe.

"I want to see if anything else was taken."

"You know his wardrobe that well?" Hawke was impressed that the two, who seemed to have been a couple already, hadn't married sooner.

"I know the expensive items. He was proud of an expensive suit he bought after he'd received a raise for helping merge two companies. And he had an expensive pair of cuff links made after his latest raise. He called them mementos of his rise up the ladder." A sigh filled the room. "They're both here."

"Everything seems to be in the safe, including the earrings." Hawke glanced up at Marion. "Someone was here looking but they didn't leave any sign other than forgetting to lock the safe." Hawke closed the door, making sure it clicked. "Either they found what they were looking for in there or they didn't and checked the whole house."

"But how did they get in? And shut off the security system?" Marion's hands were on her hips and her eyes were blazing with anger.

"I would suspect, they had Adrian's key. As for the security system…is it the same as the financial company uses? If so, someone could have called and asked for the information saying they were calling for Adrian." Hawke shrugged. "Is there anywhere else here that he might have hidden something?"

"We could check all the pockets in his suits and pants." She glanced at the six pairs of shoes. "In his shoes?"

"Let's start looking." Hawke handed Marion a latex glove and they started on opposite ends of the closet and shoved their hands into every pocket.

By the time they finished, Dani walked into the closet. "Any luck in here?"

"No. You?" Hawke asked.

She shook her head. "I didn't find anything hidden anywhere but I did notice things weren't all in their places. Almost like someone else had gone through the files and books."

"Yeah, we found the safe open. I think someone was here before us." Hawke nodded to Marion. "Grab that sweater you wanted and let's go check out your place."

"I need to put it in something. If the neighbor is watching he's going to expect me to take out more than a sweater." She grabbed a duffle bag and put a sweater in it. "Okay."

"We'll go out the back and walk down a block. You can pick us up there." Hawke motioned for Dani to follow him. They exited out the patio door.

"Do you think whoever went through this house went through your sister's?" Dani asked.

"We're not going to know until we get there." Hawke kept walking. Whoever they were dealing with was one step ahead of them.

Marion parked the car in the underground parking for her apartment building. "We need to walk around to the back of the building. My apartment is on the ground floor, and I have a key hidden on my patio."

Hawke followed his sister, with Dani by his side, out of the parking garage and into the bright sunshine. They walked down the sidewalk and up an alley on the side of the three-story building. Tenants on the second and third floors had balconies facing a small park in the middle of what looked like four apartment buildings.

At the second yard, Marion opened the gate and walked into a small area without grass, but with lots of flowers and multi-colored pathways. She walked over to a gnome and tipped him, revealing a key underneath.

She picked up the key, grinned at Hawke, and walked to her patio door. A gasp and curse had Hawke stepping around her to peer through the glass door.

The inside of the house looked as if a tornado had swept through.

"Was your house key in the belongings you left at the resort?" Hawke asked, taking the key from her shaking hand and opening the door.

"Yeah. Do you think they came over here and tore my place up looking for the proof Adrian had?" Marion stepped over the threshold. "I need to call the police but if I do, they'll arrest me." Her eyes peered into his.

117

"What do I do?"

"You need to call Adrian's sister and make sure they are safe. Whoever is looking for Adrian's proof may have already been to their house."

"But why tear my house up and leave Adrian's looking untouched?" The question almost came out as a wail.

"Because he is a murder victim and the police will go to his place, if they haven't already, and the real killer didn't want them to suspect anyone other than you of killing Adrian. While you, as a fugitive, wouldn't call the police to report this."

"But wouldn't the cops have come here looking for her or information about where she might be hiding?" Dani asked.

"I would guess they came here as soon as Pannell informed them you were a fleeing murderer. Then the person searching for the evidence came in afterward and tossed the place." Hawke waved a hand. "Is there something or a place that Adrian looked at or messed with a lot when he was here? Something that attracted his attention?"

They were all inside, shoving things aside with their feet to walk around.

"He liked the painting I purchased from an Indigenous artist. It's in the bedroom." They followed Marion through the small living room and down the hall. She opened a door on the right and tears trickled down her cheeks.

Hawke pulled her out of the room and stepped in. The mattress had been sliced open. Clothing, pillows, and knickknacks littered the floor along with stuffing. The large painting of an Indian girl's face, a horse, and the sun had been slashed.

This was more than looking for something, this was a violent act against Marion.

"Do you have a neighbor you could trust to call this in and not say you were here?" Hawke wanted this on record for when they caught the real killer. He wanted his sister compensated for her loss.

"I could ask Mrs. Walker, next door. But it would be better if you asked, as my brother. She knows I'm at a retreat. Maybe you could say you came to see me and saw the mess through the door." Marion found a small suitcase and started shoving clothing in it. "I doubt there is anything else—" She peered around the room frantically. "I need the photo of Mom and there should be one of Adrian."

Dani began digging through the clothing. She came up with a photo of a handsome man. "Is this Adrian?"

"Yes!" Marion hugged it to her chest before placing it in the suitcase. "There should be one of Mom about the same size. She sent it to me a few years ago for Christmas."

They went through the room three times and couldn't find the photo.

Hawke had a bad feeling. The killer might have taken the photo to know what Marion's mom looked like. Which meant he planned to get to her.

"Do you have the clothing you want? I don't think we're going to find Mom's photo."

Both women looked at him. He could see when they both comprehended what he wasn't saying.

"You two go to the car and call Mom. Tell her to go visit someone off the reservation. She can't tell anyone where she is going but us. And she's to stay there until we tell her otherwise. Also, see if anyone has been asking about either of us. I'm going to tell your neighbor to call the police."

Hawke waited until the two were out of sight before he walked over and knocked on the patio door of Marion's neighbor.

A woman in her sixties, with dark gray hair cut short and wearing green pants that weren't shorts but didn't go to the woman's ankles, and a bold-colored flowered shirt, stood on the other side of the plate glass staring at him.

"Hi, I'm Marion's brother," he said loudly through the glass as he pointed to Marion's yard.

The woman studied him for a bit, then opened the door two inches. "What did you say?"

"I'm Marion's brother. I stopped by to talk to her but she's not home and it looks—"

"That's because she's at a retreat with her company. If you're her brother, why didn't you know that?" The woman nailed him with a glare.

"I thought she was back. But what I'm saying is you need to call the police."

The woman's large black eyebrows rose in the middle. "Call the police? What for?"

"I'll show you." Hawke led the woman out of her yard and into Marion's. He pointed at the patio door.

The woman walked up, gasped, and held her hand to her chest. "My heavens, when did this happen?"

Hawke shrugged when the woman faced him. "I have to take off, could you call it in for me and Marion? I'll call her and let her know the police will be contacting her." He started to walk away and asked, "Do you have a key to let the police in?"

"She keeps it under the gnome." The neighbor hurried to her apartment as Hawke checked to make sure Marion had put her key back.

Chapter Fourteen

When Hawke dropped into the passenger seat of the rental car, he knew something was wrong. "Did you get hold of Mom?"

"Yes. She said the tribal police had come around to see if you were there, but didn't say anything about me. She'll be with Aunt Betty." Marion's fingers gripped the steering wheel so tight her knuckles were white.

"What else?" he asked.

"Adrian's sister isn't answering her cell or house phone," Dani said.

"Do you know where she lives?" Hawke asked, studying his sister.

"Yes."

"Then let's do a drive-by and see if there are any police. If it looks quiet, we'll see if we can get in the house." Hawke buckled his seat belt and sat back as Marion put the car in gear and left the parking garage.

It was close to forty-five minutes before Marion

turned a corner and said, "It's the third house on the left."

Hawke spotted the law enforcement vehicle. "Just drive by naturally. There's a police car sitting in front of the house."

"The lights are on," Dani said. "I saw some through a side window."

"That would be one of the girls' bedrooms," Marion said.

"How many kids does Alice have?" Hawke asked. He wanted to know the number of people someone could use to coerce information out of Adrian's sister.

"She has two girls by her first marriage and a baby boy by her second husband. He's gone a lot on oil rigs." Marion pulled over and parked on the next block. "Now what do we do?"

"Do you know which neighbor would be the nosiest?" Hawke asked.

Marion stared at him for several seconds. "Alice only ever talks about Grace. I think she's the neighbor to her left. Adrian seemed to know her as well. I think she went to school with them."

Hawke spun in his seat and peered into Dani's face. "Just in case the person sitting on the house has photos of Marion and me, you'll have to go see what you can find out from the neighbor, Grace."

Dani nodded. "Do you want me to try Alice's house too?"

"See what you find out from the neighbor and if she says they are home, see if you can get someone to answer the door so we know if they are alone or not." Hawke didn't like putting Dani in the crosshairs of either the police or the person looking for evidence against them, but he also couldn't take the chance the cop sitting in the car hadn't been shown photos of him and Marion.

"I'll be careful." Dani patted his shoulder and slipped out of the car. She stayed on the opposite side of the street until she was at the end of the next block, then crossed and walked back toward them.

"What do we do while Dani is in danger?" Marion asked in a tone Hawke had heard before.
She wasn't happy with him sending Dani to do his work.

"I'll check my messages." He pulled out his phone. "See. I've missed a call from Sergeant Spruel and Special Agent Pierce." He frowned.

"What's wrong?" Marion leaned toward him.

"Bo said they have officially stated you killed Adrian and there is a reward for information for anyone who has seen you." He sighed. "That's not good."

"Do you think the person at the Missoula airport will talk to the police?" Marion asked.

"The guy fueling up the plane?" Hawke thought about when they walked up to Dani. "He didn't really see you. I was between you and him and the front of the plane was between us and him and Dani."

But he wondered if they might not need to find somewhere else to land when they returned. He texted Bo from the burner phone. *Do you have an alternate landing strip to return on?*

No sooner had he sent the message than coordinates appeared on his phone.

Thanks.

Dani would know what the coordinates meant.

He glanced over his shoulder. She was still standing on the porch talking to the neighbor. That must be Grace.

"When we get back to Montana, you'll have to keep a low profile. I'll have Bo take us someplace more isolated than the cabin." But isolation also meant he would be farther from information.

"How can we find who killed Adrian if I'm tucked away somewhere?" Marion asked.

"We'll find a way. Right now, I'm worried about Adrian's sister." His eyes wandered to the car where the policeman sat and back to the sister's door. "How do you get your mail?"

Marion stared at him. "What?"

"Mail. How do you get it? A mailbox at your apartment building or do you pick it up?" Hawke thought maybe Adrian might have sent the information in the mail.

"I asked the post office to hold my mail while I was gone. I don't get a lot but if two magazines are put in my box at the apartment building there isn't room for anything else."

"We need to go to the post office tomorrow for you to collect your mail." It meant they'd be spending the night.

"We can't," Marion said, peering at him.

"No one at the post office will know you are a fugitive. The wanted posters don't get out that fast," Hawke said.

She shook her head. "We can't because it will be Sunday. This is Saturday night."

He'd lost track of the days since he'd been awakened by his sister's mysterious call. "You'll have to see if you can forward it then."

He called Spruel to learn what Bo had already told him.

"You need to take your sister to the authorities before the citizens of Montana decide they'd like the reward."

He knew his boss meant well and had put his job on the line helping Hawke this far. "We'll keep digging. If it's a problem for you, I'll stop contacting you."

"Not a problem, just goes against ethics. I'd rather be kept in the loop than find out you aren't coming to work because you've been arrested."

"Thank you for your help so far. I'll let you know when I'll be back to work." Hawke ended the call. There was no sense in getting Spruel in trouble because of his family problems.

Next, he called Pierce.

"Special Agent Pierce."

"It's Hawke. Anything new?"

"Not really. I did hear that your sister's place was tossed. A neighbor called it in." His voice held a hint of a question.

"Your ears only, we're in Dallas. We went to Adrian's place. Someone had already been there. Someone who had the alarm code and knew how to open the safe."

Pierce started to say something and Hawke cut him off. "We didn't touch anything and didn't find anything. We also went to Marion's. There they had maliciously destroyed things."

"That doesn't sound good. Whoever is looking for the information is out to get her. Which means they will do all they can to keep law enforcement on her." Pierce's tone was angry.

"Yeah." Hawke glanced at his sister. She was listening intently.

"We're trying to determine if Adrian's sister has been approached by Pannell or someone else asking if

Adrian gave her anything." Hawke watched Dani leave the neighbor's porch and walk over to Alice's house.

"We've had her under surveillance, as well as the local police," Pierce said.

"I spotted the local, where is your person?" Hawke asked.

"Inside."

"Then you know no one has tried to take one of her kids or harassed her?"

"Yeah. As soon as we received the letter from Adrian, an operative was put inside to monitor calls and screen visitors."

"Dani's knocking on her door as we speak." Hawke inwardly groaned.

"You sent your girlfriend to see if someone had Adrian's sister's family hostage?"

Hawke couldn't tell if Pierce thought that was genius or idiocy.

"I saw the cop out front and thought he might have photos of Marion and me." He watched Dani talking to the woman at the door. "I better text her that's FBI and they are fine."

Pierce laughed, then said, "Yeah, she'll be on our list of malcontents after this."

Hawke ended the call and texted Dani. *FBI inside. Everything is good.*

A minute later she exited the house and walked down the sidewalk to the end of the block, crossed the street, and stopped at the rental car. Once she was seated, Dani said. "I had a good conversation with the neighbor. She knew Adrian was dead. She'd been the one who consoled Alice when the police brought the news. From what I could get from Grace, Alice doesn't believe

Marion did it. When I talked, briefly to Alice, she was in shock, but she also kept flicking her gaze to the woman, I presume was the FBI. It was almost as if she didn't trust the woman."

Hawke motioned for Marion to drive. "Find us a motel for the night."

"Motel or hotel?" Marion asked.

Hawke studied her. "There's a difference?"

"Yes. Motels usually have the doors to the outside and less surveillance. Hotels, your door opens onto a hallway where there are surveillance cameras. I prefer hotels."

"Then find a hotel." Hawke shifted to peer into the back seat. "Tell me what you and Alice talked about in front of the agent."

Dani settled back in her seat. "I was only in there long enough for me to give my condolences and say I was a friend of Adrian's before you texted me. But the 'friend' as Alice introduced her, was staring at me intently. I thought maybe she was part of the finance company's people. But if she was FBI that makes sense."

Hawke had noticed lights following them ever since they left Alice's house. "Take a right at the next intersection."

"But that won't get us toward a hotel," Marion countered.

"We don't want a hotel now. We want to lose the person following us. As soon as I can't see the lights, I want you to pull into the first place that will hide the car and we'll trade places."

"But you don't know your way around." She did what he asked.

They quickly changed places. Hawke waited to see

if a car when by, when one did, he backed out and went the other direction. "Give me directions to a hotel out the east side of town. One where you can use a computer to contact the post office."

Hawke followed her directions and didn't notice anyone else following them by the time they arrived at a hotel. He paid for two rooms and they settled in.

Dani came out of their bathroom ready for bed. "Why did Marion need a computer to contact the post office?"

"She had her mail held while she was gone. If Adrian sent her information, it might be at the post office." He patted the bed beside him. "I told her to have it and the rest of her mail sent to our house. Herb has been picking up the mail since I left. If someone breaks into our house to look for it, at least while I'm gone, they won't find anything."

"What if they stake out the mailbox and see Herb take the mail?" Dani asked.

"I'll see if Spruel can have the county and the troopers go by multiple times during the mail drop off and catch anyone who is watching."

Dani nodded. "Are we landing back at Missoula tomorrow?"

He showed her the coordinates on his phone that Bo had sent him. "I'm assuming you know what to do with these coordinates when we get in the plane?"

Dani looked at the numbers and letters before typing them into her phone. After a minute of studying a map, she glanced up at him. "It's a landing strip in the middle of a wilderness. I'll need to land somewhere else to fuel up after I drop you off."

"Guess I'll have to give you my credit card." Hawke

rolled over, grabbed his wallet, and handed her the card.

"What will you use if you need something?" Dani put the card in the wallet she carried in her pant pocket.

"I have my debit card and I hope to be headed back home soon. You can drop that off at home your next trip to the valley." He kissed her and turned out the light.

Chapter Fifteen

Marion stared across the table watching her brother and Dani. They were all in the dining area at the hotel where they'd spent the night. The two had been staring into one another's eyes for the last minute. She found it cute that they weren't touching but they seemed to be connected. She and Adrian had that. It was better than lust, it was deeper and more meaningful. It was why they had planned to spend their lives together. She sighed and turned as if looking out the window. Sweeping a lock of hair back from her face, she swiped at a tear that burned in the corner of her eye. Would she ever get over the loss of Adrian? Her aching heart said no. Would she learn to live with it? She had no choice.

Gabriel said, "When we get back to Montana you can use the computer Bo gave us to dig deeper into the clients of Pannell Finances. Who would get any complaints clients might have about their accounts?"

"That would be Adele, but there are very few complaints and most of them are misunderstandings."

She studied her brother. "You don't think whoever is stealing money would be dumb enough to take money in large enough amounts to make people suspicious."

"I doubt it if this has been going on for a long time. However, someone may have become greedy and tried to get money quicker and realized they'd goofed when Adrian became suspicious."

"That could be. So that person's greed is what killed Adrian?" Marion asked, her gut twisting thinking about how Adrian had died. It had been an unnecessary death.

"I've discovered over the years greed and passion seem to be the main reasons that usually end up getting someone killed." Gabriel stood and they all picked up their packs and duffle bags.

Settled in the car with Gabriel behind the wheel, Marion gave him directions as her mind wandered.

"Take a left at the next light."

At the airport, while Dani did the pre-flight check, fueled up, and turned in her flight plan, Hawke returned the rental car. He'd left Marion sitting on a wheel of Dani's plane. She'd seen just how disrupted her life had become with the murder of Adrian and the authorities looking for her.

Marion's life would never be the same. She'd always see the man strangling her fiancé, know the company she'd worked for since college believed she'd kill someone, and never know whom to trust again. He sighed and wondered if her life had been as wonderful as she'd always made it out to be. She was quick to say she was visiting their mom when she was cleared of the murder.

He stepped onto the tarmac and spotted the two

women in the cockpit of the Cessna waiting for him. Hawke wasn't surprised when Marion didn't move out of the front seat when he climbed in. Fine by him. He could use a nap. He settled into the seat behind Dani, pulled his Stetson over his eyes, and drifted off as soon as the plane was airborne.

Hawke woke to the sound of the two women talking. He pretended he was still asleep and tilted his head to hear better.

"When this is over, what are your plans?" Dani asked.

"I want to start over. Maybe at the reservation with mom. Or maybe in Portland or Seattle." He heard the indecision in his sister's voice. "I'm not sure I want to continue being a lawyer but I'm not sure what else I could do. Or would want to do."

"Maybe something will come to you while you spend time with your mom. She has missed you." The yearning in Dani's voice wasn't missed by Hawke. He knew how much Dani missed her parents who were no longer alive. She'd told Hawke he was lucky to still have his mom.

"I've missed her too. But I felt I had to be available to the company twenty-four-seven to keep my job. There have been changes but as a woman in a corporate business, it is a lot like being an Indian in a White school. You have to work twice as hard to get noticed in a positive way. I have been fighting prejudices my whole life. I'd hoped by graduating at the top of my class and landing the job I did; things would be easier. They weren't." Marion sighed. "I don't think we will see change in our lifetime."

"I had to be three times better than the men around

me to make the same status they did. I know what you're saying." Dani's voice was hard. Hawke had heard her stories about climbing the Air Force ladder on her performance and not sleeping her way to the top.

"We're fighters," Dani said. "You'll come out on your feet and be happier."

"Thanks. I hope so."

Hawke decided it was time he 'woke up.' "Are we there yet?" he asked, stretching.

Dani laughed and said, "Leave it to a man to sleep and leave the women to get him to his destination. Look down. We've been flying over wilderness for ten minutes. We should land in about twenty."

Hawke peered out the window and saw nothing but trees, streams, rocks and mountains. His kind of country.

True to her word, twenty minutes later they were on the ground. Bo and Dog sat in a pickup waiting for them. They both exited the vehicle. Dog bounded over to greet them, and Bo walked behind him, less enthusiastically.

"Smooth landing," he said to Dani.

"Thanks. I've made a few." She turned to Hawke. "Radio when you can and keep me informed."

He pulled her into a hug and whispered in her ear, "Let Mom know what's going on. You'll find Aunt Betty's phone number in the address book in my bedside table. Don't tell her about Marion staying with her. I don't want her hopes up in case..." He left it at that and released her.

Dani smiled at Marion. "Hang in there, your brother isn't known for giving up on finding the truth." She nodded to Bo. "Nice to meet you." She walked back to the plane, and they all headed to the pickup.

Bo waited until Dani was airborne before he started

the vehicle and they drove away from the dirt and grass runway.

"Did you learn anything new?" he asked.

Hawke told him about the searched house and apartment. "Feds are keeping the sister safe."

Bo snorted. "We know how well that will go."

Hawke gave him a disapproving glance.

Marion jumped into the conversation. "What do you mean by that?"

"The Feds aren't known for keeping women safe. Especially, Indian ones," Bo said.

"Bo and I met at a search and rescue conference, and shortly after we were helping the Feds find a missing Blackfoot woman," Hawke said.

"A cousin of mine that law enforcement took too long to ask questions about her disappearance," Bo added. "The Feds said the trail was cold. Hawke and I proved them different."

"You found her?" Marion studied Hawke.

He bent his head. "Not alive. She'd been raped and killed. But we brought her home so her family could mourn." He'd been on too many of this type of tracking assignments.

Marion's face grew as sad as when she'd told him about Adrian.

"The MMIW movement is getting the word out about missing Indigenous people and getting law enforcement to work harder when a woman, child, or man goes missing. But it is still not a priority for most agencies." Hawke had been asked to talk at one of the meetings to emphasize how important it is for law enforcement to act quickly.

"What exactly is the MMIW movement?" Marion

asked, her interest brightening her brown eyes.

"It's a movement across the U.S. and Canada to help families of missing and murdered Indigenous women. It has also expanded to help families find missing and murdered children and men. Sometimes it is called the MMIP. For people rather than just women," Bo said. "It is not an organization, though there are some nonprofit MMIW groups who are working to teach safety to Indigenous people."

"How can I get involved?" Marion asked.

Hawke grinned. "Talk to our mother. She has been part of the movement for years."

"Really?" A smile grew on Marion's face. "I should have known she would be working to help others after how alone she felt with my father."

Hawke understood what she meant. Back when he was growing up, if a husband beat his wife, most felt there must have been a reason for it. The only reason his stepfather had needed was his mom not giving him all of the money she'd earned.

"Where are you taking us?" Hawke asked to change the topic.

"Where I stashed your things, the computer, and some more reports from the State Police that came to that mailbox in St. Ignatius. Not sure if they will be useful. My cousin thinks they just sent it to try and see if the mail gets picked up." He grinned. "But, of course, my cousin put fake mail in the box so it only looks fuller."

"Will there be internet service where you are taking us?" Hawke asked.

"Yes. And you won't be far from a main highway. But there aren't any neighbors to be nosy." Bo turned onto a paved road and accelerated. "I'll have you settled in shortly."

Hawke peered out the window, studying the landscape. It was his element. The outdoors.

His phone buzzed. A glance showed him it was Pierce.

"Hello, Pierce, what have you learned now?" Hawke asked.

"Are you back in Montana, yet?"

Hawke was hesitant to answer, unsure who all would have access to this knowledge. "Why?"

"I'll take that as a 'yes.' They pulled a body out of the lake. It has a strong resemblance to the man in the sketch you gave me."

Hawke glanced in the back seat at his sister. "You want Marion to make an ID?"

"I would."

"Where's the body?" Hawke didn't like the idea of Marion going somewhere she could be followed.

"It's in the Missoula County morgue. I can pick you two up tonight and we can look at it after hours when there won't be anyone but us there." Pierce was pushing this a little too hard for Hawke's liking.

"I'll get back to you." He hung up and said, "Special Agent Pierce wants Marion to look at a body they pulled from the lake. He says it resembles the man in the sketch." He glanced at Marion. "I don't like the idea. Someone could follow us after we leave the morgue."

"Where is the body?" Bo asked.

Hawke told him.

"I can lend you my truck to meet your Fed and you can face time Marion when you get into the morgue. Then when you leave, I'll have things set up for you to get away from anyone who may be following you." Bo grinned. "I like playing hide and seek with the Feds and corrupt businessmen."

Hawke laughed. For the first time, he felt they may be getting closer to finding proof Marion hadn't killed Adrian.

Chapter Sixteen

Hawke stood inside the morgue with Pierce. True to his word, the Special Agent met Hawke outside the building and led him to the morgue without anyone else being present.

As Hawke opened the app to facetime with Marion and show her the dead man, Pierce asked, "When did you leave for Montana and when did you return?"

Hawke stopped pushing buttons on his phone and glared at the man. "My sister did not kill this man. She has been with someone ever since I found her."

Pierce held up his hands. "I need to be able to tell the State Police and my people that."

"Have you been telling everyone our movements?" Hawke asked, knowing Pannell had the money to buy off anyone he thought might have information he wanted.

"Only my supervisor knows what you have told me. I can't keep all that information to myself. Then it looks like I'm aiding you."

Hawke didn't like that answer.

"Hawke? Are you there?" Marion's face appeared on his phone's screen.

"Yes. Are you ready?"

Pierce pulled a sheet off the head of the body on the table in front of them. The man's face was bloated. It would be hard for her to be certain this was the man.

"The face is distorted from being in the water. It might make it hard for you to tell if this is the man," Hawke said, turning the phone to the body's head.

"That's enough," Marion's voice trembled.

Hawke turned the screen to see her face. "Well?"

"Like you said, his face is puffy. I'm not positive. If I could see his eyes as they were when he was alive, I could say for sure…" She paused and said, "How was he killed? Drowning?"

"No, it wasn't drowning."

Hawke handed the phone to Pierce as he pulled the sheet down the torso of the body, looking for wounds. He found what looked like a gunshot wound in the man's gut area. Whoever shot him was either not a good shot or there had been a fight and the mercenary lost.

Pierce held a photo in front of the phone. "Does this help you identify the man?" Before he finished his question, Marion gasped.

"That's him. That photo is the man who strangled Adrian and tossed him to the side to come after me." Anger had replaced the fear in Marion's voice.

"It's Philip Longo. A hired mercenary," Pierce said.

Hawke studied the Special Agent wondering where he was going with this.

"Ms. Shumack, have you ever heard of this man?" Pierce asked.

"No. And I had never seen him until the afternoon he killed my fiancé."

"His name was never on any paperwork you read at Pannell Financial?"

"Where are you going with this?" Hawked asked, not liking the tone or the insinuation in the Fed's voice.

"I have someone checking the contracts and legal paperwork your sister has worked on during her time with Pannell. Philip Longo signed a contract she was in charge of two years ago."

"No. I have never dealt with this man. I would have remembered him," Marion insisted.

"Did someone bring this paperwork to the attention of your agent?" Hawke asked. It seemed too easy for this mercenary to be attached to Marion by any kind of paperwork, let alone a contract.

"Pannell's secretary was helping the agent go through Ms. Shumack's work files," Pierce said.

"She wouldn't know where to find all my work files," Marion said.

Hawke forgot his sister was on the phone. He took the device from Pierce. "You're sure she wouldn't have access?"

"Yes. Contracts can only be accessed by me, the head of legal, and Drew."

"But she is Pannell's secretary, wouldn't she have access to everything he does?" Pierce asked.

"No. When it came to legal contracts and discussions, she was never allowed in the room. It was always Drew, his legal team, the business we drew the contract up with, and their legal team. No one else." Marion said.

Hawke didn't like how the company Marion had

worked for, for over twenty years, was now throwing her to law enforcement.

"What company was the contract for?" Marion asked in a business tone.

Pierce pulled out his phone and scrolled.

"He would have had to have been with a business. That's the only contracts I dealt with. Drew's personal lawyer would have dealt with anything between Drew and anyone else," Marion said.

"There isn't a company named. Only Longo's name and you as the lawyer who drew up the contract," Pierce said.

"Then it never happened. I was only involved with companies. No single party contracts."

Hawke heard the resolve in her voice and studied her calm face. She was telling the truth.

"I'd be looking into the secretary and the personal lawyer if I were you," he said to Pierce.

The Fed nodded. "Where are you staying?"

Hawke shook his head. "Do you think I'd let anyone know where my sister is when they are framing her for killing her fiancé?" Hawke stared at the Special Agent. "Until we find the person behind these two killings, her life is in danger. I'll keep her hidden until you arrest the real killer." Hawke looked into the phone. "See you soon." He ended the call, shoved the phone in his pocket, and headed for the door.

"Hawke, I'm not trying to railroad your sister. We need to bring her in for questioning. We can keep her safe."

Hawke snorted and said, "Right. Like I can believe the federal government will keep my sister safe from someone who has enough money to buy off half of the agency. No. We're doing just fine on our own." He walked to the doors and down the corridor to the outside door.

Sitting in the vehicle Bo brought him to use for the meeting, he texted his friend. *Leaving.*

I'll put things in motion.

Hawke pulled out of the parking area and headed north. He picked out a vehicle behind him, staying its distance no matter if he sped up or slowed down.

At St. Ignatius, he pulled down into the small town and found the grocery store. He parked in the parking lot, left the keys in the ignition of the vehicle, and walked into the store. He walked through the aisles, straight to the back, where a young man smiled, handed him a key, and said, "Small red car."

Hawke stepped out into the evening and spotted the car parked at the end of the alley behind the store. He slid into the driver's seat, put the key in the ignition, and drove the alley as far as he could before turning back toward the highway.

He turned south, watching the road behind him. Nothing appeared to be following him when he turned onto Jocko Road. If he thought he was still being followed there was another switch he could make before hitting the gravel road that would take him across to Hwy 83 and Salmon Lake.

When they'd returned from Dallas, Hawke was happy to learn they were in the wilderness not far from the lake and the resort. Bo had discovered that the Pannell group was still in Montana. They'd been moved from the lake to one of the resorts in the wilderness. Bo had found them a place just off the resort's property.

Driving back to the house, Hawke went over what

they knew. The man who had killed Adrian was himself killed. That meant whoever hired him had wanted to make sure he didn't talk. That would come back to Pannell, but Hawke had a suspicion Pannell wouldn't do his own dirty work and couldn't see the man paying someone to knock off someone he'd paid to kill Adrian. That would just make a string of killings.

The secretary was looking good for this. She may not have had the money to pay the hit man after he'd taken care of Adrian. She'd been the one to lead him around at the resort and make sure he had access to the rooms to see that the computers were gone. Why?

He turned down the gravel road that led to the house where they were staying. Bo was now staying with them. He felt the urgency of getting to the truth as much as Hawke did. The lights were on as he came out of the trees. Not just a light, but all of the lights. Why would Bo use the generator to light the whole house?

Chapter Seventeen

Hawke parked the car and studied the windows. Nothing moved behind them. Where was Dog? He should have bounded out at the sound of a vehicle. It didn't feel right. But how could someone have found them here?

He parked the red car next to Bo's pickup and slipped out the passenger door to hide in the shadow of the truck. His backup weapon was in one boot and his knife was sheathed in his other boot. Armed, he made his way to the rear of the house. Two horses were tied up to a tree. Hawke went to the horses first. They were good quality but from the saddles and rigging, they were pleasure horses. Ones that would come from a Dude ranch or a tourist attraction. That meant their visitors were from the ranch resort next door.

Drawing his Smith & Wesson from his boot sheath, Hawke eased up to a window that allowed him to see into the kitchen. Bo and Marion were sitting in chairs, their

145

hands on top of the table. The man facing them was Drew Pannell. How the hell had he found them and what did he want?

The man standing guard at the door leading into the rest of the house had his back to Hawke. They were expecting him to come through the front door. What he really wanted to know was what had they done to Dog?

He moved to the back door and slowly turned the handle. He heard snuffling at the bottom of the door. Dog was sniffing the door. He knew Hawke was outside.

Hawke pressed his cheek against the door down at the bottom and whispered. "Move Dog. I'm coming in." Then he jumped up, twisted the knob, and shoved the door open, with his weapon pointed at Pannell.

"What the hell!" Pannell shouted and the man at the other door, swung around, his weapon drawn.

"Tell your man to slide his weapon over to Bo or I'll put a bullet in both of you," Hawke said.

Marion gasped but didn't move.

Hawke and the man with the gun stared at one another.

"Garth, lower your gun," Pannell said, not taking his gaze from Hawke.

"No, slide it to Bo," Hawke repeated.

"We're not here to harm anyone. You scared us," Pannell said. "Garth, slide the gun over."

The man did as he was told.

Bo grabbed the gun but he didn't aim it at anyone. "They came in here to talk to us. But when they discovered you weren't here, refused to say anything until you returned."

Hawke put his weapon back in his boot and pulled out a chair. "What did you want to talk to us about? And how did you know we were here?"

Bo placed the gun on the table in front of him and Pannell sat in the last chair. The man, Garth, stood at the door with his arms crossed.

Pannell glanced at Marion. "I want to know what you know about Adrian's death?"

Marion glanced at Gabriel. He gave a slight shake of his head.

She had always answered her boss's questions but she would follow Gabriel's cues. He had dealt with murder and murderers before, she hadn't. "I don't know anything."

Pannell smiled and leaned back in his chair. "I don't believe you. Your undergarments were found at the scene and you disappeared and have been running from the police—"

"I am the police," Gabriel said. "So, she isn't running from them."

Her boss narrowed his eyes at Gabriel, then pasted a smile on his face and returned his gaze to her. "I know your brother is with the Oregon State Police. But he doesn't have any jurisdiction here, in Montana. Or in Texas."

She studied him. He knew they'd been to Texas. How? Her body started to tremble. Was she looking into the eyes of the man who had Adrian killed? Did he have more men outside waiting to kill all three of them?

Pannell waved his hands. "I don't care about the murder. If you did kill him while in the throes of passion, you're more fiery than I thought." He gave her a smirk. "I'm more interested in what he discovered about my finances. About the money that is missing."

Marion shook her head. "I don't know anything

about missing money."

Her boss studied her. "You're lying. Lovers share secrets. What did Adrian say? That he found out someone was embezzling? Who did he think it was?"

She'd sat in on a lot of deals this man made for millions of dollars with businesses. He was fishing for answers. He knew there was money missing but he didn't know who had absconded with it. He wouldn't have had Adrian killed if he was searching for the person with his money. He would have asked Adrian to help him catch the person. It would have been a game that Drew Pannell would have enjoyed playing.

"We were going—"

Gabriel stopped her. "You don't have to tell him anything."

She stared into her brother's eyes. "I've watched him work people over during corporate transactions. He doesn't know who stole the money and he didn't kill Adrian. He would have wanted Adrian's help in finding out who was embezzling."

"You thought I killed Adrian?" Pannell studied her.

Marion peered into Drew's eyes. "We thought you sent someone to kill him. I saw the man. That's why I ran. I feared he would kill me, too, and then I couldn't avenge Adrian's death."

"He honestly didn't tell you anything?" Pannell asked.

"He asked me to marry him, gave me a ring, and then said we were going to find out where the money went when we returned to Dallas." She spun the ring on her finger. She would never take this off.

Her boss turned his attention to Gabriel. "What have you learned?"

Hawke had let Marion talk. She knew her boss better than he did. It appeared the man merely wanted to find out if Adrian knew he'd embezzled his own money. But he was still on the list of who would want to keep Adrian quiet, even if Marion thought he didn't have Adrian killed.

"How well do you know your secretary?" Hawke asked.

"Adele? She's been working for me over twenty years. I think she came to work for me only a year or two before Marion, why?" Pannell didn't look so confident.

"How would she get access to Marion's contracts?" Hawke asked.

"The FBI asked to see all of Marion's files. I sent Adele back to Dallas to get into the documents using my password. I trust her implicitly."

"Someone slipped a contract into the file written up by Marion for a man named Philip Longo." Hawke watched the man's left eyebrow raise slightly and his left cheek twitched. He knew the name.

"I've never developed a contract for an individual, it was always companies. I had never heard of the man, but I saw him the night he killed Adrian," Marion said.

Pannell stared at Marion. "Longo killed Adrian?"

"You knew the man?" Hawke asked.

Pannell ran a hand over his face. His eyes had softened as he peered at Marion. "I had Longo deal with some malcontents a couple of years ago. He didn't kill anyone, just roughed them up a bit, and I didn't have any more trouble with them. But I swear, I didn't hire him to kill Adrian."

"How did his name get on a contract drawn up by my sister?" Hawke asked.

Pannell shook his head. "I honestly don't know. My personal attorney dealt with Longo."

Hawke exchanged a look with Bo. That would be the next person they dug up information on. The personal attorney and Adele Barnes.

"We'd appreciate it if you let the local police and the FBI in charge of the murder investigation know that you believe Philip Longo and not Marion Shumack was the person responsible for Adrian Ulrick's death." Hawke stood. "It's time for you to get on your horses and leave. Also, no one better come around here looking for Marion. If they do, I'll be looking for a way to implicate you in all of this."

Pannell stood and glared at Hawke. "How would I know if someone comes here or not?"

"What he's saying is you and your sidekick better not tell anyone that Marion is here. Especially, your secretary," Bo said, picking up the revolver on the table and standing.

Pannell's face paled.

"Damn, she already knows, doesn't she?" Hawke said.

"Adele was the one who called around to all the homeowners asking if they were available to show me around on the pretense of purchasing. This place, the owners said they had a friend borrowing it. When she asked the name," Pannell's head tipped toward Bo, "his name came up. We already knew he was the one helping you."

Hawke was impressed and scared that the man knew so much. But he hadn't known about Longo and he didn't know who was embezzling his money. Or he was good at hiding the fact it was him. "We'd appreciate it if you either told her we cleared out, or that you didn't find us here. Especially if she is working with your embezzler." Another thought came to him. "When was Ms. Barnes in Dallas helping the FBI?"

Pannell reached into his pocket and pulled out a cell phone. He tapped on the screen and said, "This past Friday. She flew over Thursday night and came back Saturday."

Hawke glanced at Marion. She was there a day before they were. But how did she get the key to Marion's apartment? And why would she hold that much hostility toward his sister?

"Thank you. If we need to talk to you any more, we'll contact you. Please stop having us followed, it will only allow the killer to kill again." Hawke hoped his words sunk into the man's brain.

Pannell stared at Hawke for several seconds before his gaze landed on Marion. He understood who would be the next to die. The man nodded, and Bo handed the revolver back to Pannell's bodyguard.

Once the two had left the house, Hawke spun to Bo. "Stay or find another place?"

"I'm running out of places that are in this area. I can get you three places up north." Bo walked over and locked the back door.

"We need to stay near the Pannell company employees. If Adele is working with someone, it has to be someone in the company. She wouldn't have access to embezzle the money but she would have access to the contracts and information from Drew's meetings to tell the person whom to siphon the money from." Marion was petting Dog who had his head on her lap.

Hawke was glad his friend was here to comfort his

sister. "It would have to be someone else who worked in accounting, wouldn't it?"

Marion peered at him. "I would think so. Either an accountant or a lawyer who knew how to manipulate figures."

Hawke sat down. "What can you tell me about Pannell's personal lawyer?"

"Perry Mathers?" Marion stopped petting Dog and put her hands on the table. "I've heard he does more than take care of Drew's personal legal matters. That he is also a sounding board when Drew is thinking about taking on a new client or acquiring a business he thinks he can resell at a profit."

"Which means he knows a lot about the money side of Pannell Financial." Hawke pushed to his feet. "Bo, where's that computer you promised me that's hooked up to the internet?"

"I'll get it. You going to dig into this Mathers?" Bo walked over to a box sitting on a chair and lifted out the laptop.

"Yeah. We need to find out if he is raking in more money than his salary."

Chapter Eighteen

Marion woke to the sound of a dog barking in the distance. She sat up and studied the room she slept in. It took nearly a minute before she remembered Adrian's death, her flight, and now being hidden in this cabin in Montana. Her heart ached. She felt numb and wondered if she'd ever feel anything else again.

Her fiancé was dead, her boss thought she'd killed him, his secretary most likely trashed her apartment, and the man who actually strangled Adrian was dead. But by who? And did that person want her dead or with the real killer dead would they forget about her? It was too much to think about when all she wanted to do was curl up in a ball and stay in this bed.

A knock on the door. "Marion, are you up? I've got coffee on and muffins just came out of the oven," Gabriel called through the door.

A weak smile crept across her lips. This reminded her of when she was small. Gabriel would get up to go to school but he always made sure she had something to eat before he left. Their mom would come home from her night job as Hawke walked out the door to school. Then while Marion was at the preschool, their mom would work another four hours, pick her up from school, and they would both have an afternoon nap. Unless her father was home. Then he'd ask his wife to do all kinds of tasks that wouldn't allow her mom to get any sleep before she headed out for her night job.

"I'll be there in a couple of minutes," she called back. Whenever she looked back on her childhood before her father died in a car crash, she wondered at how strong her mom had been to endure the long hours of work and the beatings from her husband. She never raised her voice to her children and always had a smile for them. "Why did I stay away so long?" she voiced out loud. Now her heart held an ache for her mother. She wanted to see her and tell her she realized how much the woman had sacrificed for her and Gabriel.

In the kitchen, she took a seat at the table where a plate with two muffins and a steaming cup of coffee sat. Gabriel was hunkered over the laptop. "Where's Bo?" she asked.

"He went to town for some supplies and to ask questions." Hawke glanced up and smiled. "I'm glad you are thinking about staying with Mom for a while after we clear you. She'll like that. But beware, she still has all your clothing from high school in your closet."

She laughed. "I wondered how she managed to send me a retro outfit when I mentioned Adrian and I were going to a costume party." Her memories of that party flashed through her mind. It had been the first time they'd gone out in public together. They'd had a wonderful time and he'd told her he loved her that night. And said he'd wished her mom had sent her one of her regalia dresses.

Marion swiped at the tear at the corner of her eye. "I want to take up dancing again. Adrian wanted to see me dance. I'm going to dance in his memory."

Hawke put a hand on her arm. "That would be a good way to honor his life."

"Thank you for being my *pyáp*." She knew she had the best big brother in the world. She was ashamed she'd stayed away from her family for so long.

"There are reasons we live separately. And when the time is right, we realize we need family." He had a distant look in his eyes. She wondered what or who he was thinking about.

She picked up a muffin and pointed to the laptop. "What did you find out about Perry?"

"He has been living very well off since he became Pannell's lawyer ten years ago."

Marion shook her head. "Are you sure it was ten years ago? I remember seeing him around the office when I went to work there."

"As Pannell's lawyer?" Hawke asked.

She tried to think back to the few occasions she'd seen the man before he became an everyday entity at Drew's office. "I can't remember. But it was about ten years ago when I remember seeing him a lot and learned he was Drew's personal attorney."

"It looks like I need to look into him farther back than ten years." Hawke started tapping keys on the computer.

"What about Adele? Can you find a connection between Perry and her?" For some reason, in the back of her mind, she connected the two.

"Bo is out checking on a line we found about her. Seems she grew up around here. And is possibly related to the people who own the resort that is hosting the Pannell Financial Company's retreat." Hawke glanced up from the keyboard. "She would know this country well and would have the contacts to keep tabs on you, or us, in the area."

A shudder jiggled through her. "She's never been nice to me, but she's never really been nice to anyone other than Drew and his inner circle."

"Would you call her a gold digger?"

Marion studied her brother. "Drew is married. And I believe it to be a happy marriage. Are you insinuating that Adele is trying to become Mrs. Drew Pannell?" She shook her head. "I have never seen Drew treat her any different than any other employee. She might have those designs but it would never happen."

Gabriel studied her. "Of the two, who would you say would kill to keep their involvement in embezzling quiet?"

"Adele." It popped out without her having to think about it. "Drew would pay people off or find a way to make the numbers work. He wouldn't kill anyone."

Hawke nodded, that was the impression he'd been getting from the owner of Pannell Financial. He had the money and the status to make someone else fall into the embezzlement charge. He wouldn't need to have Adrian killed. He'd find a way to make it look like someone else and pay them off. Whoever paid a mercenary to kill Adrian had a lot to lose. Not only the money they'd embezzled but going to prison.

"I think we need to look into the other accountants.

156

If it wasn't Pannell ordering someone to skim and divert money, then it had to be someone who worked with the numbers. But how would Adrian manage to get hold of something someone else was working on?" Hawke glanced at his sister. She was picking at a muffin and staring into space. She'd cared for Adrian, more than anyone knew. Including her boss.

He pushed the plate with the muffins and she snapped out of her trance. "Any clue which one of the other accountants might have been skimming?"

She shook her head. He knew it wasn't in answer to his question but to clear it of the thoughts she'd been having.

"There are-were twelve accountants. All of them except for Caleb, Boyd, and Aldis were at the company when I hired on. Many of them were new hires then. I can't see one of them becoming greedy now. I'm sure they were all being paid as well as Adrian with a raise and bonus every year. You saw his home. They would all be living comfortably."

"What are the last names of the three you mentioned?" Hawke asked.

"Caleb DeLan, Boyd Johnson, and Aldis Garcia." Marion pulled a piece off the muffin. "Do you think one of them might have been skimming?"

"It had to be an accountant if it isn't Mathers." Hawke got into the police database and typed in the three names and waited to see if they ever had a run-in with the law. He stood and refreshed their cups of coffee. Marion was finally eating.

"Do you think your FBI friend can get the Montana police to stop looking for me?" Marion asked.

He shrugged. "I can't tell you what police in another

state are thinking."

"Okay, if we were in Oregon, would I no longer be the suspect in Adrian's death?" She peered into his eyes.

The sorrow in her eyes angered him. He'd always tried to make his sister's life as easy as possible before he joined the Marines. And by all accounts, it had been a good life, especially after her father had died. But this. Having her fiancé killed in front of her…He didn't know how to make it better. And his answer wasn't going to help.

"If we were in Oregon, you would still be considered a suspect. But we would be looking for others. Enough people there know my record for finding murderers and they would listen to what I had to say." He held up his hands. "Here, only Bo and Pierce know me. Bo is non-gratis with the State Police because he speaks out against the treatment of Indians and the disregard for the environment. Pierce has some pull, but he can only relay information as a third party and gather information for us to relay to the police. The homicide is in the hands of the Montana State Police."

"I could be arrested for harboring a fugitive." He shrugged and grinned. "But it wouldn't be the first nor the last time I have stuck to my instincts and worked against those who think they know better."

Marion smiled. It was a weak smile but it was better than the sorrow he'd witnessed earlier.

His phone rang. Spruel. "It's my boss. Eat and we'll do some more digging." He stood and walked outside.

"Hawke," he answered.

"How are things going there? We could use you back here," Spruel said.

"They found the man who killed Marion's fiancé.

He was pulled out of the lake with what looked like a gut shot. Either the person who shot him wanted to make him suffer or they weren't a very good shot. I'm leaning toward that. Which gives us a new mix of suspects."

"And the Montana Police? Are they thinking the same?"

Hawke sighed. "I can give Marion an alibi for the time I picked her up to present. If he was killed before I found her, then I'm pretty sure they are going to force me to give her up. But she didn't do it, damn it!" He rarely lost his cool around his boss, but he felt as if his hands were tied and his sister would suffer because of it.

"I'll see what I can find out. What does your friend at the FBI say?"

"He believes Marion didn't kill the victim. All he can do is keep feeding the information we come up with to Lieutenant Gernot and hope she sees there are more probable suspects." He shoved a hand through his cropped hair which had started to show more silver every month.

"Get this thing sorted out and get back here. We're working one man short." Spruel ended the call at the same time Dog bounded out of the trees.

"Where have you been?" Hawke asked, shoving his phone in a pocket and entering the cabin.

Marion had the computer in front of her. "Aldis had some problems with the police as a teenager, but not as an adult. Nothing came up on Caleb or Boyd but you must have put Adele in the system." Marion leaned back in her chair, and Hawke pulled up a chair and started reading.

He whistled, reading about her arrests as a prostitute in her early twenties. There wasn't mention of any other violations after she turned twenty-five.

"As high and mighty as she acts, I never would have figured her for a prostitute." Marion was staring at the cup of coffee in her hands. "What kind of life did she come from to make her do something like that?"

"When she's pulled in for questioning, when we get some evidence on her, I'll have someone ask her." Hawke pulled out his phone. "I bet none of her contacts around here know about her twenties. Those were all arrests in California. I wonder how they didn't come up when Pannell did a background check when he hired her?"

He dialed Bo.

"Hey Hawke, I've learned some more about Ms. Barnes."

"So have we. Are you headed back here?"

"As soon as I shake my tail. They picked me up outside of the coffee shop Ms. Barnes's aunt runs."

"Be careful. Pannell knows where we are. If he thought Marion was a killer, he would have had the police here before now." Hawke ended the call.

Marion stood and placed her dishes in the sink. "What now?"

Chapter Nineteen

Hawke wanted to talk to Pannell. Ask him why he hired Ms. Barnes and see if he thought one of his accountants, other than Adrian, could have been skimming money. And how much the owner knew about the whole business.

"Do you happen to know Pannell's cell phone number?" Hawke asked.

"Yeah. We were given it in case of an emergency." Marion wrote the number down on the notebook Hawke had been using to keep track of what they'd learned.

Before he could dial the number, his phone buzzed. Pierce.

"Hawke."

"Hey, I learned that the body was in the water since Friday. There is no way Marion could have killed him if she was with you." There was a pause. "Tell me she was with you on Friday."

"When she wasn't with me, she was with a friend's

relative."

"Hawke, how can I vouch for her if you weren't with her the whole time?"

"Whoever you tell isn't going to know that. You can talk to the woman who was with her when a friend and I went to the island to have a look around. You know, when we discovered the murder scene wasn't where forensics was gathered." Hawke didn't usually pour salt in wounds but he was getting tired of the whole mess. If he could work out in the open, he'd have more to go on than they did.

Pierce blew out a big breath of air.

Hawke heard it whoosh in the phone.

"I don't suppose you've come up with anything new?" the Special Agent asked.

"We learned the executive secretary to Pannell was once a prostitute and we think maybe one of the most recently hired accountants may have been helping her, or she and the personal attorney were saving up to go away together." Hawke knew this would only infuriate Pierce more.

"Now, you think it was done by either the secretary and an accountant or the secretary and the personal lawyer? Why these particular people?" he asked.

Hawke explained what Marion had told him and what they'd learned about the people from looking at the police database.

"People do change," Pierce said.

"Yeah, they do. Help me prove they have or help us find information that proves they are the ones embezzling. I was just going to ask Pannell some questions about these employees." Hawke was pretty sure Pierce would tell him to back off.

"Saves me finding him and asking. But don't pretend to be part of the police investigating the homicide."

Pierce giving him the go-ahead surprised him. "Ok. I'll let you know if I learn anything vital to the case." Hawke ended the call, still puzzled over Pierce being so lenient.

"What's the matter?" Marion asked.

Hawke turned his attention to his sister. "You're off the hook for the death of Longo. He was killed on Friday. You were with someone all day. I told Pierce that. The police may want to talk to Bo's cousin when Pierce fills them in." He pulled the notebook with Pannell's number over to him and it clicked. Pierce thought Hawke would see the man in person. They must have law enforcement at the retreat to see if he showed up and they would either apprehend him or follow him back to Marion.

He grinned and punched in the numbers for Pannell.

"Pannell," the man answered before the ring had gained volume.

"This is Trooper Hawke, Marion's brother. I have some questions for you. Are you alone or will someone hear your answers?"

He heard footfalls and a door.

"I'm outside. Why the secrecy?" Pannell seemed genuinely curious. Hawke had expected the man to hang up on him.

"Marion and I have been talking and wondered what you knew about Ms. Barnes before she came to work for you?"

There was a long pause. Pannell cleared his voice. "You learned about her prior occupation."

"Then you knew she'd been arrested for prostitution

in California?" Hawke asked.

"Yes. That's where I met her. She was the one and only time I was with a woman besides my wife. Unfortunately, I said more than I should have and she showed up at my company demanding a job or she'd tell my wife about how we met." The man's voice grew angrier as he talked. "The best way I could keep tabs on her was by making her my executive secretary, which made her think she had the upper hand." There was another pause. "Adele doesn't know it, but I confessed the encounter to my wife five years ago. She forgave me and is ready when Adele decides to try and get between us."

"Would Ms. Barnes have access to the information that would help someone embezzle from the company?" Hawke asked.

"She is greedy. That's why I don't let her have access to anything that I feel she could abscond with. That's how little I trust her."

"What about your personal attorney? How friendly is he with Ms. Barnes."

The long pause made Hawke believe this could be the couple that was causing all the trouble at Pannell Financial and for Marion.

"I know they were acquainted before he became my personal attorney. But after I pulled him out of the small law firm he was working for, he's been loyal to me. I know exactly when he cut ties with Adele because she was a bitch for several weeks and did very little work. Just sat at her desk, scowling and snarling when someone approached her. I had a temp taking my calls."

"Has she been friendly with any of your younger accountants?" Hawke asked.

"Who are you suggesting?" The man sounded skeptical.

"Caleb DeLan, Boyd Johnson, or Aldis Garcia."

"Aldis has a juvenile record but he has been an exemplary employee. As well as Caleb and Boyd. Caleb and Adrian were friends. I'm sure Adrian would have asked for a meeting with me and Caleb if he had discovered he was the one embezzling."

"I don't think Adrian had gotten that far. He knew something was wrong but he wasn't sure what. I think he might have said something to someone other than Marion. That's why he is dead. They wanted to stop his investigation before he exposed the real embezzler."

"What do you mean real?" Pannell asked.

"I would bet that whoever the real embezzler is has been scrambling to make up something to point to someone else, so they can grab the money they skimmed and disappear." Hawke couldn't see someone who had Adrian killed and then killed the person they hired, just walking away. They'd want the money they'd killed for and they'd want to make sure someone else was convicted. "They could be setting it up to look like it was you all along."

A burst of foul language buffeted Hawke's ear.

"Whoever has the balls to do that will find themselves on the streets." Pannell's tone left Hawke believing the person would never find work again.

"You need to have someone in accounting that you trust check into all the accounts. Specifically, ones that came to your company when the three I mentioned started working for you. I would venture whoever is doing this, has been since they started working for Pannell Financial. To have an amount accumulated that would get two men murdered, it's got to be a large sum, which would have had to be dribbled into over the years to not raise suspicion."

"I have just the two people to work on it."

Before the man could end the call, Hawke said, "Please let me know if you come up with a name. My sister's future depends on catching the person responsible for Adrian's death."

"I will. I'm fond of your sister. She's been a hard worker and never backed down when she knew I was in the wrong. I don't want her to suffer for something someone else has done."

The line went silent. Hawke glanced up.

Marion stood in the doorway to the kitchen. "How did that go?"

"Better than I'd expected. He's going to have some people he trusts look into the accounting." If Adrian had sent information to Marion about his suspicions, her forwarded mail wouldn't arrive at his mailbox until the middle to end of the week. That was a long time to wait and wonder if anything would show up.

The sound of the front door opening shot Hawke to his feet.

Marion swung around.

Dog ran out of the kitchen toward the front of the house, his tail wagging.

Bo walked up to the kitchen door and motioned for Marion to enter the room. They both walked in and sat at the table.

Hawke poured coffee for Bo and sat down. "What did you learn?"

"Ms. Barnes isn't very well-liked around here. It seems she planned to go to California to be an actress."

Bo sipped his coffee.

"She ended up being a prostitute," Hawke said.

"Really!" Bo laughed. "There are a few people around here who would love to know that. Seems after saying she was going to be a star; she came back here saying she went to business college and was now the owner of Pannell Financials' right hand. Which no one can believe."

"I had a talk with Pannell. It seems she blackmailed her way into being his executive secretary. His process is to keep his enemies close." Hawke watched Marion over the rim of his coffee cup. She had been more withdrawn today. He wasn't sure what was going on in her head.

"Blackmail isn't very far from embezzling," Bo said.

Hawke nodded. "I think she's either blackmailed someone else into helping her get the money or she found out about the person and cut herself in."

Marion glanced up from the cup she'd been staring at. "From what Adrian said about his colleagues in the accounting office, there would only be a few who would do anything that would hurt the company or Drew. While many people in the business world don't care for Drew, he has always been good to his devoted employees. If you work hard and bring good results, you are rewarded well."

"Does that mean you don't think anyone from the company, other than Ms. Barnes, would try to steal from Pannell?" Hawke asked.

"No. But there would be a small pool of people who would be upset enough to go against Drew."

"I imagine the personal attorney would have the

information about any employees who might have been disgruntled?" Hawke studied his sister. She had been staring past his head but her gaze met his.

"I think it's time I call Louise. She could look up all the employees who have lodged a complaint against the company." Marion seemed to be thinking, then shook her head.

"What was that about?" Hawke asked.

"Louise is not a fan of the company, but I can't see her colluding with anyone to steal money. She is mad because no one took her boss's sexual harassment seriously. And I can't blame her. But she would take the problem to the courts not embezzle money."

Hawke handed Marion the burner phone. "Give her a call and ask her to look into disgruntled employees and see if she's learned anything new."

Marion took the phone and found the number she'd called before to contact Louise. She wondered how calling Louise this time seemed natural. The phone rang three times and a male voice answered. She pushed the off button and peered into Hawke's eyes. "We need to check on Louise, a man answered the phone."

Chapter Twenty

Marion stood at the door still arguing with Hawke. "I'm the reason something could have happened to Louise. Let me go with you. I could stay hidden somewhere on the outskirts of the resort."

"We can't risk that. Since Pannell isn't answering his phone, I'm going to drive over and see if I can talk to Louise."

"You could be arrested for harboring me. What difference does it make if I go? Maybe I need to be arrested so they can find out I didn't do it and look for someone else." She crossed her arms and let the grief and anger of losing Adrian and possibly causing someone else pain unfurl on her brother.

"You will not turn yourself in. The chances of us finding the real killer and the law giving you justice, I'll side with Bo and me over justice anytime."

"That's the truth," Bo said. "Look at how many times since the Whiteman set foot on our land that they screwed us over. The only people we can depend on are our own. We'll make sure the real murderer is caught and you never get put in jail."

Marion sighed. She did know about all the lies and deceit that had been dealt to the First People of this continent. She'd studied all about it in law school along with her other studies. "Fine. But I don't like always being left behind."

"Bo and Dog are being left behind," Hawke said, opening the door of Bo's pickup.

"Yeah, but they like it," she retorted and spun around to enter the cabin. She hated being hidden away and left behind, but she also understood their reasoning. She spun back around. "As soon as you learn anything you call Bo. I want to know that I didn't put Louise in danger." She gave her brother the best 'do as I say' glare she had.

"I'll call as soon as I talk to her." Hawke entered the pickup and drove into the trees.

Marion glanced at the man beside her. "Do you think I'm overreacting?"

The man shrugged and motioned for her to enter the cabin.

"Do I have to be in the cabin all the time? Can't I go for a short walk? I'll take Dog with me. What kind of trouble can we get into?" She pleaded with Bo.

"Maybe after we hear from your brother, I'll go for a walk with you." Bo walked over to a cupboard and pulled out a box. It was a puzzle. "Let's work on this to take our minds off things."

"How about you tell me everything you learned, and I'll write it down for Hawke."

Hawke had a bad feeling about a man answering Louise's phone. You would have thought he'd have told her someone called, she'd see the number, and have called back. But he had the phone and so far, no one had called.

It took thirty minutes by road to reach the resort. He drove up to the large log building where the Pannell group had moved to from the island. There were smaller cabins sprinkled around the lodge. A nice corral filled with horses, an attractive barn, and outbuildings rounded out the dude ranch aesthetic. Just the place people with money would go to pretend they were cowboys and cowgirls.

He walked up to the lodge entrance and that's when he spotted a Montana State Police uniform. No sense in making a run for it or drawing attention to himself. Hawke entered the lodge and went straight to the registration counter.

"Hi, I'm looking for Ms. Beltane. Do you have a way of contacting her and letting her know I'm here to see her?" He smiled at the twenty-something woman dressed in tight wranglers and a t-shirt with the lodge's logo on it.

"I-we-"

"Hawke, how the hell did you find out so quick?" Pierce's voice sent a chill down Hawke's back.

Damn! How was he going to tell Marion the woman was dead? He turned toward the voice.

"Find out what?" he asked as innocent sounding as he could muster given his mind was buzzing with who had been the person to answer the woman's phone. And would he figure out that Marion had been the one calling?

Pierce cricked his head toward the stairs and started up them.

Hawke followed, glancing around to see if he knew any of the people in the lobby. He didn't, but that didn't mean one of them wasn't one of their suspects. Pierce had called him by name which meant the killer would know he was Marion's brother.

He followed the Special Agent into a room at the top of the stairs. A female lieutenant with the State Police stood talking to a woman wearing a jacket with the word 'Coroner' on the back. Hawke grasped Pierce's arm. "Is that Lt. Gernot with the coroner?"

Pierce nodded. "It's about time you two met in person." He pointed to a woman lying on the floor with a pool of blood behind her head like a dark red halo.

"Who is this?" Hawke asked.

"The woman you were asking for downstairs." Pierce turned to him. "Why were you asking for her?"

Hawke ran a hand over his face. This was going to make Marion want to turn herself in. She hadn't wanted the woman to get involved in case something like this happened. "Because Marion called her to ask her a question and a man answered her phone."

Pierce peered into his eyes. "Are you saying this woman has been giving you information and now she's dead?"

Hawke didn't want to voice what was pounding in his head, but he nodded, one quick movement. "Marion is going to turn herself in over this. She said she didn't want anyone to get hurt trying to help her prove her innocence." He turned from the body. "It was my idea to see if there was someone at Pannell who would help us find out what was being said over here about Marion and

Adrian."

"I take it you are the man harboring my suspect," a woman's voice said from behind him.

"She isn't a suspect, because she didn't kill anyone. You should be looking harder at the murder of the man who did kill Adrian Ulrick and this woman." Hawke spun around and nearly bumped noses with the slender, dark-haired lieutenant.

She appeared to be in her late forties, fit, and her green eyes were narrowed into slits. Anger glittered in their depths. "I don't take orders from a Fish and Wildlife officer from another state."

Pierce chuckled behind him.

"Listen. Marion had nothing to do with Ulrick's death. She gave you the sketch of the man who did kill him. Now he's dead which means whoever hired him wanted to make sure he didn't talk. And it wasn't Marion, she was with someone all day Friday when the man was killed."

"How do you know..." Her gaze drifted over his shoulder. "You have been feeding him information." Now her green-eyed glare was focused on Pierce.

"And he has been giving me all the information he has gathered. Which was the sketch of the man who was pulled out of the lake and other information that I have passed on to you." Pierce's tone was so soft it sounded like a caress.

Were he and this lieutenant involved? Hawke took a step back to draw the two of them into his field of vision. Nope, the caressing tone hadn't softened the lieutenant's glare one bit. In fact, it almost looked angrier.

"We, Marion and I, had asked Ms. Beltane some questions about what people here were saying about

Ulrick's death. We also asked her to listen to conversations and that we'd contact her again. That's what brought me here." He went on to tell Lt. Gernot about the phone call and the man answering.

"What time was that call?" she asked.

Hawke pulled out the phone and looked at the time. "Ten-thirty-two. After Marion hung up, we discussed it and decided I needed to come over and see if she was okay." He hung his head. "I'm really sorry to have brought this woman into our battle to prove Marion's innocence."

Pierce started searching the room. "There's no cell phone in here. Is that what you called?"

"Yeah. Marion had her number." Hawke also started to move around the room.

"You," Lt. Gernot, pointed at him. "Get out of our crime scene or I will arrest you for harboring a fugitive."

He was tired of being on the receiving end of her glares. She might be halfway good-looking if she wasn't constantly glaring. He stepped out of the room but not before he caught a glimpse of the back side of Adele Barnes.

Hawke hurried down the hall, catching up to the woman. "Ms. Barnes, we met before." He put a hand on her arm, stopping her.

The woman shifted a step away before facing him. "Yes, you were snooping around in Adrian and Marion's rooms at the island lodge." Her tone insinuated he wasn't welcome.

"I was looking for clues to who killed Adrian and framed Marion." Hawke stepped into her space and quietly said, "I know how you blackmailed your way into this job and what you did before. If you don't answer my questions honestly, I'll have my friend who lives in the area let everyone around here know what you really did when you went to California to be a star."

The woman's eyes widened as she sucked in air.

"Come on." Hawke grabbed her by the arm and hauled her down the hall. "Do you have a room in here or are you in one of the cabins?"

"My room is the other side of Louise's." The woman didn't sound so high and mighty.

"Is there someplace in this lodge where we can talk?" Hawke loosened his grip on the woman's arm.

She nodded and led him to the stairs. At the bottom, she entered a hall and walked into what looked like an old-fashioned library. Hawke closed the door as Ms. Barnes walked over to a stuffed chair and collapsed into it.

Hawke grabbed a straight-backed wooden chair from the roll-top desk and sat in front of Ms. Barnes. "Are you involved in the embezzling that Adrian found?"

She stared at him her lips a tight line.

"Ms. Barnes, this isn't some game of keeping a friend's secret that teenagers play. There have now been three people killed. If you know anything, it would be in your best interest, if you want to stay alive, to tell the police everything you know." Hawke peered into her face. "After the mercenary killed Adrian, whoever hired Longo—" the woman flinched at the name "—killed him, and because Louise was gathering information for Marion and me, she has been killed." He let that sink in for a few beats and said, "What makes you think you aren't the next person to end up dead? The person who embezzled is ready to take their money and run. But they'll have to clean up all the loose ends that can point fingers at them first."

"What makes you think I know anything?" Ms. Barnes asked, with none of the haughtiness she'd exuded before.

"Because you are in the right position to help someone. You blackmailed your way into your job, you have access to every part of the business, and I'm pretty sure you have a talent from your previous job that can make a nerdy accountant feel like he can take on anyone, including his boss."

A seductive smile crept onto the woman's lips as he'd talked about seducing an accountant.

"But you may have unleashed a greed that even you can't control. When you started this, did you think the person you picked would be capable of killing anyone, let alone a mercenary and now a woman you both knew?"

The smile disappeared and fear dimmed Ms. Barnes's eyes.

"If you tell us who you've been colluding with, I'll make sure you aren't charged with accomplice to the murders." Hawke knew he couldn't promise her anything, he wasn't on the case or in Montana law enforcement. But at this moment, if he could get her to tell him who they were dealing with, he didn't care.

The door opened.

Ms. Barnes could see who entered, but his back was to the entrance. She smiled. "I told you, I have no idea what you're talking about. If you say Marion didn't kill Adrian, I guess you would know better than anyone else. But I don't know who killed Louise." She smiled. "Was Marion accounted for?"

Hawke wanted to shake the woman. She would have made a good actress because whoever she wanted to hear that little bit wouldn't have known she'd been fearing for her life just moments before.

"Trooper Hawke, what are you doing here?" Pannell asked.

Standing and facing the man, Hawke studied him. Had the woman been fearful of the man because he'd killed three people and embezzled from his own company or had the woman spoken those bold words to not let her boss know she was part of his problem?

"I came to speak to Louise." He'd leave off why.

Pannell bowed his head before returning his gaze to Hawke. "I'm beginning to think this retreat was a bad idea. It had been several years since we'd had a retreat. I thought it would help bring us together but all it has done is make everyone suspicious of each other and now two of my employees have been murdered." He turned his attention to Ms. Barnes. "Adele, I need you to find the phone number for Louise's parents, please. I need to call them."

"The police will notify the family," Hawke said.

"They are, but I want to tell them how sorry I am and how much of a valued employee Louise was." Pannell studied him as if he were waiting for Hawke to criticize his desire to give the family comfort.

Hawke nodded. "I need to be leaving."

Ms. Barnes had hurried out of the room as soon as Pannell had asked her for the phone number.

Before he left, Hawke needed to let Pierce know what he'd said to Ms. Barnes. And see if the man could get someone to watch her. She had to meet up with the accomplice at some point.

He also wondered if his three young accountants were here. At the registration desk, he asked the young woman if the three men were registered.

She shook her head. "Mr. Garcia didn't come with the rest when they transferred from the Island to here. Mr. Johnson was here but left this morning. Mr. DeLan is scheduled to leave tomorrow."

"Thank you." Hawke went in search of Pierce.

Chapter Twenty-one

"What do you mean you had a talk with Ms. Barnes?" Pierce asked as the two sat in the dining room of the lodge sipping coffee.

Hawke's phone buzzed. It was Bo. He sighed. He'd avoided checking in to be there when he told Marion. Hawke held up a finger and texted. *Feds and State Police are here. Not good. I'll tell you both more when I get back.* He knew Marion would figure out the woman she'd asked to help was dead. He let out a long sigh.

"Trouble in your love life?" Pierce asked.

"I wish. No, this is family. Marion is going to be busted up about the victim's death. She hadn't wanted to involve anyone for this very result. I doubt she'll trust me about anything again." Hawke stared into the cup of coffee. He'd just gotten his sister back and he'd screwed up their relationship.

"If it's any consolation, we discovered she had been keeping a very detailed diary of what people said and who she saw talking to whom." Pierce slid an opened thin journal across the table.

Hawke read the top line. *Mr. Pannell has been on his phone more since we came to the mainland lodge than he is at work in Dallas.* Hawke glanced up. "Do you think he was clearing up the accounting mess or covering his tracks for killing someone?"

"Skip down to the next to last sentence."

I saw Adele slipping into her room after 2 am. She only had a robe on, it slipped as she was unlocking her door. Who was she entertaining?

"I accused her of sleeping with an accountant to get him to steal money." Hawke looked across the table at the Special Agent. "Does this lodge have any surveillance cameras?"

"Lt. Gernot is having a look at the night in question right now." Pierce pulled the book back. "Go to your sister. Comfort her. With this book and some surveillance footage, we'll get to the bottom of this soon." Pierce finished off his coffee and stood. "I don't want to see you around here again. We have this covered."

Hawke's gaze was still on the book. "Could I take photos of the pages in that book?"

Pierce studied him. "What do you think you'll find that we don't already know?"

Hawke shrugged. "Just because one person was slipping into her room, doesn't mean she was having a clandestine meeting with someone. I'd just like to see what all Louise jotted down."

"Knock yourself out." Pierce tossed the book on the table between them.

Pulling out his phone, Hawke flipped to what

appeared to be Louise's first spying efforts. He took a photo of each page until the last entry about Ms. Barnes.

"Thanks." Hawke nodded, stood, and headed to the front door.

"Hold up!"

He turned and found Lt. Gernot striding toward him.

"Yeah?" he asked when she stopped in front of him.

"Walk outside with me." She strode past him and out the lodge entrance.

Hawke followed, figuring she had something to say that she didn't want anyone else to hear. He hoped it wasn't a reaming for harboring a fugitive and getting in the middle of her homicide.

She stopped over by the horse corrals. The lieutenant peered into the corral before facing him. "I understand your need to protect your sister. But we have been doing everything in our power to find out who killed Mr. Ulrick, Philip Longo, and now Louise Beltane. With the fact all three homicides are connected and your sister wasn't near the latter two when their deaths occurred, I am taking Marion off the list of suspects." She crossed her arms, "But I am sending a letter of reprimand to your superior for your lack of trust in Montana State Police to bring about justice, harboring a fugitive, and for interfering in our investigation."

Hawke laughed.

The woman glared and held up a hand as if that would stop his laughter.

It didn't. He laughed harder before getting his mirth under control. "Lieutenant, I know you have to do all of that to show your superiors that I was uncontrollable, but if you look at the information you have obtained, and the information I have presented to you, you'll notice that I was closer to the truth than you were."

She opened her mouth and uttered, "Don—"

"But I will concede and let you get to the bottom of this. I'm taking my sister home and you can contact her through me at the Winslow Oregon State Police Headquarters." He touched the brim of his Stetson and walked over to Bo's pickup. He started it up and hummed as he drove back to the cabin.

While Marion was going to be sad about her friend, she should be happy he would take her to their mom's so she could start healing.

He emerged from the trees and the cabin came into view. He'd only been gone three hours but the empty feeling that settled on him at the sight of the cabin gave him a chill. That's when he noticed the little red car he'd used to escape whoever had followed him from the morgue sat lower to the ground. He slowed, creeping up to the house and car. The tires spread out under the wheels resting on deflated rubber.

He slammed the pickup into park, shoved the door open, and ran into the cabin, shouting for Marion.

Scratching and barking at a bedroom door, sent him running down the short hall to the room at the back. The one where Marion had slept.

He opened the door, and Dog slammed into his chest whimpering.

"What's wrong boy?"

That's when he spotted Bo's crumpled body on the floor. "Shit!"

Hawke dropped to his knees and felt for a pulse. There was one. It was faint. He searched for injuries and found a large knot on Bo's head. Helping his friend onto the bed, he dialed Pierce.

"Hawke, calling to tell me you and Marion are headed home?" Pierce answered.

"No. Have Pannell bring you to the cabin where he talked to Marion and me the other night. My friend is unconscious and has a lump on his head. He needs care. I'm going after whoever has Marion." He hung up, put a glass of water and aspirin within reach of Bo, and gathered up the camping equipment he could find around the house. Shoving the camping gear in his duffel bag with his clothes, he also grabbed whatever food wasn't perishable and the box of dog biscuits he'd purchased for Dog.

"Come on, Dog. We're going to go find Marion."

<><><><><><>

"Get moving!" Caleb yelled at her as Marion fell and shoved up to her feet.

"Why are you doing this?" she asked again for the hundredth time since Caleb had taken them by surprise, hitting Bo hard with a board when he'd stood in her bedroom doorway asking if she wanted to go for a walk.

She'd been surprised at how well Dog had behaved when she'd told him to stay with Bo. She'd feared Caleb would kill Dog if he tried to save her. But the dog had stayed and she'd closed the door of the bedroom and followed Caleb out of the cabin. She didn't want anyone else to get harmed because of her. She knew Louise was dead. She could tell by the way Bo had told her what Gabriel had texted.

"I need to know what Adrian knew. We're going to stay up here in the wilderness until you tell me." Caleb who had always looked nerdy and scholarly was dressed in jeans, flannel, and hiking boots. He carried a heavy-looking backpack and hadn't shown any signs of struggling under the weight or the pace they'd been keeping.

"Have you been out in the wilderness before?" she asked, more for information than to tell him she knew nothing.

"I spend all my weekends in the mountains. I love hiking and the outdoors. No one cares if you subtracted wrong or said something inappropriate to the wrong person. I like being alone."

This man sounded like her brother, only Gabriel wouldn't kill people for money or for any other reason.

"I haven't been hiking out in the woods very much the last twenty years," she said and sat down on a log. She knew if she could stay alive long enough, Gabriel and Dog would find her.

"Get up. We have to keep moving." Caleb didn't touch her, but his eyes, without his glasses, looked large and wild.

"I'm tired, my feet hurt. These aren't exactly the best hiking shoes." She held up her foot showing off the soft canvas sneaker with a thin sole. "I feel every stick and rock with these things."

"If you just tell me what Adrian told you, I'll leave you here. You can find your way back, and I'll keep going." He held a water bottle out to her.

If Caleb had Adrian killed and then killed the murderer and Louise, she didn't want to eat or drink anything he gave her. And she found it hard to believe he would just leave her out here in the woods if she told him the truth. He'd kill her. But she had to stay alive and stall. It was the only way Gabriel would find her alive.

She grasped the water bottle and was pleased to find it was still sealed. That meant he would keep her alive until she told him what he wanted to know. If only she knew the answer.

"Thank you." She drank a quarter of the bottle. "Why did you have Adrian killed?"

Caleb's face darkened in color. "I didn't kill him."

"I didn't say 'why did you kill him?' I said why did you have him killed? There's a difference." She took another swallow of water, watching Caleb.

"Technically, I didn't." Caleb motioned to her bottle. "Do you want me to carry that?"

"No."

"Then get up and let's get moving. I want to get to a certain spot by tonight." He grabbed her arm, dragging her to her feet, and then prodded her along in front of him.

When the push of his hand became irritating, Marion swung around. "Stop pushing me!" She put her hands on her hips and glared at the man.

Caleb smirked. "I'll leave you here if you tell me what Adrian learned and who he told."

She held up her hands. "I don't know. He didn't tell me anything. All he said was when he got back, he was going to look into the discrepancy he'd found."

Caleb shook his head. "He knew more. I saw him copy files and put them in a large envelope. When I asked Jerry in mailing what Adrian sent, he said Adrian sent out three envelopes. One to himself, one to you, and one to the FBI. The envelopes weren't found at your place or Adrian's. I need to know what he sent the FBI."

"Because you were named in the papers?" Marion asked. While she hadn't thought him capable of murder when they all arrived at the Island Resort, she did now. He was no longer the glasses-wearing geek that she'd always appraised him as. He looked like a man who could survive in this wilderness and one who would kill to survive.

"That's what I want to know. Why wasn't the envelope found in your apartment?" he asked.

"Because I had my mail held while I was away. It's probably sitting in the post office waiting for me to pick it up." Maybe he'd take her to Dallas to get the mail. The envelope wouldn't be there, but in civilization she'd have a better chance of getting away from him.

"That means you and no one else can get the mail?" He seemed to be talking to himself as he thought.

"See, I don't know anything. Can I go back to the cabin now?" She walked around him as if heading back the way they had come.

A hand grabbed her arm and swung her around. "You're not going back until I'm sure you don't know anything and I'm far enough away no one will find me."

He pulled her through the trees and underbrush.

Marion dragged her feet, hoping it made a clear trail for Gabriel to follow.

Chapter Twenty-two

Hawke and Dog found the trail within fifteen minutes of starting their search. Hawke had given Dog a piece of Marion's clothing to sniff and soon they were headed through the trees and brush at a good pace.

He found a spot where Marion and her abductor had stopped. It didn't appear as if Marion was in any distress. She'd sat on a log. He could tell her sneaker print from the hiking boots of the other person. He believed the person was a man by the size of his feet and weight. He was either a large man or he had on a well-stocked backpack. By the strides the man took, Hawke believed he was an average-sized man with a heavy pack.

That meant he was prepared to stay out in the wilderness. Hawke wondered what clothing Marion had on. Would the person give her adequate clothing for the cold nights? He picked up the pace after surveying the area where they'd stopped. Not soon after that, the two had stopped again.

"Good girl," Hawke said out loud. Marion was slowing them down so he could catch up. After this stop though, her feet were dragging and the other prints were alongside hers as if she were being pulled along.

"Damn, either she's injured or she said something that pissed the guy off." He peered into Dog's eyes. "Come on. We can't be that far behind them."

The cabin Bo had acquired for them was at the edge of the Lolo National Forest. Whoever had Marion was headed deeper into the wilderness and possibly over the Continental Divide. If he was the person who'd killed three people, that would be the perfect place to get lost and head off to enjoy the money he'd embezzled. The basalt and granite cliffs would hide his trail.

He needed to catch up to Marion and her abductor before they reached the Divide. The person wasn't going to take Marion with him which meant he would either leave her to die in the wilderness or kill her. Hawke didn't like either of those scenarios.

He continued following their trail until dark. The prints had ended at the edge of a rock escarpment. The lack of sunlight would make it hard to find their trail unless Dog could sniff it out. However, walking around on the rocky terrain in the dark was dangerous. He had a flashlight but feared if he was gaining on Marion and her abductor, they might see the light and keep going rather than stopping for the night.

As Hawke fed Dog a handful of dog bones and ate jerky and a granola bar, he wondered at the miles they had covered. Either the man who had Marion knew this wilderness or he was a skilled outdoorsman. Thinking of the people whom they had thought embezzled the money, he could only think of one person who might be well-versed in wilderness hiking—Pannell. He would have the money and the means to go hiking whenever he wanted. Had he picked Montana to have the retreat because he knew it well and had planned a way to escape should things go wrong? But Pannell would have had to have ridden a horse at top speed to the cabin to have abducted Marion before Hawke arrived. There hadn't been a horse around the cabin or footprints other than the two sets from the night Pannell and his guard had visited.

Hawke peered up the rocky side of the mountain where he camped and wondered if Marion's abductor had taken her up or planned to continue using canyons to make his way up and over the Rocky Mountains.

Marion sat as hunched as she could to use her core body temperature to warm her extremities. There had been a time when she'd thought Caleb was a sweet, but geeky, young man. Now she loathed him. The sun was starting to lighten the area under the rocks where he'd insisted they had to spend the night.

Once they'd made it to the shelter, he'd lit a battery-operated lamp and she noticed there was no way anyone on the outside of their rock hideout would see the light. Caleb had also lit a Sterno pot and placed a metal stand he'd unfolded over the top of it. He'd tied her hands and feet while he left the area and returned with water in a pan. He placed that over the Sterno and started asking her questions.

Between the odor of the burning Sterno, her wondering when Gabriel would catch up, and Caleb's insistent questions about what Adrian had told her, Marion had a hard time swallowing the meal in a bag he'd cooked in the pot of water. She was pretty sure if she'd just been hiking on her own, she would have devoured it, but even though her stomach was grumbling and she knew she needed energy for the following day, she couldn't swallow more than four bites.

When Caleb saw she wasn't eating, he'd taken the packet from her, ate it himself, and tossed her a blanket.

She'd spent the night with tied hands and feet, curled as tight as she could get under the thin blanket while he slept in a thick sleeping bag on top of a thin pad.

She needed to pee. Struggling to sit up, she kicked Caleb's foot inside his sleeping bag.

He sat up quickly and stared around the rock enclosure before his gaze landed on her.

"I have to pee," she said, unceremoniously. Maybe he'd take her bindings off and she could try to make a break.

He rubbed his eyes and stretched his arms before moving toward her on his knees. "I'm going to untie you. Go on outside and do what you need to do, but if you aren't back in a reasonable amount of time, I'm coming after you. When I catch you, I don't care if you have information, I'll tie you to a tree and let the animals have you." His eyes held a coldness she'd only seen once before. They were the eyes of the man strangling Adrian.

She nodded and shivered as he untied her hands and feet and motioned toward the opening between two boulders that he'd used the night before to go out and get the water.

Marion's body was stiff from her curled-up position and the cold. Once she was outside of the rock enclosure, she scanned the area for a place to pee. She noticed the small spring where Caleb must have filled the pot with water the night before.

Staying away from the spring, she walked over behind a large rock and squatted. When she was finished, she walked to the spring, scrubbed her hands in the water, and washed her face. The water was cold and invigorating. Now she scanned the canyon they were in. Would Gabriel find the wrapper she'd dropped after they'd walked a while in the rocks and then came back down and continued up the canyon? She hoped an animal hadn't found it and packed it off before he came to it.

If he didn't catch up to them today, she would know he lost their tracks.

"Here, this is all I'm giving you since you won't eat the M.R.E.s," Caleb said, walking toward her with his pack on his back. "Let's go. I plan to get across these mountains in three days, with or without you."

"Then just leave me here. I can't help you. I don't know anything. Adrian only told me he found some money missing. If you hadn't kidnapped me, I wouldn't have known it was you." She threw that at him. Showing him he'd made more than one mistake following his greed.

"No, we're still close enough that you could find your way back. I plan to leave you up where you don't know which way to go." He pushed her upper back. "Get moving. Just stay at the bottom of this canyon."

A flash of brown to her right had Marion stopping and staring into the pine trees. Moving branches revealed a bull elk. He moved gracefully through the trees, his antlers deflecting the branches around him.

"Move!" Caleb insisted.

The bull elk took off at a run, his antlers clattering against the trees.

Marion wanted to turn around and tell the man to

relax and enjoy what the Creator had put on this earth, but she knew he would just tell her to move. She started forward on sore feet, praying that Gabriel caught them today. She needed to doctor her blistered and punctured feet as well as would like something warmer to wear. As they slowly climbed higher and higher the air grew cooler. She'd spotted patches of snow in areas that didn't get a lot of sunlight.

Hawke woke before the golden glow of the sun crept over the forest. He'd stood in the dark in the middle of the night when he'd gotten up to pee. Staring up the side of the cliff, he'd tried to see anything that would tell them if Marion and her abductor were going straight up.

After a handful of jerky, a granola bar, and water, he refreshed Dog's memory of Marion's scent by having him smell the sweatshirt he'd brought with him.

Dog sniffed the shirt inside and out and stuck his nose to the ground, running back and forth before he started up the rocks as Hawke had feared. They went fifty yards up the rocky cliff and Dog made a quick right and headed down again.

"Damn, I should have known, they'd take the easier route," Hawke said, following Dog down the rocky cliff and into the narrow canyon. It was rocky on one side with a small stream, trees, and brush at the bottom.

From Dog's trot, Hawke judged they were getting close.

Dog disappeared to the left and before Hawke caught up to him, spotted the animal standing on a rock outcropping above the stream.

Hawke made his way toward the rocks. Dog disappeared.

Before Hawke reached the rock grouping, Dog darted out from between two of the boulders. Hawke saw the opening and entered. If Dog had run in and out without so much as a shout, there wasn't much chance that anyone was in there. But he might learn something.

Whoever had Marion knew this wilderness. He'd picked the perfect place to spend the night without anyone finding them. The area inside the ring of boulders was twenty feet in diameter. He noticed a rectangular area where the grass and small plants had been flattened. Not far from there he found an area shaped like a crescent. It appeared the abductor slept well while Marion slept cold.

Anger heated his torso and clenched his fists. He would make the person who treated his sister like a prisoner pay. He didn't see anything else in the small area.

Back out in the canyon, he found their footprints. He'd judge them to only be a couple of hours ahead of him. "Come Dog. We'll move quickly and quietly."

Dog put his nose to the ground and trotted up the canyon. Hawke jogged behind him. He could tell by the marks Marion made she was doing all she could to move slowly and deliberately, making as many marks in the ground as she could.

Chapter Twenty-three

"If you don't start moving faster, I'm going to drag you," Caleb said, in a tone that a week ago, Marion would have said wasn't Caleb but someone else.

"I told you these shoes aren't made for hiking. I have blisters and every time I step on a broken stick or pointed rock it bruises my feet. They hurt. Being dragged would be a blessing," Marion said. She held one of her sneakers in her hand, pulling out a small stick that had punctured the sole and poked her in the foot.

When Caleb turned to peer up the canyon, Marion piled small sticks in a formation pointing up the canyon.

She was replacing her shoe when he faced her.

"Get moving. At this pace, we won't be as far up the canyon as I'd planned for tonight."

Before she could reply, something brown and gray flashed out of the trees and across to the other side of the canyon.

Caleb spun, following the animal's movement.

Someone tackled him from behind.

Marion recognized Gabriel's hat that fell to the ground during the tackle. She jumped to her feet and looked around for a stick to help him. The two men rolled around on the ground. Caleb had maneuvered out of his heavy pack. When they stopped moving, Gabriel was the one on top. He had Caleb's arm behind his back and the younger man's face pressed into the dirt, sticks, and, Marion cringed, elk droppings.

"I knew you'd find us today," Marion said, as Dog walked up to her.

Hawke glanced at his sister. She looked dirty and pale. "Did he hurt you?"

"Not physically, but he marched me up here in improper shoes and clothing." She glared at the man Hawke had on the ground.

"I want to see who this is." Hawke had pulled the string from the hood of Marion's sweatshirt he'd been using for her scent, as he'd watched Marion take a stick out of her shoe and the man with her was staring up the canyon. He'd had his back to Hawke so he'd yet to make an identification of the man.

After tying the abductor's hands together behind his back, he pulled him up to his knees. "Stand."

The man remained on his knees.

"Stand up. Anyone who can carry that heavy pack can get to his feet with his hands tied behind his back." Hawke grabbed the back of the man's jacket and jerked him to his feet.

Hawke stopped his jaw from dropping when he recognized Caleb DeLan. The young man who had been so helpful when he was searching Adrian's room at the resort. "You were on my list but we hadn't put it all together yet," Hawke told the young man.

Caleb just stared ahead, saying nothing.

"Oh, now you're quiet. I could have used more of that during this hike you took me on," Marion said. "Can I go through his pack and see if he has another pair of shoes in there?"

Hawke nodded. "Take any clothes out of there you want. I have one of your sweatshirts over at my duffel bag. I was using it for scent."

"You can follow scent?" Caleb asked.

Hawke stared at the man and laughed. When he stopped laughing, he said, "For Dog. He followed her scent and I followed him."

Caleb glared. He didn't like being treated like a dummy. Hawke put that information away for later.

Marion walked back toward them wearing her sweatshirt and carrying Hawke's duffle bag. He'd worn it like a pack with one strap over each shoulder. She dropped his bag next to Caleb's pack and started digging through it. She pulled out a pair of wool socks, waterproof pants, and a pair of athletic shoes.

While she put all of these on, Hawke studied Caleb. The accountant looked different dressed like an outdoorsman and giving him an overconfident stare.

"I don't suppose you want to tell me why you paid to have Adrian killed and then killed the man you'd paid for the job?" Hawke asked.

The man didn't bat an eye.

"Then when Louise Beltane overheard something, I'd say you and your accomplice talking, you killed her, too."

The man's gaze flickered a moment.

Was it the mention of an accomplice or Louise's

death that had caught his attention? "Care to share who your accomplice is?" Hawke asked.

Caleb remained quiet.

"He kept asking me what Adrian had told me. He wouldn't believe me that I only know that someone was embezzling and Adrian was going to get to the bottom of it when we returned," Marion said.

"What were you going to do with Marion?" Hawke asked, pretty sure he'd planned to kill her when he'd reached the other side of the mountains.

It was as if the man's lips had been sewn shut. He didn't mutter a sound and stared straight ahead. Almost as if he'd been taken in by the police before. Funny that hadn't come up in background checks.

"Marion, slip that duffle on like a pack. It's not very heavy. I'd like to make him carry his pack but I don't want to untie his hands to get it on him." Hawke shouldered Caleb's pack and then he grabbed the man by the arm, leading him back the way they'd traveled.

They'd only hiked about an hour when Hawke heard Marion's stomach growling. "Stop. I've got some food in the duffle," he said.

"There's a lot of food in Caleb's pack," Marion offered.

Hawke slid it off his shoulders. Maybe he'd find some climbing rope to use on Caleb. He didn't trust the string he'd pulled from the sweatshirt hood.

"Sit on the ground," Hawke told the other man, giving him a downward push with a hand on his shoulder.

Caleb sat on the ground. He hadn't uttered a word as they hiked.

Digging through the man's pack, Hawke found

M.R.E.s, granola bars, dried fruit, jerky, and water purification tablets.

He handed dried fruit and a granola bar to Marion. Then he handed a bar to Caleb.

The younger man looked at him as if to say, "How do I eat with my hands tied behind my back."

Hawke held the bar out to Marion. "Open that and hold it while he takes bites."

She did as he asked. Hawke grabbed jerky for himself and shared it with Dog.

After about a fifteen-minute break, Hawke pulled the pack back on and motioned for Caleb to stand. "Let's get going. I'd like to be within phone service by tonight."

They hiked another hour when Dog's hackles rose along his spine and he lowered his head, peering into the trees.

"Hey, Boy, don't start anything," Hawke said, staring into the trees in the same direction as Dog.

Marion moved closer to Hawke. "What is it?"

"From the way Dog is acting, I'd say it's a cougar or a bear." Hawke still didn't see anything. "Let's keep moving, but keep an eye to your right in case whatever it is decides to charge us."

"I'm not going to get myself eaten because you think you can outsmart a wild animal," Caleb said.

Hawke stared at the man who hadn't said anything for hours. "I'm not trying to outsmart it; I'm showing it doesn't scare me. That I won't hurt it."

"With my hands tied, how can I run from it if it does chase us?" Caleb asked, his shoulders shrugging as he moved his hands behind his back.

"You won't have to run." Hawke grabbed the man's arm and started moving forward. "Marion, get in front of me and keep alongside the stream."

They started forward.

Tree limbs snapped and the sound of beating hooves growing closer came from behind them. Hawke shoved Caleb to his right and pulled Marion behind him, making a path for what sounded like elk stampeding their direction.

They'd barely made it into the timber when the first cow elk galloped by. She was followed by fifteen cows and calves.

"They're magnificent!" Marion said in a voice laced with awe.

A large bull brought up the rear running at top speed. From the tufts of hair sticking up on his rump, Hawke believed he had tried to battle with a cougar before following his herd.

When the sound died away, Hawke turned his attention to his sister and… "Damn!" Caleb had taken off while he and Marion stared at the elk running by.

"He can't be far," Marion said.

"No. I'll take you back to Pierce and you can tell him everything you learned from Caleb." Hawke didn't like going back without the person who abducted Marion, but she was his first concern. She needed to be back in civilization. She'd never taken to the outdoors like he had.

"That's crazy. If you take me back, are you just going to turn around and come back up here looking for Caleb?" She put her hands on her hips and stared at him.

"Most likely, yeah." He wasn't going to lie. He wanted Caleb for ruining his sister's life.

"Then why waste time? I'm dressed better now and we have all the supplies. Let's catch him. He said he was headed to the other side of the Rockies. I think he was meeting someone."

Hawke studied his sister. She had determination on her face and a fire in her eyes. She wanted the man who had Adrian killed.

"Okay." He held up a hand. "Don't move. I need to find his tracks." Hawke stepped to the spot where he'd last seen Caleb. He spotted the displaced and cracked twigs where he'd stood. Using this as a starting point, he scanned the ground and found a footprint. He stepped forward and studied the ground for another one. He went about twenty feet and found the string that had tied the man's hands. He'd managed to stretch it and wiggle out. Hawke had been afraid of that and should have tied him better the first chance he had. But his main thought had been to get the two of them down to authorities.

"This way," he said, motioning for Marion to follow him. From the displaced debris on the forest floor, Caleb had taken off at a run. At least with him running his tracks were easier to see.

Chapter Twenty-four

At dark, Hawke had to concede the man they were following knew all the tricks to hide his tracks. Once Caleb had stopped running, he'd used a limb to brush away his footprints, he'd crossed several rocky areas, and even walked in a stream. Which would have left him with cold wet feet unless his hiking boots were waterproof.

Hawke was still on his trail, but wouldn't be able to follow him without light to show all the deceptions the man was using. "We'll camp here tonight." Hawke slid the heavy pack off his shoulders and moved his arms to get circulation back in his shoulders.

"Do you want to put some of the items from that pack into the duffle bag?" Marion asked.

"No. I'll get used to it by tomorrow." Though he knew after his extended stay in the mountains in December that he no longer had the stamina and strength he did ten or even five years ago. "Let's find a good spot under the cover of a rock overhang or a large pine."

"Why do we need a roof over us?" Marion asked, walking over to a large tree where they could stand up and barely touch the lowest branches.

"I like to have a bit of a buffer from any wind or precipitation that might form during the night." Hawke followed her and knelt beside the pack. He pulled out the Sterno burner, a pot, and three MREs. He listened and heard a stream trickling nearby.

"Go ahead and get my sleeping bag out and the one in the pack. Place them close to the tree trunk. I'm going to get water to boil our dinner."

Marion nodded and unzipped the duffle as Hawke walked out from under the tree in the direction of the stream. Dog bounded up beside him. "Go back to Marion. Keep her safe," Hawke said, motioning for the animal to go back to camp.

The animal stared in the direction Hawke was going and then back at the camp.

"Go on. I'll be fine." Hawke motioned again, and Dog trotted to the tree.

Knowing Dog was keeping Marion company eased his mind. He could think about Caleb's flight. The young man was taking a lot of paths up the face of cliffs and rock walls. It had been hard in a couple of places for Hawke to keep going with the heavy pack, The younger man had nothing but his own weight. However, he would be hungry and cold tonight. That should slow him down a bit tomorrow.

Hawke found the stream, filled the pot, and headed back the way he'd come. He heard the snuffling sound before his eyes made out the large dark shape moving through the trees toward Marion and Dog. It was late spring, early summer, if that was a sow bear she could have cubs following her which would make her meaner.

Hawke moved as quickly and quietly as he could toward the tree and their camp. Navigating around the creature heading in the same direction.

He ducked under the tree from a different direction than he left, startling both Dog and Marion. They were staring in the direction of the oncoming bear.

"What do we do?" Marion whispered.

"Toss the package of jerky in Caleb's pack as far as you can to the right. Then pick up the duffle and one of the sleeping bags. I'll grab the pack and the other sleeping bag. Then go out behind the tree and keep going. I'll be right behind you."

Marion did as Gabriel asked, even though her knees and hands were shaking. She'd never been this close to a bear. And it wasn't a small cute bear. The thing was huge. She kept on jogging, using the adrenaline to keep her going. A large boulder blocked her way. Or at least that's what it looked like in the darkness of night.

"What do we do now?" she asked, turning back and listening to Gabriel's labored breathing behind her.

"I don't think the bear will keep following us. We gave it the food that gives off the most scent." Gabriel dropped the pack and sleeping bag at his feet and dug into the pack. He straightened with a flashlight in his hand. The beam bounced off a boulder the size of a van. The light moved to the right and reflected off a wall of rock.

"It looks like we have found the base of a cliff. This will be where we spend the night." Gabriel grabbed the sleeping bag off the pack, laid it out, and fished his hand into the pack. He held out a granola bar, water bottle, and dried fruit. "We'll heat up MREs for breakfast when we have better light."

He sat on the sleeping bag and opened a granola bar.

Marion had spread out the sleeping bag she'd snagged and sat on it as she ate their meager meal. Her stomach continued to growl after she'd eaten. She knew it was from all the hiking she'd been doing and not enough calories. Finishing off the bottle of water, she wandered into the darkness and peed before slipping into the sleeping bag and trying to go to sleep. Her last thoughts were, how far away from Caleb's trail were they? She was beginning to believe they would not catch up to him and would be better off going back to Bo and the FBI agent and see if they could get him on the other side of the mountain range.

Hawke woke feeling stiff and pissed. He should have gone back to Pierce, had Marion tell him everything she knew, and then worked on the angle of an accomplice working with Caleb. Now that they knew he was the one who moved money around and was willing to kill to keep it, they needed to find out if Ms. Barnes hired Longo and falsified the contract between him and Marion. Ms. Barnes was the person who had access to everything even if Pannell was too blind to see that. He thought she only knew what he wanted her to know, yet she had access to anything she wanted in that company. The other people didn't know she wasn't trusted by Pannell. All she had to say was Mr. Pannell wanted an update on whatever and they would give her the information.

He stood. His joints popped and he cursed under his breath. Fifty-five wasn't that old, but he wasn't as young as he used to be. This prolonged hiking was for younger people. He'd much rather be on his horse.

With daylight, he could see they were in a large valley with a long high bluff of limestone in their path if they kept going east. He wanted to get to a place where he could contact Bo to retrieve them or find an easy trail to get back to the authorities. But first, he wanted water to make something warm to drink.

"Gabriel, I found a stream down that way."

He turned at Marion's voice and realized her sleeping bag was rolled up, and she wasn't wearing the rain pants anymore. She had a small coffee pot in one hand.

"Is there coffee in Caleb's pack?" he asked, thinking this day might not be so bad after all.

"Yes." Marion placed the pot on top of the Sterno stove she'd already lit and tossed in a white packet. "It's a good thing I picked this up and put it in the pack before our bear showed up or we wouldn't have anything to heat up water."

"Why did you do that?" Hawke studied her.

"I didn't want to wait for water to boil to eat." She laughed sarcastically. "And then we had to take a long hike before we even were able to eat."

Hawke shook his head. "But it worked out for the best this morning."

"How are you going to find Caleb's trail?" Marion asked.

"We're not. We're going to try and find a trail back to Bo and Pierce. Caleb is probably on the other side of the mountains by now. The next best thing is to find his accomplice."

Hawke pulled the pot off the Sterno when the water started boiling. He pulled three MREs out of the pack and opened them one at a time, breaking open the heating pouch and placing the food pouch inside. When the food and coffee were ready, he handed Marion a cup of coffee and an MRE along with a multipurpose utensil.

He dumped the contents of one MRE on a rock for Dog and then dug into his packet.

It was quiet as they ate. As soon as Marion finished, she asked, "How do you plan to find a trail headed back?"

"This looks like it could be a popular place. We'll go along the bottom of this cliff and see if we find any signs of a human trail." Hawke hoped there would be a trail that would take them west to a trailhead or lookout where he could use a radio to contact Bo.

Within fifteen minutes, they had their packs on and were walking north along the cliff. To the west was a small lake. Three different camps were set up along its shore.

Hawke walked up to the first camp which had a couple and two children. "Hi. We came to the cliff from a southern direction and wondered if there was a trail around here leading out to a trailhead?"

The man studied them. "There aren't very many trails to the south."

Not wanting to worry the couple since he was sure the only people Caleb would harm were those who would put him in jail, he kept they were following a fugitive to himself. "We nearly got ran over by a herd of elk and lost the trail we were on and then last night we had an encounter with a bear that put us further off course." He glanced at Marion who nodded her head.

"I see." The man pointed. "Go straight that way and you'll come to a trail. Follow it south and then west."

"How far is that?" Hawke asked, shifting the heavy pack.

"About twelve miles, maybe a little more."

"Thanks." Hawke shifted the pack and walked in the direction the man told him.

Marion caught up to him. "Are you sure you don't want me to take some of that or at least go through and leave behind what we don't need? If we're going to get to a ranger station today, we don't need the extra food."

"I'll concede we can get rid of some of the clothes and whatever else it looks like we don't need." Hawke slid the pack down his arms, and they both knelt beside it. He untied the top and started pulling items out. The sleeping bag first, then the Sterno stove, coffee pot, and pan.

Marion pulled out a tin. "This has the coffee." She added it to the pile of other items they would need.

Hawke also placed all the granola bars and dried fruit in the pan to save. And the six MREs that were left. "I don't see a need for these clothes." He pulled out two pairs of pants with lots of pockets like Caleb had been wearing. Two more flannel shirts, two t-shirts, four pairs of socks and boxer shorts, a sweatshirt, and a nice jacket.

Looking at the clothing, Hawke shook his head. There was nothing in this that should make the pack feel so heavy. "I don't understand why the pack felt like I was carrying more than this."

He grasped the empty pack. It was heavier than any empty pack he'd ever carried. "It's still heavy." He pulled it closer and felt the outside pockets. They were empty other than some fishing line, lures, hooks, and snare lines. Caleb had everything he needed to survive in the mountains in his pack. Hawke wondered how he was faring without it. But that didn't answer why it was heavy. He pulled his knife out of his boot sheath and pried the top off one of the metal tubes that made up the frame of the pack.

"Hand me that flashlight," he said, holding a hand out to Marion. She placed the flashlight in his hand and he flicked it on. Shining the light down in the aluminum tube, it illuminated something metal wedged in the tubing.

"I need something that will fit in here that's about five inches long." His knife blade was wider than the opening.

Marion looked through the duffle bag she'd been packing before digging through the pile of items they planned to keep. "All I can find are the eating utensils." She handed them both to Hawke.

He opened the Swiss knife-like utensils to the knife on both sets and tried to pry the object out of the frame. It wasn't easy. What he wouldn't give for his own Swiss Army knife with pliers right now. But that had been left behind in his pack in his truck somewhere in Ronan.

After what felt like hours, he finally wiggled the metal out of the tubing. "Damn! It's a twenty-gram bar of gold." He pulled his gaze from the gold bar and studied his sister.

"That's why this is so heavy. It has the money he embezzled, converted to gold." Hawke glanced at the items in the leave pile. "Let's just take the food, cooking utensils, and sleeping bag."

Marion nodded as she picked up the clothing. "Shouldn't we at least put this alongside the trail when we get there so someone can make use of them?"

"If you don't mind carrying them that far," Hawke

said, knowing that leaving the clothing would lighten the pack only a little. The riches in the frame of the pack were the real weight. And now it wasn't just physical weight it was mental as well. He didn't for one minute think that Caleb ran off and left this. He had been leading them to some place where he could ambush them and get the pack back when the bear had chased them off course.

Caleb was most likely backtracking and looking for their trail. All his trying to hide his tracks had been just a ruse to keep Hawke's attention on the ground.

"Let's hike as fast as we can. I want to get to a radio and contact Bo." Hawke shouldered the pack and stood.

Marion had shoved the clothing in the duffle bag. She pulled it over her shoulders. "I'm ready."

Dog went ahead of them. Fifteen minutes later they came across an easy-to-see trail. Hawke headed south. It was faster walking on the cleared trail than it had been moving through the forest and climbing rock cliffs.

They stopped once to eat granola bars, drinking as they hiked. By four in the afternoon, Hawke spotted what looked like a campground and trailhead. Hawke asked the first person he saw to borrow their phone.

"The service out here isn't very good," the man said.

"I'd like to give it a try," Hawke said, thinking if nothing else he could dial 9-1-1 and have the dispatch contact Pierce.

He dialed Bo's number and the man answered. "Who's this?"

"It's Hawke. We're at the start of trail one-twelve and we need to be picked up ASAP."

"You have Marion?" Bo asked.

"And more. Come soon." Hawke ended the call as it started to crackle. He handed the phone back to the man.

"Thank you."

Then he led Marion over to an area where they could sit in the trees and keep an eye on the trailhead.

"What are we going to do?" Marion asked.

"Put this up a tree and sit here to wait for Bo. If Caleb comes down the trail, we'll tell him I ditched the heavy pack to get out of there quicker." Hawke unloaded the sleeping bag, food, and cooking utensils out of the pack, leaving it beside the duffel bag where they'd keep watch. He walked to a large pine thirty feet farther into the forest. He used the climbing rope from Caleb's pack to hoist it twenty feet into the air.

Once that was secured, he smiled at Marion. "We'll be out of here in a few hours and can start working on finding Caleb's accomplice."

They walked back to the area where they would wait for Bo.

"What if he didn't have an accomplice?" Marion asked.

Chapter Twenty-five

Marion sat staring at the trailhead. She wondered if Caleb would be so angry that he'd lost his gold that he'd use violence to get it back. She'd observed the crazy in his eyes when he was dragging her out into the wilderness. Knowing that what he'd killed for was only thirty feet away hanging in a tree made her stomach cramp. Gabriel had made them MREs but she couldn't stomach the dehydrated food even if she felt as if she hadn't really eaten in weeks.

She glanced at Hawke who appeared to be napping with his hat pulled down over his eyes. Wasn't he scared? Then she noticed his hand on Dog's back. The animal was staring at the same spot she had been. That's when she realized how much her brother relied on the animal to be his eyes and ears. She'd witnessed the devotion between the man and animal since the first time she'd met them.

The sound of helicopter blades slicing the air, made

her look up into the sky. Out of the corner of her eye, she caught Gabriel raising his hat and studying the aircraft. A smile tipped his lips, and Dog's tail started wagging. She had a hunch she'd be meeting Dani again.

Gabriel stood. "Gather up our stuff and meet Bo and Dani at the helicopter. I'll cut down the pack and join you."

Marion shook her head. "I think we should go together to get the pack. Or better yet, step out and show yourself to Bo and the two of you can cut it down. We don't know that Caleb isn't lurking around waiting for us to show ourselves."

His grin grew. He rubbed a hand over his face, sobering his expression but his eyes danced with merriment. "I believe you have become as skeptical as me in a short period of time."

She laughed. "Let's go get Bo."

They stepped out of the trees as Bo walked out from the helicopter. Dani sat in the pilot's seat.

Marion ran over to Bo. "Gabriel needs your help."

He studied her but strode over to her brother.

Marion continued to the helicopter. She opened the door, tossed the duffle bag in, and crawled up into the seat.

"You'll have to crawl back there and sit," Dani said, tossing the duffle bag between the seats to an open area behind.

Marion peered into Dani's eyes. "Thank you for coming." She meant each syllable of every word.

"I heard you were kidnapped. Bo radioed me in as soon as Hawke took off after you. Only we didn't have a clue which way he went." Dani patted her shoulder. "Move on back, here come the boys."

Marion grinned at Dani calling the two men, who were more macho than any man she'd ever met before, boys. She settled in one of the back seats as Dog leaped back beside her. Then the pack was shoved between the seats. She pulled it on back, and then Bo appeared between the seats. He grinned and took the other seat.

Gabriel settled in the seat beside Dani and the helicopter rose, leaving a small group of people on the ground watching. Marion scanned the people and sucked in her breath. They'd just made it out in time.

She tapped Gabriel on the shoulder and shouted, "Caleb was down there watching us leave."

He nodded.

How long had he known that?

<◇><◇><◇>

Hawke felt a huge relief when Dani landed the helicopter at the Missoula Airport and he spotted Pierce and Lt. Gernot waiting for them. Dani had radioed ahead for the two to be there when they arrived after Hawke had told Bo and Dani what had happened and what was in the frame of the pack.

He climbed out of the helicopter after the propellers stopped turning. Hawke helped Marion out and Bo handed him the pack. By that time, both the special agent and the lieutenant were standing by the aircraft.

"Hawke, wasn't sure if we'd see you again," Pierce said, by way of greeting.

"Why's that? You know I always find my way back." Hawke held out the pack. "I don't know how much gold is shoved in the frame of this pack, but I'd bet it is the embezzled money from Pannell Financial."

"Where did you get the pack?" Lt. Gernot asked, reaching for it.

213

Hawke kept it out of her reach and handed it to Pierce. "Caleb DeLan had it on when I caught up to him and Marion. We were in the process of bringing him back when he got away, without the pack. I'll tell you the rest when you have this secured and we've had a decent meal."

He motioned for Dani, Marion, and Bo to keep walking.

"Wait a minute. Ms. Shumack needs to give a statement, and I want to know more about what happened," Lt. Gernot said.

"Hawke, call me when you're rested and we'll schedule a time to interview you and your sister," Pierce said.

Hawke raised a hand in acknowledgment and smiled. The federal agent knew him well. He wouldn't answer any questions until his sister was fed, cleaned up, and rested. He looked out for the innocent.

When they were all seated in Bo's truck, Dog sitting between the women in the back seat, Marion asked, "Do you always disregard authority?"

Dani and Bo laughed. Hawke gave them both a glare and said, "No. Only when I know someone, namely you, need to eat and rest before you get bombarded with questions. And don't you talk to anyone without me or Bo present."

"Will they allow that?" Marion asked.

Hawke shrugged. "We'll find out. Bo, where's the closest place to get something to eat, then a motel with a good shower and soft bed, please."

Marion studied her brother's profile. He had a quality about him she liked. He always was there for her, making sure she wasn't hurt. Did he do that for everyone he helped? She glanced over at Dani. The woman was petting Dog and staring at the back of Gabriel's hat with a soft smile tipping up her lips.

Bo drove them to a chain restaurant that served breakfast all day. Gabriel had the largest breakfast platter they made. Dani chided him for eating so much when he'd been putting little in his stomach for days.

Marion had half a sandwich, soup, and salad. She was full before she could eat the salad. But the green fresh vegetables looked so good, she forced them down. Stuffed, her eyelids got heavy and she wanted to take a nap.

"Let's go find a place for a nap," Gabriel said, as they all left the restaurant. When they entered the truck, Hawke handed Dog a sausage rolled up in a pancake.

"You are going to kill him early with all the people food you give him," Marion said.

"No, he works hard and deserves all the people food he wants," Gabriel replied, scratching Dog behind the ear and smiling at him.

Marion rolled her eyes and settled back in the seat.

The next thing she knew the truck had stopped and everyone was getting out. She'd dozed off after they'd eaten. The hotel was a nice one. She felt conspicuous walking in looking like a homeless person, in borrowed clothes carrying a duffle bag. Dog even was hesitant, as if he didn't think he'd be allowed.

"Get two rooms, I'm going to go see what I can learn from my sources," Bo said. "I'll be back for you in the morning."

"Thanks. I'm going to owe you an elk hunting trip in the Wallowas for all you've done." Gabriel put out his hand and the two men shook.

"I'll make sure you do that." Bo smiled at Marion and Dani. "Get some sleep. Everyone is safe now."

Marion smiled. "Thank you for all your help." She gave him a hug.

Bo's cheeks reddened. "You're welcome."

He disappeared and Gabriel turned to the clerk at the registration desk.

"Two rooms next to each other or with an adjoining door, please." Gabriel pulled his wallet out of his pocket.

She was going to owe him a lot for all the things he'd been paying for since Adrian's death.

"Dogs aren't allowed in this hotel," the clerk said.

Gabriel put a hand on Dog's head. "He's my service animal. He can detect when I'm about to get angry."

The clerk's gaze moved to the dog, up to Gabriel's face, and back down to the animal. "I don't see a service vest on him."

"I don't like people to know I have a problem." Gabriel stared at the man without giving away that he was lying.

He was good, Marion thought waiting to see how the whole thing played out. Bo had left and there was nothing they could do with Dog except take him up to the rooms.

"You'll have to pay an extra hundred in case the dog makes a mess," the clerk said.

"He won't," Gabriel said, signing papers.

The clerk looked dubious but handed Gabriel two packets with keys. "You'll be in rooms three-eleven and three-thirteen."

"Thank you." Gabriel motioned for her and Dani to walk to the elevator. Dog followed them, entered the elevator, and they rose to the third floor.

"That wasn't very nice lying about Dog being a service animal," Marion said.

Gabriel studied her for a couple of seconds. "He is a service dog. He helps me with my job all the time. If I were a canine officer, he would be a police dog and therefore in the service of a law enforcement agency."

She grinned. Learning more and more about her adult brother was becoming interesting.

He handed her a key packet. "You get lucky number thirteen," he said with a mischievous smile.

"It sums up the last couple of weeks pretty well," she answered, unlocked the door, and walked in. That's when she remembered she had the duffel bag with Gabriel's and Caleb's clothes. She'd dig out a new set of clean clothes for her and hand the bag over through the adjoining door so Gabriel would have his clothes.

Digging through the bag, she pulled out a pullover and a pair of cargo pants. She'd never worn this type of pant before, but she could see the need for all the pockets when one was working or hiking. She found a pair of socks and decided to wash her underwear and use the blow dryer to dry them.

She walked over to the adjoining door and knocked.

Dani opened the door. "Yes?"

"I thought Gabriel might want his duffle bag with his clothes. I took out the ones we pulled out of Caleb's pack so I'd have something clean to wear." Marion held out the bag.

"Thanks. Hawke's in the shower. He'll be happy to have some clean clothes. Sleep well." Dani closed the door and Marion left the clothes hanging over the chair and went into the bathroom. She was ready for a shower.

Chapter Twenty-six

Marion rose at the sound of knocking on the adjoining door.

"Marion, wake up. We need to get breakfast and go talk to Pierce," Gabriel called.

"I'm up," she said, rubbing her face and stretching her legs. She'd crawled into bed without a stitch of clothes on after the shower and promptly fell asleep.

Padding on bare feet to the bathroom, she plugged the hair dryer in and started drying her bra and panties hanging over the shower rod. She'd been too tired last night to dry them. They had dripped dry fairly well but still felt damp. While she dried the garments with one hand, she ran her fingers through her hair, untangling the strands that fell to the middle of her back.

Now there was pounding on her outside door.

"Hold on, I'm getting dressed," she called out, pulling on the panties and hooking the bra. She jogged into the main room, donned the pullover, and grabbed the pants, drawing them up and realizing they were about four inches too wide at the waist. She'd lost a lot of weight in the last two weeks.

Marion walked to the door, holding the pants together at the waist. She flung the door open. "You don't happen to have an extra belt in your duffle, do you?"

Gabriel, Dog, and Dani walked into the room. Dani closed the door behind them.

Gabriel placed the bag on the bed and dug through it. He came up with what looked like a shoestring. "Turn around."

She put her back to him and felt him pulling the loops on the pants together in the back, taking up the slack.

"It's not fashionable, but it will keep your pants from dropping to your feet," he said.

"Thanks," she said, sarcastically. Marion sat on the bed, pulled on the socks, and shoved her feet into Caleb's athletic shoes. "Any chance we can stop somewhere and get me some clothes that fit better before we leave Missoula?"

"I'm sure we can find the time once we've talked to Pierce." Gabriel walked to the door. "Let's get some food and get the interviews over with."

Marion couldn't agree more. They walked out of the hotel and to her surprise Gabriel walked over to a large silver SUV with its motor running. He opened the back door and motioned for Dani to get in. She did.

"This is some Uber," Marion said as she slid into the vehicle. Glancing at the driver's seat she discovered the FBI agent.

"Good morning, ladies," he said and smiled.

Gabriel closed Marion's door and sat in the front passenger seat.

"Where to?" Pierce asked.

"Breakfast," they all three said at the same time.

The agent smiled and put the car in gear.

Marion felt something poking her in the thigh. She shoved her hand between her leg and the seat but didn't find anything that could be poking her. Wiggling, she felt it again. But it wasn't the seat, it was in a pocket of the pants. Flipping up the flap on the pocket, she shoved her hand in and wrapped her fingers around what felt like a flash drive. She eased her hand out of her pocket and looked at the object while holding it down by the seat.

It was a flash drive. Not a cheap one. 1TB was inscribed on the plastic cover. Wanting to make sure she had a witness to the discovery, she shoved it back in her pocket and would pull it out at the restaurant, acting surprised.

Hawke leaned back in the bench seat at the restaurant. He was full and felt better than he had since getting the call from Marion nearly a week and a half ago. He'd noticed Pierce giving his sister the side eye, which was the only way he could study her considering they were sitting on the same bench. He couldn't tell if Pierce was interested professionally or personally.

Marion had been very quiet all during the meal, only speaking if asked a question. He could tell something was going on in that head.

Dani slid from the booth. "I'm going to the restroom."

Marion's gaze lit on Dani and she shoved out of the booth, too.

When the two women disappeared through the restroom door, Pierce asked, "Is your sister always this quiet?"

Hawke shook his head. "Something's going on. I don't know what. She spent the night in the next room, and she was sleeping hard. I checked on her twice and she was out. But it took her a long time to get dressed."

"I imagine she had a hard time putting those clothes on. I could tell they aren't hers."

"Yeah, they're actually clothes that were in the pack I handed over to you."

"They belong to our suspect?" Pierce asked.

"Yeah. He dragged Marion out of the cabin with flimsy shoes, inadequate clothing, and no coat. When we had him captured, I told her to dig through his pack for warmer clothes. Then when he ran, and we were trying to make his pack lighter, she took some of the clothing out and put it in my duffel." Hawke shrugged. "I didn't see any harm in her wearing clean clothes today."

"Maybe she was having trouble putting on the clothes from her abductor," Pierce said in a speculating voice.

Dani and Marion walked up to the booth. Dani motioned for Marion to sit and then she placed a flash drive on the table in front of Pierce.

"Marion found this in the pocket of these pants when we were in the Suburban," Dani said, sitting down on the bench beside Hawke.

Hawke studied his sister. "Why didn't you say something when you found it?"

Her gaze slashed to Pierce and back to Hawke. "I was afraid he'd think I made it up and had it with me all along. I was going to pull it out while we sat here but I couldn't think of a nonchalant way to find it."

"It does look suspicious that you withheld the knowledge of this for as long as you did, Ms. Shumack," Pierce said, all in your face Fed.

"I know. I should have said something as soon as I found it. But you have it now and that's all that matters." Marion's eyes were downcast as she'd behaved when chastised as a child. It was interesting to Hawke that he remembered so much about his sister as a child.

"Let's go give our statements. Pierce can have someone look at this while we're talking to him," Hawke said,

"I'm afraid, Lt. Gernot will also be in on the interviews," Pierce said.

Hawke groaned and Dani laughed.

"Let's get this over with." Hawke scooted along the bench, pushing Dani to her feet. "Come on," he said to Marion, urging her to her feet and out of the way so Pierce could get out.

Walking to the agent's vehicle, Marion again apologized for not mentioning it sooner.

"We'll talk about it during the interview," Pierce snapped.

Hawke wondered at the Special Agent's abrupt change of tone with Marion all the way to the FBI office.

They were met at the entrance by Lt. Gernot and Bo. Hawke nodded at his friend and introduced the lieutenant to Dani.

"Do you want to interview Trooper Hawke or Ms. Shumack?" Gernot asked Pierce.

"I thought you were doing these interviews together," Hawke said. He wasn't worried about himself, but he didn't want Marion to get shoved in a corner and respond in a way that would make her look guilty.

He'd already asked Bo to sit in with Marion, but still. She barely knew him.

"It will expedite things to have you both interviewed at the same time," Lt. Gernot said.

"I'll take Ms. Shumack," Pierce said.

Hawke studied his friend. There was a hint of defiance in his tone. What was he planning to do? "Bo will sit in on the interview."

Both the lieutenant and the special agent studied his friend.

"That's not protocol," Lt. Gernot said.

"She doesn't have legal counsel," Hawke said.

"She is a lawyer," the lieutenant countered.

"I'm corporate. I don't know anything about criminal law. At least Bo, having been a state trooper, knows enough legalities to let me know when I'm being harassed." Marion had finally broken out of the pity party she was having over the flash drive.

At least that's what Hawke figured.

Pierce shrugged. "I don't care as long as he doesn't answer or ask questions." He glared at Bo.

"I know my place," Bo said.

Pierce motioned for the two to follow him.

Hawke turned to Dani who had Dog on a leash. "Take Dog for a walk."

She nodded and the two walked out the entrance.

"Let's go," Hawke said to Lt. Gernot.

She studied him for a few seconds and motioned for him to follow her down the same hall where Pierce had taken Marion and Bo.

<><><><><><>

Marion's mouth felt like she'd been gnawing on a

stuffed pillow. It was dry and she found it hard to speak.

Pierce repeated his question. "Tell me everything that happened the afternoon of Adrian's death."

"Could I have a glass of water?" she asked.

Bo rose and left the room.

She swallowed and cleared her throat. "I'm sorry. It was...I don't like remembering seeing..."

Bo returned with a bottle of water. He unscrewed the cap, and she drank half the bottle before she felt as if she could speak.

She was to the part of the day where she'd gone to the cabin to call Hawke when the door opened. Perry Mathers stood in the doorway.

"Don't say anything else until I can confer with you."

Marion glanced at Bo then Agent Pierce.

"Who the hell are you?" Agent Pierce asked.

"I'm Ms. Shumack's attorney." Perry looked more steadfast than she'd ever seen him.

"I don't need a lawyer," she said. "I'm only being interviewed to give my account of being abducted by Caleb—"

"She isn't being held on any charges. I'll have to ask you to leave," Agent Pierce cut in.

Marion studied the agent. He hadn't wanted her to say anything about Caleb. Why? Now her curiosity was piqued.

"She has the right to an attorney," Perry argued.

"If she needed one," Agent Pierce said.

Bo stood. "Would you like me to escort this man out of the building?"

The agent eyed Bo for a moment.

"No, I can do it myself." Agent Pierce peered into

Marion's eyes. "I'll be right back."

She nodded and sat with her hands clasped around the water bottle.

Perry argued loudly all the way down the hall.

"You're doing fine," Bo said. "Just stick to the facts and don't add in any of your thoughts."

"Thanks." She glanced up at Gabriel's friend. "How did Perry know I was here?"

Agent Pierce stepped through the door and closed it. "I was wondering the same thing." He studied her before sitting down across the table from her. "Did you call anyone last night?"

"No. I took a shower and went to sleep. I didn't even get out of bed until Gabriel was banging on the adjoining door this morning." She raised her hand. "I don't have a phone."

"There are phones in the hotel rooms," he said.

"You can check. I didn't use it."

Chapter Twenty-seven

Hawke sat across the table from Lt. Gernot. She asked all the questions he'd expected and he'd given all the answers he had.

They had both stopped to listen when someone in the hall was yelling something about rights. He'd heard that before from people who were suspects and usually ended up being convicted of the crime.

"Like I've told you from the beginning, Marion had nothing to do with her fiancé's death other than seeing the man who killed him. She ran fearing for her life. Then when we were getting close to discovering more about the embezzlement, that man and another employee of Pannell Financial were killed. And yet another employee abducted my sister. I found him but because I didn't have handcuffs, he got away during an elk stampede."

The woman's eyebrow rose. "An elk stampede allowed the man to get away and then a bear chased you and your sister off his trail?" She tapped a pencil on the tablet she'd been scribbling on in front of her. "That seems a bit unique to me."

"I don't make up stories when it comes to catching suspects. I tell the truth. You can ask any person I've ever dealt with." He shouldn't let this woman get to him. He had to keep telling himself, she didn't know him. Didn't know his record of catching murderers or the fact he couldn't let a track or puzzle go without following it to a good conclusion. He hated anything left unfinished.

"Have you contacted Drew Pannell and asked if any of his employees have gone missing?" Hawke wondered if there was someone else, like Adele Barnes, who had left the retreat early. That was who he figured was in on the embezzlement and who probably talked Caleb into changing the numbers around.

"No. Until you came back and told us about Mr. DeLan, we didn't have any need to check on his employees."

Hawke studied the woman. "Two Pannell employees have been killed and one was running for her life and you haven't been touching base with the owner of the company?"

The woman's cheeks grew red. He couldn't tell if it was embarrassment over not doing her job or if she had a connection with Pannell.

"You can bet if we let word leak out that we have the money from the embezzlement, people will start scurrying to cover their tracks." Hawke thought he saw a flicker of fear flash in the lieutenant's eyes before she lowered her lashes as if looking at the tablet.

A knock on the door drew their attention away from the conversation.

The lieutenant stood and opened the door. Pierce walked in trailed by Marion and Bo.

What was up? Hawke stood, thinking they were taking him out of here.

"What are you doing in here? We will confer when I'm finished," Lt. Gernot said to Pierce.

"You're finished." Pierce motioned to Hawke. "Someone tipped off Pannell we were interviewing Marion today."

Hawke glanced at the lieutenant. "I figured that out during the interview."

Pierce's gaze swung so fast toward the lieutenant that his face was a blur. "What all have you told Pannell about this investigation? It's no wonder he's been one step ahead of us every time we find something." He took three steps to back the woman into the corner of the room. "Have you been working for him from the start?"

She stood tall and attempted a glare, but it wavered. "He is a large benefactor for the Montana State Police. I was asked to keep him in the loop and keep him happy."

Hawke rolled his eyes. They should have known the millionaire would have paid for privileged information.

Pierce cursed under his breath before saying out loud, "I'll make sure the State Police don't get any more of our findings." He swiped his hand and picked up the notebook Lt. Gernot had made notes in during Hawke's interview. "And I need the notes from your interview with Oregon State Trooper Hawke." He emphasized Oregon.

"You three remain. I'll see that Lt. Gernot is escorted out of the building."

When the door closed behind Pierce, Hawke turned his attention to Bo and Marion. "How did you learn Pannell knew about these interviews?"

"Perry Mathers showed up saying he was my

counsel," Marion said.

Hawke studied her. "Pannell's personal attorney?"

She nodded. "And he was acting pushier than I've ever seen him. I mean, even when he'd be dealing with the hard case attorneys for Pannell, he always acted like you could squeeze him like a marshmallow. You know, soft and pliable. And that was working for his paycheck."

He caught the drift of what his sister was saying. "You think he was there to find out what happened to the gold? Like it was his."

She shrugged. "All I know is he has never acted like he had a spine. This morning he did."

"Maybe Pannell told him to grow a backbone or be tossed," Bo said.

"Or he's being paid well like the lieutenant to keep Pannell apprised of this investigation. But why? To get the embezzled money back or because he paid DeLan to embezzle it." Hawke was studying the expressions on his sister's and friend's faces when Pierce opened the door and entered.

"Pannell paying large sums of money to the Montana Police should have come up when we checked his financials." Pierce dropped down onto a chair. He shook his head slightly and peered at Hawke. "Dani said to tell you she and Dog caught a ride back to the hotel."

Hawke nodded. This looked like it was going to be a longer interview than they'd thought. "Has the gold all been pulled out of the frame yet?" he asked.

"No. They don't want to damage the bars, they're evidence. That makes the process slower."

"It would be good to know the exact amount that was embezzled and the amount the gold comes up to,"

Hawke said thoughtfully.

"Why?" Marion asked.

"To see if we can get the perpetrators to start fighting amongst each other if the FBI let's slip to say, Lt. Gernot or Pannell himself, that the amount of money missing is more than the gold that was converted." Hawke locked gazes with Bo.

His friend smiled. "Make someone think the other stole from them."

Pierce shook his head. "The FBI can't leak false information."

Hawke studied the Special Agent. "No, but we could."

"Let me go see if the agents in accounting have discovered the true amount that was embezzled. At least you would have the correct number to make your leak sound plausible." Pierce left the room.

Marion had watched the agent leave the room. She shifted her gaze to her brother and Bo. "You're really going to start a rumor that someone, whom the person would think is Caleb, stole money from them? You'd be putting him in danger."

Gabriel stared at her. "He put you in danger. He was willing to kill you to get over those mountains and meet up with his accomplice to live the good life for the rest of his years. He killed the man who killed Adrian and possibly killed Louise. Putting him in danger is worth learning who his accomplice is."

She shuddered. Caleb, a man she had always thought of as nerdy and soft, had shown her a completely different side. One she didn't like. "Who do you think his accomplice is?" she challenged.

He shrugged. "Pannell, Ms. Barnes." He seemed lost

in thought.

Just as she was going to ask another question, he blurted, "The lawyer who showed up this morning."

"Why him?" Bo asked.

"He is Pannell's personal lawyer. Marion said he had access to everything. He was the person who wrote up the contract between Longo and Pannell before. He could have easily made up the one between Marion and Longo. He'd have access to her signature and all that his client learns about the embezzled money."

Marion nodded. "He rarely sat in on business dealings, but I'm sure Drew would have talked them over with him. And if not him, he could have gotten information about clients from anyone at the business just saying he was asking for Drew."

Gabriel held his hand out to Bo. "I need to borrow your phone." He handed it to Marion. "Call Pannell and thank him for sending his lawyer here this morning. Let's see if he knew anything about it."

Marion's hands were shaking. She didn't know why; Drew had never made her nervous before. She waited while his private line rang.

"Hello?" he questioned, in an irritated voice.

"Drew, it's Marion. Thank you for sending Perry to the FBI headquarters in Missoula to represent me. It was thoughtful but I don't need him. I'm not a suspect anymore."

"He what? I don't know anything about what Perry was doing this morning. But hearing you aren't a suspect is good news. When will you be back to work?" The man was all business as usual.

"I don't know. I'm going to use my vacation time to visit with family and make a decision." She glanced at

Gabriel. He raised his eyebrows.

"Decision about what?" Drew asked with a harshness to his tone that said he wasn't in the mood for someone to be manipulating him.

"Whether or not I want to continue in corporate law with Pannell Financial. I'll send you an email when I get settled." She ended the call. She didn't want her very persuasive boss to make her change her mind.

"This side of the conversation was interesting," Gabriel said.

She smiled. "He didn't send Perry to my rescue this morning. Or he didn't want us to think he did."

Chapter Twenty-eight

While Gabriel, Dog, and Bo went to retrieve Hawke's truck, Marion and Dani went shopping for clothes. They used an Uber to rent a car they used to drive to the thrift stores. By the time they had hit all the stores, Marion had enough clothes to last her until they returned to Oregon. She hoped it was soon, but Gabriel couldn't give her a time frame when she'd asked.

"Do you think Bo and Gabriel will be able to draw the accomplice out with their story about the amount of the gold not matching the embezzled money?"

Dani was driving the rental car. She shrugged. "I'm sure it's going to make someone angry enough to do something. What, we don't know. But that's what your brother is good at. Watching people and telling what they're thinking or their intentions. Since I've met him, he's figured out every puzzle that's come his way. Granted he didn't like some of the results, but he knew that going in."

Marion jumped to the question she'd been dying to ask this woman. "How did you and Gabriel meet?"

Dani glanced over at her. "That will require a stop at a coffee shop."

From the wrinkles on Dani's forehead, Marion feared the meeting wasn't what shaped their future together.

In his own truck and following Bo in his, Hawke thought through what he and his friend had come up with. Bo still had connections in the State Police. He was going to ask one of those connections to mention to Lt. Gernot that he heard the gold the FBI found in the Bob Marshal Wilderness didn't match up with the figures suspected of being embezzled. Even if Bo's friend only managed to get half the information to Gernot, enough would make it to the people who mattered to put things into motion.

He planned to have dinner with Dani and Marion and then send them back to Oregon while he and Bo continued their quest to find out who, besides Caleb DeLan, was involved in the murders. He could care less about the embezzlement. It was one person taking another person's life that bothered him. Especially when it was good people. From what his sister said about Adrian, there needed to be more like him in this world. And Louise had been helping find the truth when she came to her end.

Bo pulled off the highway and into the parking lot of a restaurant. Hawke parked beside him and rolled down his window.

"I'll go talk to my friend. Best if I do it face to face. Then I'll do a reconnaissance of the resort and see if our suspects are still there. I'll expect to see you around ten?"

"Yeah. As soon as I have dinner and put them on Dani's helicopter, I'll head your direction." He held up his phone. "Now that I have my rig back, I have my phone. Call if you need me sooner or the suspects have left."

"Roger." Bo rolled up his window and headed out of the parking lot.

Hawke glanced at his watch. Four. It wouldn't hurt to have an early dinner and get the two women off to Oregon before dark. He dialed Dani's phone.

"Hey. You must be in your truck to be using your phone."

It beeped. Sergeant Spruel was trying to call him. "Yeah. Meet me at the restaurant near the hotel and we'll have an early dinner. I'll be there in twenty."

"See you there."

He hung up and answered his sergeant's call. "Hawke."

"Why haven't you been returning my calls?" growled his superior.

"I didn't know you'd been calling. My truck and phone have been out of my reach." Hawke felt that was better to say than, I've been using a burner phone to avoid talking to you.

"Why have you been away from your vehicle and cell?"

Hawke gave Spruel the condensed version of his time since his visit to the morgue.

"It sounds like Lt. Gernot wasn't much help."

"No," Hawke agreed. "Her actions mucked up things. But Pierce and I have a plan that we hope will get us results in a couple of days."

"Why don't you just leave it for the FBI to do?"

Hawke inwardly groaned. He wasn't going to tell his boss that this wasn't really sanctioned by the whole FBI. "I know things that can push buttons. You know how that goes?" He hoped that would be enough to not have Spruel tell him to head home now.

"In other words, you are going to be in the middle of the plan to force the accomplice out in the open."

Hawke sighed. "Yes, it was my idea and I do know the suspects better than anyone else involved in this investigation."

"Get it wrapped up and get back. And don't expect to ask for any time off in the near future." The call ended.

The gruff exchange at the end was Spruel's way of saying he'd used up comp time helping his sister.

Hawke drove to the restaurant where he was meeting Dani and Marion. He patted Dog on the head. "Stay put and I'll bring you a burger. We'll have a long night ahead of us." He exited the truck, locked the doors, and walked into the restaurant.

Dani and Marion were sitting in a corner booth.

He walked over and sat by Dani. "How did your clothes hunt go?"

"I found enough clothes to get by for several days and washing them I can manage for as long as we need." Marion sipped on a fruity-looking drink.

He waited until they'd ordered before he said, "I'd like the two of you to fly out of here tonight. As soon as we finish eating."

Both women stared at him as if he'd just asked them to take off all their clothes in the middle of the restaurant.

"I lost my fiancé because of the person you are trying to find. I'm not leaving here until I can look them in the eye and call them a killer," Marion said, her voice lowered, making the words come out sounding like a hiss.

"She has a point," Dani said, sipping her beer.

Hawke shook his head. "No. I want you both out of here. It will be easier for me to keep tabs on the suspects without worrying about where you two are and if anyone is using you to get me to back off."

Dani nodded. "Okay, I see your point. Marion has been abducted once already." She glanced across the table at his sister. "It's best we do as he says. He needs to be able to work without worrying about us on the sidelines. We can go to Wallowa County and use the computer to dig up what we can on the suspects." She smiled at Hawke and said, "Does that make you happy?"

Narrowing his eyes, he studied the woman he knew almost as well as he knew himself. She was giving in too easily and being a bit too smarmy. He didn't trust her.

"I'll take you two to the helicopter after we eat." He continued to hold Dani's gaze. When she just smiled and stared at him, he finally broke eye contact and studied his sister. She still looked pissed. This wasn't a good sign, but he had other things to think about once he put them on the helicopter.

<><><><><><>

Hawke drove straight to the road leading into the resort after kissing Dani, hugging Marion, and watching the helicopter liftoff.

"I'm beginning to think that DeLan was the only person in the embezzling. You would have thought someone should have heard something from Gernot by now." Bo's voice was coming from the speakers in Hawke's truck. He had called the man for an update and had it on speakerphone.

"Unless she finally realized how she'd compromised the investigation and is now keeping her mouth shut." Hawke had worried that would be the case when they came up with the plan.

"If so, we need to get the information to someone who would get things rolling," Bo said.

Running all he remembered about the investigation through his mind, Hawke had several ideas come to him. "I think Pierce can help us with this one. Keep watching. I'm going to make a phone call." Hawke ended that call and dialed Special Agent Pierce.

"Hawke, anyone take the bait?" Pierce answered.

"That's what I'm calling about. I don't think Gernot relayed the message as we'd hoped. I thought maybe you could call the accountant that helped the Feds work on the books and mention that you'd recovered gold from the embezzler and you wanted to make sure the amount was the same. When he tells you the amount, if it's the same, pretend it isn't but if it's different, you won't have to pretend." Hawke knew Pierce was a by-the-book Fed but he also liked to get the bad guys.

"I see where you're going with this. He'll call Pannell to tell him only part of the money has been found. He'll discuss it with his lawyer and perhaps someone else, like Ms. Barnes, will hear them and we'll have snagged the three suspects into the ruse." Pierce sounded like he was enjoying this game of cat and mouse.

"Yeah, something like that." Hawke wondered if that word would get around tonight at all. It was now eight. "Call me back and let me know how the call goes."

"Will do." The call ended.

Hawke called Bo back. "Pierce is going to work a different angle. I'm wondering if we should just call it a night and be here at first light. I don't know that the message will get—"

"You'll never guess who just arrived," Bo said, interrupting him.

"Lt. Gernot?" Hawke said.

"Man, how did you know that?"

Hawke grinned. "She's the only one you would have been excited about."

Bo laughed and said, "True."

"Now we wait and see what happens. I'm just turning off on the resort road. I think I'll pull off at the first place I see. You let me know who leaves when and I'll decide if I need to follow them."

"Roger."

The call ended and Hawke found what he was looking for. A side road that saw little traffic. He drove down it until he found a good place to turn around. Once turned around, he drove back toward the road, staying just far enough back passing headlights wouldn't catch his vehicle.

Half an hour passed and Hawke wondered where Dani and Marion were. Surely, they were nearing Wallowa County. He hoped if Marion's mail was there, they opened anything from Adrian and took it to Sergeant Spruel. He'd know the fastest way to get it to the Feds.

Dog stretched and looked out the window.

"Do you need to take a pee?" Hawke asked, opening his door, and letting the dog jump over him.

His phone rang. Pierce.

"What did you find out?" Hawke asked.

"The amount that the accountant has come up with is nearly a hundred thousand more than was calculated in gold."

Hawke grinned. "So someone, possibly DeLan, did skim from his accomplice. He's probably already out of the country knowing we have the gold and it won't cover all that was stolen."

"I have a watch for him at all borders and airports. He'll be picked up," Pierce said.

"Lt. Gernot did finally turn up at the resort. Bo's going to let me know—" His phone beeped. "That's him. I'll catch you up later."

"Yeah, what's happening?" he asked, answering Bo's call.

"Gernot left about ten minutes ago and the lawyer just left in a hurry behind her. I'd say follow him. I'll hang out here and see if anyone else decides to take a drive tonight."

"Sounds good." Hawke ended the call, whistled for Dog, and waited for the first car to go by. With his lights off and the distance, he couldn't see her, but Bo had said she was ahead of Mathers.

Not five minutes later, another vehicle. A sporty car that looked out of place on the gravel road shot by.

Hawke didn't turn his lights on. He used the moonlight and the rear lights on the sports car to follow. He didn't want to turn his lights on until they arrived at the highway.

Once they were on the highway with more vehicles Hawke turned his lights on and followed the man. He appeared to be heading to Missoula.

His phone rang. Bo.

"More action on your end?" Hawke asked.

"Yeah. Pannell just took off in a suburban."

"Are you following him?" Hawke wondered if he was going to meet up with Mathers.

"Yeah. We're headed toward Seeley."

"Keep me posted where you end up," Hawke said, following the sports car off the highway near Missoula.

"I will. It's interesting they are going different directions," Bo said.

Hawke continued to follow the lawyer. "It looks like the attorney is going to the airport."

At the airstrip, the sports car didn't turn into the regular parking lot.

"It looks like he's going to charter a plane. I'll hang back and then find out where he's chartering it to."

"Roger. Want me to try and talk to Ms. Barnes?" Bo asked.

"No. I think the people who are on the move are the ones we want to check out. Keep your distance and let me know where you and Pannell end up." Hawke ended the call and slowly crept along the road leading to the hangars. He waited for Mathers to park and walk into a hangar before he parked and followed.

Easing in through a side door, Hawke listened for voices. Footsteps echoed before voices greeted one another.

"Is the plane ready to go?" one man asked.

"I checked all the fluids and did regular maintenance yesterday. I didn't think Mr. Pannell would need it after calling for his helicopter," another voice said.

"He authorized me to use it. Get it out on the tarmac and ready to go." The first man who spoke said. "I want to lift off in thirty minutes."

Footsteps faded out of the hangar moments before

another pair ran in and low voices could be heard. Then the sound of rubber rolling on the cement floor rumbled through the hangar.

Hawke eased his way along the side of the building to see what was happening. Two men were maneuvering a Learjet out of the wide opening with a dolly. He knew from flying with Dani that Mathers would need to share a flight plan. He'd wait until the man was in the airplane and ask the hangar attendant where he could find out that information.

Chapter Twenty-nine

Marion was worn out when Dani flipped the lights on illuminating the house she and Gabriel shared.

"It's beautiful!" Marion exclaimed. For some reason in her mind, she'd expected the ex-Air Force pilot and her long-time single brother to have four walls and a roof over their heads. Nothing fancy or nice.

"We haven't had it a year. In fact, we're still working on getting our own furniture. But that's a long story. Right now, we need sleep. Then we'll check in with Herb and Darlene in the morning to pick up all the mail."

"Who are Herb and Darlene?" Marion asked, carrying the small suitcase she'd purchased at the thrift store over to the end of the hallway and setting it down.

"They were your brother's landlords for a lot of years and now they are our neighbors." Dani glanced at her. "You'll get to see where Hawke lived and who took care of him until I came along."

243

Marion laughed and then asked, "Why does everyone call him Hawke? His name is Gabriel."

Dani shrugged. "It's what he tells everyone to call him. I guess he thinks Gabriel is too sissy for a cop."

Marion laughed again, then put a hand over her mouth. She hadn't laughed much until Adrian came into her life, and now, he was dead. She shouldn't be laughing. It must be because she was exhausted.

"Take the guest room. It's at the end of the hall to the left. There's a full bath right next door. Make yourself at home." Dani started down the hall and her phone rang. "Yes, I'm in the house. No there's no need to come over."

Marion watched as the woman bobbed her head and said, "Yes, breakfast when we pick up the mail would be nice. Thank you." She listened. "No. Not Hawke. It's his sister." She smiled. "Yes, I'm sure you are anxious to meet her. See you at seven."

Dani turned back to Marion. "We are having breakfast with the Trembleys at seven in the morning. What time would you like me to wake you?"

"Who are the Trembleys?" Marion asked, wondering why Dani had been so easily persuaded to be somewhere at seven for breakfast.

"The neighbors who have the mail." Dani smiled. "Take a shower or whatever you want. I'm going to bed."

"Good night." She took two steps. "Hey, how did they know you were home?" she asked Dani.

The woman smiled. "Because Hawke had cameras installed so they could keep an eye on things when we're both gone."

"Oh." Marion thought about that as she ambled to bed.

Keeping an eye on the Learjet from inside the hangar, Hawke watched as Mathers climbed into the pilot seat and fastened his seat belt. It appeared the attorney knew how to fly.

Hawke went in search of the hangar attendant. He found the man putting away the fueling hose.

"Hi," he said, walking up to the man.

"Hey! What are you doing out here? This is off limits to anyone who doesn't work here or have an airplane here." The man straightened and put his hands on his hips.

Hawke flashed his badge. "I wondered if you heard where that man said he was flying to?"

"Nope. He and Pannell never tell me anything. Just put the plane in the hangar and tell me to take care of it. Then they return and tell me to get the plane out and fuel it up."

"Then can you direct me to where he would have had to go to file his flight plan?" Hawke had a feeling the man would be more than generous with his help considering the tone he'd used while talking about Pannell and Mathers.

"I'll call air traffic control and see where he's headed." The man pulled out a phone, poked at the screen, and then said, "Hey Charlie, the Learjet that just left here N-Nine-three-six-C where did the flight plan say it was going?"

The man listened and his face grew red. "What do you mean he didn't give you a flight plan? He said that was where he was going while I fueled up the plane. No, I believe you. Thanks." The man turned to Hawke. "He and Pannell are going to get a piece of my mind when I see them again."

Hawke studied the man. "To your knowledge has he ever done this before?"

"Not that I know of. And if he had, they wouldn't have been able to land here."

Hawke found that telling. There had to be a reason why Mathers didn't want anyone to know where he was headed. Could it be to meet up with DeLan? And he knew his accomplice had withheld money. Or had DeLan been paid the hundred thousand to help?

They needed to find DeLan before anyone else. "Thanks for your help." Hawke started to walk away then spun around and asked, "How far can he go on a tank of fuel?"

"About two-thousand miles depending on the headwind."

With the information, Hawke called both Pierce and Bo, then headed to catch up with Bo who was sitting outside of a house near Seeley Lake waiting for Pannell to come out.

Marion was surprised the next morning when after she'd dressed, Dani told her to bundle up and then they walked out to an ATV and Dani swung her leg over.

"Come on. This is the quickest and easiest way to get to the Trembleys."

Marion swung her leg over and sat behind Dani. On a faint road through new grass and mud, between several pastures, Dani pointed out Hawke's two horses and a mule.

"All of my horses and mules are up at the lodge. We just started our summer season."

"Don't you need to get back up there soon?" Marion

asked, worrying she was keeping the woman from her livelihood.

"I have a married couple who are my wrangler and cook/housekeeper. Their daughter helps with cleaning cabins and in the kitchen and my nephew helps out in the summer with the horses and trail rides. I'm just the one who takes care of the books and flies the clients in and out."

They rumbled over a narrow cattleguard.

"Now we are on the Trembleys' property."

They drove up to an older style farmhouse that looked as if it had been built in the last ten years. When Marion mentioned it, Dani shook her head. "This is Herb's family's homestead. The house was built in the early nineteen hundreds."

"It's been well preserved." Marion studied the structure with awe.

"The people who live here love it." There was a sadness in Dani's voice.

"Is it wrong for them to love the house and the land?" Marion asked.

"There were many families who loved this land before Herb's family homesteaded." Dani peered into her eyes. "They were our ancestors."

Marion nodded.

"I am glad that the Trembleys love this place and take such good care of it. But in my heart, I wish it hadn't been stolen from us."

"I read a lot about the broken treaties and laws that were made to keep us down." Marion put a hand on Dani's shoulder. "But look at us. You were a woman pilot in the Air Force. I am a corporate lawyer, and Gabriel is a State Policeman. We are slowly getting our power and our country back. It's slow, but it is happening."

Dani smiled. "I like you."

The door to the house opened and a smiling man with a face Marion instinctively liked, invited them in.

Dani made the introductions and they all sat down to a wonderful breakfast of French toast, homemade strawberry jam, bacon, and coffee.

"Mrs—" Marion started.

"It's Darlene. I feel like we're family, we've heard so much about you from Hawke." The woman smiled, rose, refilled their coffee cups, and sat back down. All with a smile on her face.

"Darlene, this is the best breakfast I've had in a very long time. Thank you."

"You're most welcome. This is one of Hawke's favorites," the woman said.

"Did he actually board in your house?" Marion asked.

"No, he rented the apartment over the arena. But he and Dog never passed up an invitation to a meal." Darlene laughed and Herb joined her.

Dani grinned and shrugged.

"Can we get the mail?" Marion asked.

The older couple stopped laughing and stared at her.

"I'm sorry, but I'm sure you noticed some of the mail was forwarded from Texas. That was Marion's mail. She's anxious to see if something is in it," Dani said, giving Marion a look that said, 'cool your jets.'

"Yes. When I realized I'd be coming here for a while, I had my mail forwarded." Marion smiled, hoping the couple wouldn't think she was pushy.

"I have it in a box." Herb rose and walked into

another room.

"Darlene, thank you so much for the breakfast and for you and Herb watching out for our place," Dani said, rising.

"You're leaving so soon?" Darlene asked.

"Yes. Once I get Marion settled in over at our place, I need to check in with the lodge and see if I'm needed to fly anyone in or out."

Herb entered the kitchen. "When will Hawke be back?"

Marion and Dani shared a glance.

"I don't know for sure," Dani said. "Soon I hope."

"Thank you, again," Marion said, taking the box and following Dani out to the ATV.

"If you need anything, you know where to find us," Herb said, as Marion waved and Dani started up the 4-wheeler.

Back at Gabriel and Dani's house, Marion put the box on the kitchen table and the two started going through it. Dani piled their mail to one side and handed Marion the mail with her name on it.

Halfway down the box, Dani pulled out a padded envelope. "This is addressed to you."

Marion knew who it was from as soon as she saw the handwriting. Tears welled in her eyes as she took the parcel. Her finger traced her name on the front. She flipped it over and put a finger under the tape securing that the envelope didn't open.

Inside, she found a note and a flash drive.

Marion, If you are reading this, then my discovering embezzlement at Pannell Financial has gotten me killed. And if that is the case, please find justice for me and the people who lost money. But first and foremost, stay safe.

You are the shining light your people need. Leave Pannell and Texas and use your knowledge to help your people. I've seen you light up talking about your heritage. Continue to learn and protect those you can. You were the first and only woman I've loved. Thank you for giving me your love in return. Adrian

It was several minutes later that she realized her tears were soaking the note. She swiped at her face and eyes, trying to stop the flood. Finally, she put the note on the table and peered at Dani. Tears glistened in her eyes.

"He sounds like he was the perfect man for you. I'm so sorry for your loss," Dani said, opening her arms.

Marion fell against her, clutching the woman, crying and wailing. Officially grieving for the man she loved.

When Marion was spent, Dani settled her onto a kitchen chair and brought her a cup of tea.

While Marion pulled herself together, Dani gathered a laptop, a pen, and paper, and sat down at the table. She picked up the flash drive. "Do you want to be the person who looks at this?"

"Go ahead. I'm not sure I'd understand it all anyway." Marion didn't want to admit, while she wanted to find the person responsible for Adrian's death, she didn't care that they were stealing from one another. That was the side of the company she worked for that she hadn't understood.

Dani pushed the small drive into the slot on the side of the laptop and started clicking the mouse. "Okay. It looks like he copied files." She clicked around some more. "And some emails."

Marion sat up. "Who were the emails between?"

"Drew Pannell, Perry Mathers, and someone with an email that isn't a name." She spun the laptop around and

Marion studied the email address. It didn't make sense.

"All of this needs to go to the FBI person Gabriel knows," Marion said.

Dani pulled her cell phone out of her pocket. "He put all of Special Agent Pierce's contacts into my phone yesterday." She started typing and then looked up. "I need to use the radio to contact the lodge. Why don't you either go for a walk or take a nap."

Marion studied the woman. What was she trying not to say? "Are you trying to get rid of me? I wouldn't have thought talking to the people running your lodge would be top secret."

Dani's face deepened in color.

"Ahhh, you were going to give Gabriel a report and wanted to talk about me." She stood. "Go ahead. I'm going to take a nap." She plucked the note from Adrian from where she'd dropped it and went to her room. Behind the closed door, she curled up on the bed, clutching the note, and cried herself to sleep.

Chapter Thirty

Hawke rubbed the kink in his neck and picked up a cold fry. Dog hung his head over the seat and Hawke's shoulder as if he'd been waiting for him to pick the cold potato up all night.

"Yeah, I'm tired of sitting here too," Hawke said, giving the greasy fry to his friend. Who wouldn't complain that it was cold or greasy.

His phone beeped. Pierce.

Before he could say anything, Pierce said, "That house you're sitting on belongs to Adele Barnes' parents."

"Is she still at the resort?" Hawke asked, tossing all the reasons Pannell would be at Ms. Barnes' parent's house all night.

"As far as my agent can tell, she is in her room."

"Have your operative check to make sure. Something is off. Why would her boss spend the night at her parents without her?" The only thought that popped into Hawke's head was the man was trying to get information out of them. He didn't like that idea. "Call me back with what you learn." He ended the call, opened the driver's door, and told Dog, "Come on."

He walked over to Bo's vehicle and rapped on the window. Bo had followed the man to this house and Hawke had arrived to let Bo catch some zs.

"Yeah, what?" Bo said loud enough, Hawke heard him outside the vehicle. The man stared at the house for several blinks then shifted his attention to the window and Hawke. He rolled the window down. "Yeah, he on the move?"

"No. Something's up. Pierce called. This house belongs to Ms. Barnes' parents. I don't like that he was in there all night. And according to the Feds, Ms. Barnes is tucked away at the resort. Doesn't make sense."

Bo rubbed a hand over his face. "Yeah, this whole damn thing hasn't made any sense."

"Let's see if we can peek in the windows." Hawke headed to the house. He doubted anyone was watching for someone approaching. Not if Pannell was busy trying to get information out of the older couple.

He went to the left and Bo went to the right. Hawke peeked in a bottom corner of a window of the older log-style house. It was the great room, as they were called in log houses. Or so Dani had told him. He didn't see anyone.

Moving along the wall of the house, with Dog on his heels, he slid around the corner and peered in a window on the end. It also looked into the great room. Nothing. The next window appeared to be a bedroom. The bed was made and nothing in the room suggested anyone was using it. The next window was high and frosted. A bathroom, no doubt. There was another window near the end of the house. He looked in and found a bedroom that had been turned into an office/den. The papers were scattered all over the desk and floor. Someone had been looking for something.

He slipped around the corner and found Bo staring into a window at the other end of the backside of the house. Hawke hurried over and peered in.

Pannell looking frantic, was pacing back and forth in front of an older couple who were sitting in chairs, their heads bobbing as if they were sleeping.

"What do you think?" Bo whispered.

"We have two choices. Call Pierce and wait for him to round up Feds or locals to come stop this, or we stop it and suffer the consequences." He peered into his friend's eyes and knew what he thought.

"Let's go."

They moved to the back door. Looking through the window in the door, it appeared to be an enclosed porch. Hawke tried the door knob. It turned. Either Pannell had never tried to get information from someone or he had been confident no one would find him here.

Hawke opened the door quietly and they crept through the room, following the sound of Pannell talking about needing to find Adele, and he wasn't leaving until one of them told him where she was.

At the door to the bedroom, Hawke's phone buzzed. Shit! He motioned for Bo to get to the other side.

Pannell opened the door before he could do anything. Bo grabbed Pannell by the arm, getting him in a restraining hold.

Hawke answered his phone. "Bad timing," he said to Pierce.

"Adele isn't in her room. By the looks of things she cleaned out and left sometime before we started watching her." By his tone of voice, someone was going to get an earful from the Special Agent.

"We just restrained Pannell. He was here trying to find out where Adele went by threatening her parents." Hawke motioned for Bo to take the shouting man into the great room. Pannell was blustering that he would have the two of them put in jail for breaking and entering. "You want to send someone to pick him up for questioning?"

"Yeah. I'll be there in twenty." The call ended.

Hawke walked into the great room. Bo had Pannell seated in a dining chair with his hands zip-tied behind his back. He was working on zip-tying his legs to the chair.

"Nice." Hawke said with appreciation.

"I always have half a dozen ties in my pocket. You never know when you come across someone unruly." Bo stood. "Better check on the old people."

Hawke pivoted and headed back to what appeared to be the couple's bedroom. He told them he was a friend and would they like a cup of coffee.

"I want to use the bathroom," the woman said.

"Go right ahead. We have Pannell tied up. The FBI is coming to take him away." Hawke helped the woman to her feet.

"Are you one of Adele's friends?" the old man asked.

Hawke hesitated then said yes.

"Then you know she's getting married. She wanted a destination wedding and we just couldn't see the sense in us traveling all that way." The old man had tears in his eyes. "She never wanted us around her much anyway so

I suppose she planned the wedding knowing we wouldn't make it."

"I'm sorry. I could take you if you'd like." He knew if they agreed he'd be spending his own money to take them to watch their daughter be arrested, not married.

"No. A flight to where they are going is too expensive. We'll just be happy if she or someone else," he smiled at Hawke, "sent us some photos."

Hawke got the hint. "I'll see what I can do. I'll go make that coffee and bring it in here to you and your wife. I'd prefer you didn't have to speak to Mr. Pannell."

The man nodded. "He didn't hurt us, just kept going on and on about money and how our daughter was, well, he called her all kinds of names."

The woman came out of the bathroom. "He did too hurt us. He hurt our hearts the things he was saying about our daughter. Nearly tore my heart in two the names he called her, and him being her boss."

"I'll get that coffee." Hawke left the room making sure to close the door.

Bo already had the coffee pot gurgling. "What did you find out?"

"They know where Caleb and Adele are," Hawke said in a low voice. "I'm going to text Pierce so he can get someone looking for them." He nodded toward the bedroom door. "I told them I'd bring in a cup of coffee. They didn't say anything to Pannell about where Adele is, but I didn't want them to slip now that they feel safe."

"He's pissed. Called me every dirty word for Indian he could think of." Bo glared at the man struggling against the zip-ties and shouting how he was going to get them both locked up for a very long time.

"It appears he either cares about his business

256

reputation or he was the one skimming and someone else came along and stole his money." Hawke poured coffee into two cups and carried them to the bedroom.

"Mr. and Mrs. Barnes, I brought you coffee but forgot to ask if you took it black."

"Yes, just black," Mrs. Barnes said, taking a cup. "How did you know that bully was holding us hostage in our own home?"

"My friend followed him here. We didn't realize this was your house until it was late and we thought he was here with your daughter." Hawke handed the other up to the man.

Mr. Barnes scowled. "Our Adele with that man? No, he's too pushy. She'd never put up with a pushy man. She likes to run things."

Hawke wanted to learn more about the man their daughter was marrying. But since the man thought he was a friend... "So you two like the man Adele is marrying?"

The woman puckered her mouth and wrinkled her brow before saying, "You couldn't really say like, but he seems to love our daughter."

This caught Hawke's attention. "Doesn't she love him?"

Mrs. Barnes shook her head. "I don't really think so. The one time she brought Caleb with her, I caught Adele on the phone giggling and saying she loved someone else."

Hawke took in the information. Caleb had been used to skim the money and someone else was running off to marry Adele. His first thought flashed to Mathers not filing a flight plan.

"I'm sure they'll honeymoon where they are getting

married," Hawke thought maybe the woman would come up with the name of where the wedding was taking place.

"Oh, yes. She said the South Pacific Islands are beautiful this time of year," Mrs. Barnes said.

Hawke smiled at the woman. "I'm sure they would be. I'm going to go back out and make sure my friend isn't having any problems with Mr. Pannell." Hawke left the room, smiling. He knew where the woman was headed.

Bo sat at the small table in the kitchen eating toast and sipping coffee. Pannell had finally stopped yelling.

"Learn anything else?" Bo asked, shoving the plate of toast toward Hawke.

Dog appeared at Hawke's side. He gave the animal a half slice of toast and held the other half in front of his mouth. "I know where they are going and I think Mathers is using Pannell's plane to get them there."

Bo grinned. "Those two have guts, I'll give them that."

"But they don't have the gold."

Chapter Thirty-one

Pierce arrived, took down all their statements and had another agent haul Pannell off. The three of them, Pierce, Bo, and Hawke, stood by Pierce's vehicle discussing what was happening next.

"Dani sent me the files on a flash drive that the first victim sent to your sister. It shows where the money was taken from. There were also copies of emails that had Pannell and Mathers' work emails but were really between Ms. Barnes, DeLan, and a third person whose email we are checking. There was never a name attached to that email."

"You'll probably find it to be Perry Mathers, the personal attorney for Pannell," Hawke said.

"From what you told me about him taking the plane and no flight plan, I'd say you are probably correct." Pierce scratched his head. "If they are using a private plane to get to the South Pacific it will be harder to stop them. And that will be a lot of fuel stops between here and there. The only country I can think of down there that we don't have extradition treaties with is Vanuatu."

"How do you know that?" Hawke asked, awed that the FBI agent was versed in extradition countries.

"We have to know where a person can hide and not be brought back. We need to get them before they arrive in that country." Pierce slid into his SUV and pulled out his phone.

"You going home?" Bo asked Hawke.

"Nothing else I can do until they catch DeLan, Ms. Barnes, or Mathers."

"And then you'll not be allowed to interview them. The Feds will have their case and no longer need your assistance." Bo slapped him on the back. "Once again, an Indian saved the government's ass and no one says thanks."

Hawke shrugged. He didn't need thanks. He'd just wanted to clear his sister of the murder charge and find the person who did kill Adrian and subsequently Longo and Louise.

"As long as Marion is safe, I'm happy with the outcome."

"True there." Bo walked over to his vehicle.

Hawke's phone rang. It was Dani. "Hello," he said, thinking it would be good to get home.

"We have been looking around in social media and there is a photo of Caleb and Adele snuggled together and the caption, Our hideaway in Montana. I'm sending the photo to you."

Hawke called to Bo. "Wait a minute!"

His friend did an about-face and walked back over to him.

Hawke put his phone on speaker and opened the

message Dani sent him. "Does this look familiar?" he asked Bo.

"Did you find anything else interesting?" Hawke asked Dani.

"Adele's social media is pretty sparse. I think she's the brains of the two. But Caleb has photos of them posted all over his sites."

"We think she was using him." Hawke thought a moment. "Can you find Perry Mathers on social media?"

"What are you two doing still here?" Pierce asked, walking up to them.

"I'm pretty sure this was taken on the other side of the divide. That is the east side of Fairview Mountain in the background," Bo said.

"Perry's goes back a long time," Marion said. "Oh my! And in one he is marrying Adele."

Hawke shifted his attention to Pierce. "Did you do backgrounds on Mathers and Ms. Barnes? Didn't their marriage come up?"

Pierce had his phone out typing. "I'll ask the agent who pulled that material together."

"Are there any more photos of their hideaway?" Bo asked.

"There were three more in the same post, but they aren't in them," Dani said.

"Send them over," Hawke said. "You two are good sleuths," he added. His phone dinged and he and Bo studied the photos.

"I think I know where this is. Want to see more of Montana?" Bo asked Hawke.

"Sure." Hawke glanced at Pierce. "We'll let you know what we find."

The FBI grunted.

Hawke glanced at Bo. "Your rig or mine?"

"Mine. Grab your gear."

Hawke whistled for Dog and grabbed his duffle and the sack of dog food out of his truck and tossed that in the back of Bo's. Dog hopped into the cab, sitting in the middle as they drove away from the Barnes place.

"This could just be us wanting badly to get these guys," Bo said. "They are probably long gone."

"Or, they could be hiding out waiting for law enforcement to stop looking for them so they can sneak out of the country." Hawke pulled up the area Bo thought the pictures were from and studied the map on his phone. "Tell me what is in the area."

As Bo pulled into a gas station, Hawke's phone rang.

"It's Dani."

Hawke answered the phone. There was poor reception. "I can only hear bits and pieces," he said, standing outside the pickup as Bo fueled and Dog relieved himself on the back tire.

"Grandparents property…" crackling sounds and, "Fletcher."

"Are you saying one of the people we think stole the money has grandparents named Fletcher with property around here?" he hoped she could hear him.

The line went dead.

Shit! It was worth a try to go in the gas station and ask about the Fletchers. Just as he stepped into the store, his phone buzzed. A text from Dani.

Caleb's grandparents, Fletcher, have a place near Willow Creek Reservoir. We think that may be where the photos were taken.

Hawke glanced at a topographical map hanging on the wall. He typed back. *We're in the area and will check it out. Thanks.*

Bo walked in and Hawke showed him the text message. Then they walked over to the map on the wall and discovered they had stopped in the area Dani had mentioned.

Hawke walked up to the person behind the counter and asked, "Can you give me directions to the Fletcher place?"

The middle-aged man scanned the length of him and then glanced over his shoulder to Bo. "Why you want to know?"

"We're friends of their grandson, Caleb. He asked us to stop in and say, hi."

The man narrowed his eyes. "The Fletchers are gone on a trip and they don't like anyone messing around up there when they're gone."

"Caleb didn't say anything about that. Thanks." Hawke walked over to the drink section and grabbed a bottle of water and iced tea.

Bo put his purchases on the counter and asked, "Is there an airstrip around here?"

"You don't look like a pilot to me," the man said, ringing up the items Bo had set on the counter.

"I have a friend who wanted to join us and is going to fly his plane in."

The man looked from Bo to Hawke and back to Bo. "You two seem to have a lot of friends for bein' off the reservation. Eight-sixty-nine." The man held his hand out.

Hawke put the drinks down on the counter a little harder than necessary. "I've been off the reservation nearly forty years keeping your ass safe." He pulled his badge out from under his shirt. He nodded toward Bo. "Him more so than me since he's retired Montana State Police."

The man's face reddened. He didn't say another word as he took Hawke's money and counted out the change.

Bo quietly asked, "Is there an airstrip around here?"

"Yeah, five miles north of here. It's just a small strip with a few hangars."

"Private?" Hawke asked.

The man nodded. "Someone from out of state."

"Draw a map for how to get to the Fletchers and the airstrip, please." Hawke said, opening his tea and drinking while the man hunted for a piece of paper.

Bo nudged him and grinned.

The man came back with a pen and paper. He drew a dot. "This is where we are." Then he drew a line. "This is the road out there." He pointed to the road in front of the gas station. "Go three miles, turn west, then about ten miles, and you'll see an archway made of river rock and logs. That's the Fletchers." He moved his pencil to the spot he detoured off the highway. "Back on the highway, go another two miles, and turn to the west. About a mile in from the highway there's a meadow that has been made into an airstrip."

Hawke picked up the paper. "Thanks."

At the pickup, Hawke poured the water into a bowl for Dog and handed him a piece of jerky. "I say we go see if the Pannell Learjet is at the airstrip before we go check out the Fletcher place. That way we'll know if Mathers is there as well."

"Makes sense to me." Bo slid in behind the steering

wheel, and Hawke slid in picking up the empty water dish.

Hawke held his phone in his hand wondering if he should let Pierce know what they'd found out. He decided to wait until they knew if the Pannell plane was at the airstrip.

Bypassing the road to the Fletcher place, Hawke stared up the gravel path that disappeared into the trees. Who was down that road? Had Caleb made it to his grandparents' home? Would Adele and Mathers kill him because he lost their money and could blackmail them about their scheme?

Bo turned to the left and a mile down the road was an asphalt runway and three hangars. He parked the vehicle and they got out followed by Dog.

"Let's check the hangars and see what we find," Hawke said.

Bo nodded and they walked up to the first one. The door was locked and there weren't any windows.

"You can wander off or look the other way," Bo said, pulling out a lock-picking kit.

"It's not my jurisdiction," Hawke said, watching his friend pick the lock.

Bo opened the door and they stepped into darkness beyond the light shining from the open door.

Hawke felt along the wall and found a light switch. Bo closed the door.

A small prop plane stood in the middle of the hangar. They left the building making sure the door was locked behind them. At the next hangar, Bo picked the lock and they stepped inside. It smelled of fuel and grease. A flick of the light revealed tools, barrels of fuel, and no plane.

They moved on to the last hangar. Hawke wanted to find the Learjet but that would mean there would be another person to consider when they checked out the Fletcher place.

Bo unlocked the door and swung it open. Hawke stepped through and flicked on the light. Sitting in the middle of the hangar was the Learjet. It even had the number the mechanic at the Missoula airport rattled off to the air traffic controller.

"Mathers is here. Most likely at the Fletcher place." Hawke walked up to the aircraft and opened the door. Since they were here it wouldn't be a bad idea to check it out and see if Mathers left anything behind that might give them a clue as to what they planned to do.

Hawke climbed into the plane and began looking in every nook and crevice for something that might have been left behind. The plane was clean. Almost as if it had been thoroughly cleaned for a reason.

Chapter Thirty-two

Hawke, Bo, and Dog were hunkered down outside the Fletcher house. There were lights on and there appeared to be two people moving around inside. Hawke was anxious to know which two.

"We need to figure out a way to get in there or at least see in there," Hawke whispered.

Bo nodded. "I could go to the back and make some noise. While they are focused on that, you could pop up and peek. Or even get inside."

While it was risky, they couldn't call law enforcement in until they knew who was in there and what was going on. "I'll try to slip in and call you with my phone and put it somewhere. At least then we can hear what they are saying."

"As long as they stay in that room," Bo said skeptically.

"Yeah, it's a chance, but it's all we have at the moment other than one of us getting caught by them."

"That's not a good idea considering how many people have been killed so far." Bo pointed to the front door. "Just get your phone in there and get out." He crept along the front of the house and disappeared down the side.

Five minutes later there was the sound of garbage cans crashing.

Someone in the front room said something and footsteps pounded toward the back. Hawke popped up and found the room empty. He tried the front door. It was locked. Then he pried the screen loose at the bottom of the window and pressed his hands against the glass to shove the window up. To his surprise, it moved. They might have made sure the doors were locked but they hadn't checked the windows. He dialed Bo and dropped the burner phone down onto the floor in front of the window. Then he closed the window and eased away from the house, meeting Bo back at the pickup.

"Did you get to see who is in there?" Hawke asked.

"I didn't see the woman but I heard her. I couldn't tell you if it was Ms. Barnes or not. But the man wasn't Mathers."

Hawke studied his friend. "Was he average height, slight build, and red hair?" If that was DeLan and Ms. Barnes arguing, where was Mathers? He had flown the plane out of Missoula.

"I couldn't tell the hair color but he fit the rest of the description."

"Hear anything on your phone?" Hawke asked.

Bo pushed on the screen with his finger and DeLan's voice, though distant, said, "It must have been a bear. You're too jumpy. No one knows we're here."

"How can you be sure? It's as if they know

everything we're doing before we do it." It was a female voice, but Hawke had to agree with Bo, it didn't sound like Ms. Barnes.

"We'll lay low here for a week or two and then we'll head to Mexico and become husband and wife."

"They aren't going to the South Pacific," Hawke said. "And the voice doesn't sound like Ms. Barnes. It is DeLan, the man who abducted Marion and lost the gold."

"Why hasn't Drew called us back?" the woman said in a whiny tone.

"That's got me worried. I'm sure he wouldn't go to the police, but, after the mess this has all become, he might have."

"If he doesn't pay for Perry's release, what will we do?" the woman asked.

"They have Mathers." Hawke was confused. "And it sounds like they're holding him for ransom from Pannell. Why would he care about an attorney enough to pay ransom to the people who stole and lost his money?"

"Then we'll take what we do have and get out of here."

Hawke pulled out his phone and texted Pierce. *Do you still have Pannell in custody?* The couple in the house didn't know that Pannell had been arrested for threatening Ms. Barnes' parents. If he could get Pannell to get the message and respond, they might have a chance of keeping the two here long enough for Pierce to get here and arrest them.

Yes. The interview isn't going anywhere.

Give him his phone. We've found DeLan and a woman. They are talking about ransom money from Pannell for Mathers. If he starts up a dialog with them, you will have time to get here and arrest them before they take off.

Hawke's phone buzzed.

When he answered Pierce asked, "What are you talking about?"

Hawke told him about finding out the Fletchers were DeLan's grandparents, finding the house, and how they were overhearing the conversation going on inside. And about finding the plane in the hangar only three miles from the house.

"Okay, I'll hand him the phone and tell him with his cooperation on this we'll talk lesser charges. I'll also assemble a team to head your direction ASAP."

"We'll be outside waiting." Hawke hung up. "What else have they said in the house?"

"Not much food. He's sending the woman to the nearest town because no one will recognize her."

Hawke perked up. "Then we'll get a chance to see who she is."

They had the pickup parked in the trees to the side of the road before the archway leading up to the house. Hawke wanted to get closer to get a good look at the woman.

"I'm going to go back up toward the house and try to get a look at her when she comes out of the house." Hawke told Dog to stay and jogged back up the road as the lights on the garage next to the house came on.

He headed to the nearest tree and hid behind it as a Range Rover slowly pulled out of the garage. The driver stopped long enough to make sure the garage door closed and then they proceeded in Hawke's direction. He had his phone out typing in the Texas license plate.

As the vehicle passed, he couldn't see in. The windows were tinted.

He texted the license plate to Pierce.

His finger still lingered over the send button when Pierce replied.

That's one of Pannell's personal vehicles.

Hawke stared at the tail lights going through the archway. If Pannell was in custody, that left his wife to be driving around in their personal vehicle.

He jogged back to Bo. "I think I know who the woman is."

"You saw her? Those windows were tinted."

"I wrote down the license plate and sent it to Pierce. He said it's one of Pannell's personal vehicles." He raised both eyebrows.

Bo's brows nearly touched before his eyes widened. "You mean Pannell's old lady has been working with the accountant to steal from her husband's business?"

"It seems so." Hawke leaned against the pickup. "Anything else from the phone?"

A grin spread across his friend's wide face. "He told the woman to go to the place where we got directions."

Hawke returned the grin. "Let's go detain the woman. It will make the Feds job easier."

Bo drove the truck down the gravel road and out to the highway. Hawke called Pierce updating him on what they knew and their plan to detain the woman.

"Thanks. It will be easier if he only has one hostage," Pierce said.

"And detaining a woman is less likely to get us killed," Hawke replied, ending the call.

Marion paced the floor. It had been hours since they'd heard anything from Gabriel or the FBI agent.

"You need to sit down and eat something," Dani

said, putting a big plate of nachos on the kitchen table.

"Why haven't we heard anything?" Marion asked, plopping onto the seat. She caught herself. It had been years since she'd acted this way. Straightening her back, Marion chided herself. She was forty-five for heaven's sake, the least she could do was act like it.

"They are either in an area where there isn't any service or they are busy. Your brother will contact us when he has some news." Dani plucked a tortilla chip topped with ground beef, salsa, sour cream, and dripping with cheese, off the pile and popped it into her mouth.

Marion picked up a chip and bit off a corner. How did the woman calmly go about her day knowing the man she loved was in danger? Deciding to ask rather than wonder she said, "How can you sit so calmly knowing Gabriel could be in danger?"

Dani stared at her for a moment then said, "I was in the Air Force. I flew into some highly volatile places. But I knew I could fly in and fly out because I'd been well-trained. The same goes for your brother. He's been well trained and he has three decades of on-the-job training. I know he is equipped for any situation he comes up against. And because of that, I know to sit tight and wait for his call. It will come when he has taken care of things. If I were calling him all the time, he wouldn't stay focused on keeping alive."

The woman believed every word she'd said. Marion saw it in her bright eyes and the slight smile on her lips.

Marion scooped the toppings onto a chip and ate it. After licking her fingers, she said, "Did Gabriel say if I could call Mom?"

"He said it would be best if you didn't until everything is settled." Dani's eyes softened. "I know you are anxious to talk to her. She is a good listener. That's why she is so well liked by the young people she babysits for."

It felt awkward to have a woman she'd just met tell her about her own mother. A woman she should know everything about but didn't because she had put her career first. A career that had ended up killing her fiancé and branding her a murderer.

Hawke walked into the convenience store. He nodded to the man behind the counter helping a woman who clearly had to be Mrs. Pannell. She had on high topped boots that fit her legs like her skin. So did the pants, what he could see below the thigh-length jacket she had on. This view reminded him of someone else he'd seen lately.

Hawke went to the drink coolers and grabbed a bottle of water for Dog and a soda for himself.

Bo walked through the door as the woman turned from the counter. The realization hit. This was the woman DeLan had been in a deep discussion with at the Island Resort. She had been at the resort during Adrian's murder and possibly the killer's. Bo held the door for Mrs. Pannell and headed to get himself a drink.

Placing his items on the counter, Hawke nodded to the outside. "Do you know who she is?"

The man studied him. "What do you want to know for?"

"She and a man are staying at the Fletcher place. We followed her down here hoping to learn something." Hawke paid for his drinks.

"Never seen her before," the clerk said.

Hawke spotted the woman studying the tire Bo had

let the air out of. "She's going to be coming back in here to get help. When we offer to help her, you're going to vouch for us without letting her know we are law enforcement." He peered into the man's eyes.

He frowned.

"There's a man's life at stake if you give us away," Bo added.

The man appeared puzzled, but he nodded. Hawke stood halfway between the counter and the door as Bo paid and Mrs. Pannell huffed back into the store.

"Where can I find a tire store?" she asked.

"About an hour to the north and east. Two hours to the south and west," the man said, flitting a glance at Hawke.

"What's the problem?" Hawke asked, staying where he was.

She spun on him, her eyes narrowing.

He wondered if she'd seen him investigating Adrian's death.

"These two could help you. They're pretty handy with tools," the clerk said.

"I don't need tools, I need a new tire," the woman said, haughtily, as if the clerk hadn't a brain in his head.

"Do you have a spare?" Bo asked.

"Spare? As in change? No! I don't give handouts to worthless people like you." She tipped her chin up and stared down her nose at Bo.

Hawke laughed. He couldn't help himself. She was going to be in for a shock if she and DeLan did get out of here. He'd have her grubbing in the mountains and going for a week without a shower. Her long, manicured talons would soon be short and ragged.

She swung around, glaring at him. "What's so

funny?"

Hawke stifled the laughter. "Nothing. We weren't asking for change. Bo wanted to know if you had a spare tire. We could change out the flat one with a spare."

"I don't know. My husband makes sure my vehicle is in proper running order." Her gaze slid from his face down his body and back up. "You look like a manual laborer. Do you know where the spare tire would be?"

Bo held up his phone. "I just looked it up."

She spun to the clerk. "Are these two people you would trust to change a tire for your wife?"

"I don't got a wife," the clerk said.

"I can believe that. Well, then. Can you vouch they won't take me out somewhere and kill me?"

The man nodded.

"I need a firm yes or no."

Hawke was puzzled. This woman hadn't been so forceful when they were listening to her conversation with DeLan.

"They will not take you out and kill you," the clerk said.

"Fine. Come take care of my tire." She led them outside.

Bo showed Hawke the video of where to find the spare.

"We need you to open the back," Hawke said.

She held out her hand. "Show me the video. I'm not falling for you two throwing me in the back of my car and driving off with me."

Bo handed her the phone with the video he'd found.

The woman sniffed, handed the phone back, and unlocked the back door of the vehicle. There were half a dozen suitcases that needed to be unloaded before they could get to the hatch in the floor to pull out the tire.

The woman was on her phone, texting.

Hawke figured it was DeLan she was letting know she had a flat tire.

As he and Bo slipped the easy lift-out strap onto the tailgate of the vehicle, his phone buzzed. A quick glance showed a text from Pierce. *They found Mathers. DeLan wasn't there.*

"Shit!" he said.

"Is there something wrong with the spare?" Mrs. Pannell asked.

"No. It's fine," Bo said, cranking the jack and raising the vehicle.

Hawke rolled the tire over to where Bo was taking the lug nuts loose. He showed Bo the text. They both turned their heads studying the woman now absorbed in her phone.

"We have to find a way to stay with her until someone picks her up," Hawke whispered.

"Are you sure you know what you're doing?" the woman demanded from about twenty feet away.

"Yes." Hawke pulled the flat tire off while Bo used his knife to put a slit on the inside of the spare tire.

They put the spare on, tightened the lug nuts, and let it down on the ground.

"You're all set," Hawke said, putting the flat tire back in the vehicle and placing the suitcases in just as they'd been.

The woman didn't say thank you before speeding off toward the Fletcher place. Hawke and Bo climbed into the pickup and followed as Hawke texted Pierce that they were following Mrs. Pannell up the road and she would have another flat soon. Better that the Feds pick her up than he and Bo come to her aid again. They were headed to the Fletcher place to see if they could pick up a trail for DeLan.

When Mrs. Pannell didn't turn at the Fletcher drive, Hawke knew where she was headed. "I bet she knows how to fly that plane."

Chapter Thirty-three

A mile before the road to the airstrip, Mrs. Pannell stopped her Range Rover. Bo had to make a quick dive onto a barely visible road to keep her from seeing they were following her.

Hawke and Dog leaped out of the pickup. "We'll head for the airstrip and see if she was meeting DeLan there. If DeLan is at the airstrip, I'll let Pierce know."

He headed through the trees directly toward the hangar nearly two miles away. Dog raced along ahead of him as if he knew where they were going. Hawke whistled, calling the animal back when he felt like they should be getting close. He stopped to catch his breath since he'd jogged most of the way, trying to keep Dog in his sight.

"Let's do a slow approach. We don't know if he's alone or has a weapon." Hawke patted Dog on the head.

Keeping his ears on alert for any sounds out of the ordinary and peering beyond the trees, bushes, and boulders in the immediate area, Hawke advanced as if he were sneaking up on an enemy.

The sound of the hangar door rolling up announced they were close. Seconds later he stepped through brush and found himself on the backside of the building housing the aircraft. He tapped Dog on the head and pointed to the opposite side of the building. The animal trotted to the end and glanced back.

Hawke motioned for him to go as he started walking along the opposite side of the building. At the front, Hawke peered across to see Dog waiting for a command. Hawke put up a hand to stay. Then he eased to the side of the open door and slowly looked inside.

DeLan had his back to the opening as he pulled on the plane dolly. It was apparent whoever owned this strip hadn't purchased the newer electric version. If there was a better time to catch the man off guard, he wouldn't have it.

Hawke quietly walked up behind the man and put a hand on the middle of Delan's back.

The man turned around swinging. Hawke wished he'd pulled out his weapon and pressed that to the man's back as he ducked a right cross and countered with a punch to his attacker's stomach.

DeLan folded but righted himself almost instantly. Recognition and anger flared in his eyes.

"You took my money!" he yelled and rushed Hawke, knocking him to the hard concrete.

Wind whooshed out of his lungs as his back and head cracked against the floor. Stars twinkled before his eyes.

The man straddled Hawke, landing a blow to his already muddled head.

A fierce growl sounded before DeLan cried out and fell to Hawke's right side.

"Stop! Stop!" yelled DeLan.

The growling and screaming didn't help the ache that started at the back of Hawke's head and lanced down his neck.

"What is going on in here!" shrieked a female voice.

Hawke opened one eye to watch Mrs. Pannell approach the dog and man beside him. She had a revolver in her hand.

He couldn't let her shoot his best friend. Ignoring the pain, he shouted, "Dog! Run!"

The animal shot out of the building, leaving Hawke to look up into the barrel of the weapon.

"You! Who the hell are you?" the woman shrieked.

Hawke wondered if she'd listen if he asked her to speak quieter. He doubted it.

DeLan sat up, hugging a bloody arm to his stomach. "That dog nearly chewed my arm off."

"Who is this man?" Mrs. Pannell demanded.

"He's Marion Shumack's brother. The one I told you about who took our money." DeLan shoved to his feet. "What did you tell me you wanted to do to the man who stole our money?" The man goaded the woman.

Hawke had a feeling she'd threatened to kill him and now she had him in a position to do that.

"This is the out-of-state trooper who found his sister and followed you all over the mountains?" Her eyes narrowed.

Hawke was having trouble keeping his eyes open to watch them. A bout of nausea hit. He rolled to his side to throw up. The boom of a gun echoed through the building before the woman screamed.

Hawke swiped at his mouth and watched a blurry image of Dog, standing on the woman's back, her face inches from the pool of vomit.

DeLan kicked at Dog and caught the woman in the stomach as she rolled. The characters of the play in front of him were all blurry, wobbly, and making so much noise he felt like he was going to hurl again.

Another shot rang the metal siding.

"Dog! Off!" Bo's voice broke through the chaos.

A warm soft tongue licked Hawke's face as he heard sirens. Then everything went dark.

"I see. Yes. I can have us there in two hours. Thank you."

Marion studied her brother's partner. "Who was that? What did they say?"

"It was Bo. He said Hawke is at the Missoula hospital. He has a concussion. We need to get over there so you can give your official statement to the police and FBI and can drive Hawke back here." The woman was tidying up the kitchen as she talked.

"I'm ready." Marion stood up, carrying her empty coffee cup to the sink.

"Pack clothes for a couple of days." Dani swiped a finger across her phone. "And meet me in the Jeep." She started walking toward the front door.

Marion jogged down the hallway to the room where she'd been staying. She tossed enough clothes in the small suitcase she'd purchased at a thrift store and hurried to the front of the house. Dani already had the vehicle running.

"Please fuel up my plane right away. I'll be there in twenty minutes. Also file a flight plan for me to

Missoula, Montana." She listened. "Yeah, it has been a frequent place lately and no, I'm not picking up clients that far away." She ended the call and tossed the phone on the seat. "Asshole."

Marion stared at the woman as she backed out and headed to the highway. When they brought Gabriel home and she was settled with Mom, it would be fun to get to know Dani better. She had many different sides to her. Right now, Marion just kept her mouth shut and watched the scenery flash by. But when they were up in the air headed to Missoula she'd see if Dani knew any more about what had happened than Gabriel was in the hospital and she needed to give a statement. They must have caught the people responsible for Adrian's death. Tears burned her eyes, but she wasn't going to let them fall. Not yet. Not until this was all over and she could properly mourn.

<><><><><><>

Hawke woke up with a splitting headache and stared at the white ceiling. Reaching into his memory, he struggled to remember how he came to be in this room. Easing his head sideways, his gaze took in the right side of the room. He was in a hospital.

Hell, he didn't remember getting shot. The only thing that hurt was his head and neck. Raising a hand, he discovered a neck brace. Shit! He wiggled his toes and rotated his feet back and forth, then raised both hands in front of his face. Relief replaced the fear that had taken hold in a split second. He'd thought he was paralyzed. Nope, just this shitty aching in his head.

Flashes of running through the forest with Dog. He whistled and wished he hadn't when his head started a new beat to offset the one that had been softly playing.

That was stupid. They wouldn't let Dog in the hospital.

The door opened and Bo's smiling face appeared and the sound of a lightweight chain. Hawke dropped his hand over the edge of the bed and a wet, warm tongue licked it. His lips curved into a smile. And that's when what happened flooded into his brain.

"You saved my life. Both of you," he said, staring into Bo's round smiling face.

"Yeah, you're going to owe both of us a big juicy steak when you're out of here." Bo put a hand on his arm. "When I heard that gun go off, I ran out of the trees and there you were lying on the floor. Dog landed in the middle of the woman's back and sent her face first into your vomit." He laughed. "That was pretty funny but I didn't have time to laugh. That guy was holding his arm and trying to get to the gun she'd dropped."

Dog put his front paws on the bed and stared at Hawke.

"You did real good, boy." Hawke swallowed the lump of emotion in his throat and stroked the wiry hair on Dog's head. He peered up at Bo. "Both of you. I couldn't move from the smack I took falling backward on the concrete. I should have gone in with my gun in my hand, but I was trying to be a good out-of-state cop and not use a weapon."

Bo laughed. "Since when did you care about being good?"

"Since I didn't want anything to get those two off with any technicalities. Please tell me they are in custody and they are singing."

"They are in custody. From what Pierce told me they are waiting to get Marion's statement so they have some evidence about Adrian's murder to go at them with to try and get one to turn on the other."

Hawke tried to sit up and pain shot through his head and neck. "I need to call Dani."

"I already did. She and Marion landed about two hours ago. Dani insisted if you were still out she should go with Marion to the Feds to give her statement. That would be what you would want." Bo raised one eyebrow.

Hawke smiled. "Dani is correct. Marion has never been in trouble a day in her life. She needs someone tough with her when the Feds question her."

Chapter Thirty-four

Marion sat in a room with Special Agent Pierce and a woman agent. Dani had insisted, since Hawke couldn't be there, she would be sitting in. Pierce had frowned but allowed her to enter the room. She sat behind Marion.

"Ms. Shumack tell us exactly what happened the day Adrian Ulrick died and how you were kidnapped by Caleb DeLan," Special Agent Pierce said.

Marion swallowed, drew in a deep breath, and then told the events of the day exactly as she'd told Hawke and this agent the first time he'd questioned her.

The Special Agent's gray eyes were unnerving at first. But as she talked and became agitated having to retell how she'd run away leaving poor Adrian, she felt he empathized with her. This helped her to continue. Until she stopped after having called Hawke.

"I'm sorry you were there to witness the crime against your fiancé," Special Agent Pierce said. Before today, she would have thought he was patronizing. But she'd felt as if he really did care that she'd had to go through all of this.

"Thank you. I would give anything to have Adrian back and not have lived through what I did. The only good is it is taking me home and I realized I am not cut out for the business world."

His eyes lit up. "Going home?"

She nodded. "Back to Nixyáawii. Home."

<<>><<>><<>>

Hawke sat in the passenger seat of his pickup. Dog sat beside him while Marion drove. The doctor let him leave the hospital but he had to not drive for several more days. He was glad Dani had brought Marion back to give her statement and drive him home. He was ready to leave Montana.

"How did the questioning go?" he asked. Dani had said she'd struggled but Special Agent Pierce had been good about letting her deal with her feelings and tell the story. He had seen a bit of that side of the special agent but had been surprised all the same. He came across as a pretty by-the-book type of Fed.

"It went okay. Each time it gets a little easier." Marion didn't take her gaze off the road.

"Dani said Pierce was helpful."

She glanced over at him. "He was nice. I hadn't expected that from my memories of the FBI who showed up at Umatilla."

"That animosity is slowly changing. But it will take more Feds like Pierce to make it happen."

"And Indigenous people like you?" she glanced over at him.

He shrugged.

"Did they ever get Caleb and Mrs. Pannell to

286

confess?" Marion asked.

"I don't know. No one has said anything to me. I asked Bo to see if he could find out. I would think they have enough against the two to put them away for a long time." He rubbed his forehead. "What I don't get is why Pannell would pay ransom for Mathers, his attorney?"

"He's so alpha you wouldn't know it, but Drew and Perry are lovers. I always thought Stella didn't care as long as she had all the money she wanted." Marion shrugged.

Hawke stared at his sister. "You knew this all the time and didn't tell me?"

"I didn't think it had anything to do with Adrian's death."

"How many other people in the company know about this?" Hawke was still wrapping his mind around the take-charge man he'd dealt with having a fake marriage and letting that shrieking woman spend all his money. Pannell had enough money and clout he could have come out about his love for another man and no one would have cared.

"All the people who have been around as long as I have."

"Adele Barnes?" It clicked. "I wonder if that is really what she was blackmailing him about?" Hawke's head was hurting worse. "But why pay? Why not just come out and get rid of that nasty wife?"

"Everyone has their reasons for doing what they do. We don't know what Drew's might be." Marion glanced over. "Go to sleep. I'm sure I can find my way to Wallowa County."

<◇><◇><◇>

Hawke woke to the buzzing of his phone in his shirt

pocket. They were coming down Minam Grade and he was going to lose whomever the caller was anyway, so he closed his eyes and slowly allowed his body to wake. When he felt fully awake, he opened his eyes again and glanced over at his sister. He smiled. It had been a long time coming, but she was finally back where she belonged.

"When Dani and I landed in Alder a few days ago, I couldn't take my eyes off the beauty of this land," Marion said. "I can see why our ancestors loved it so."

"I agree. That's why I am still working here and haven't taken any promotions." He watched the Wallowa River rage by as the snow melt rushed from the mountains and on to the Grand Ronde, to eventually end up in the Columbia River and Pacific Ocean. The path that carried the salmon and other fish their people used to sustain them.

"As a grown-up, I can understand. As a child, I didn't want to be an Indian. I didn't want to stay on the reservation. But now, having been gone and feeling my heart and soul healing each time I set foot back in Oregon... I want to stay and make it so the children who wish to rush from the reservation will come back. To help their elders and to teach the young."

"That's good to hear." Hawke watched as she slowed at the Eagle city limits. Her gaze scanned the town.

"I don't remember seeing this much signage before for a Nez Perce interpretive center. And here, what is Tamkaliks?"

"There is an arbor and land owned by the Nez Perce. Tamkaliks is the annual powwow held the week before Chief Joseph Days. Dani and I didn't make it last year but we plan on going this year with Mom. You should come with us."

Marion nodded. A sad smile barely tipped her lips. "I promised Adrian I would dance again. I will dance in his memory."

Hawke put a hand on her shoulder. "That would be a wonderful tribute." Again, he cursed the people who took Adrian from his sister's life. The man sounded as if he would have brought her back to her roots and to them without the tragedy.

He directed Marion to the turnoff to his house. Sage and Tuck's pickup was there, along with Herb and Darlene's car.

"Why are there so many people here?" Marion asked.

He explained to whom the vehicles belonged. "I'm sure they just want to all make sure I'm alive." He slowly exited the passenger side. Dog came bounding out the door and down the steps. Dani had flown him home with her.

"Hey, boy. I still owe you a steak." He'd bought Bo a steak dinner the night before. He would forever be grateful to his Montana friend.

His phone buzzed again. He answered as Marion grabbed their bags out of the backseat of the pickup.

"Hawke," he answered.

"It's about time you answered. Tell me you didn't drive yourself home," Pierce said, in his usual stick-up-his-ass tone.

"Marion drove me home. Which is where I just arrived and would like to go in and see my family and friends." Hawke didn't want Marion to enter the house without him. They had a surprise for her.

"I'll quickly tell you that DeLan and Mrs. Pannell met at a company event, started dating, and she was the one that told him about her husband skimming money. Together they moved the money he skimmed into an account they could access. Adrian made the mistake of asking DeLan if he'd seen any discrepancies in an account he handled. That's when they decided to bring in Longo. Mrs. Pannell had heard her husband talking about him to Mathers. Then she was the one who killed Longo when she was meeting him on the premise of asking him to find Marion. It happens that Louise overheard DeLan talking to Mrs. Pannell at the resort. When she questioned him, he killed her. So they are both murderers and will both be going to prison. And Adele Barnes discovered what they were doing and blackmailed them out of a hundred grand. That's what she used to disappear. She wasn't getting married to anyone in Vanuatu."

"Good to hear Mrs. Pannell and DeLan are going to pay. Sounds like Adele hit the jackpot. Bye." Hawke ended the conversation and hurried up the walk to the house. Marion was on the porch waiting for him.

"You didn't have to run," she scolded him.

"I wanted to catch up. And that was Pierce. They are both going down for Adrian's hired murder. Mrs. Pannell for Longo's and DeLan for Louise. Oh, and Adele was blackmailing them. That's where the missing one hundred thousand went."

Marion bit her lip as her eyes glistened with tears. "I wish Adrian were here and poor Louise."

"They were both trying to do what was right. They are heroes." Hawke reached around her and opened the door. "Someone wants to see you." He stepped back as she studied him.

"Go on." He motioned for her to walk through the door.

The door swung open and all the people he held dear were standing in the living room, smiling. They parted and his mom stood in the middle of the room.

Marion dropped the bags and ran into their mom's arms.

Hawke kicked the bags in ahead of him until Kitree picked them up.

"You don't look very good but that's a big smile on your face," she said.

He put an arm around the child's shoulders and hugged her. "My head hurts like a son-of-a-gun but my heart is overflowing."

She laughed. "You can't hurt too bad if your heart is full."

He glanced down at the now twelve-year-old. "You have always been too smart."

Dani walked over. "Kitree, why don't you put those bags in the laundry room? Hawke needs to give his mother and sister a hug."

Hawke thanked Dani with a kiss on the top of her head and walked over to wrap his arms around the two women he'd protected as a child and would go on protecting until he was no longer upon this earth. Mama Bear and Small Bear were safe now.

Thank you for reading *Bear Stalker*. I hope you enjoyed Hawke's latest story. Please leave a review where you purchased the book and at Goodreads and/or Bookbub. Reviews are how an author's book gets seen.
Other books in the series:

Murder of Ravens - Book 1
Print ISBN 978-1-947983-82-3

Mouse Trail Ends - Book 2
Print ISBN 978-1-947983-96-0

Rattlesnake Brother - Book 3
Print ISBN 978-1-950387-06-9

Chattering Blue Jay - Book 4
Print ISBN 978-1-950387-64-9

Fox Goes Hunting - Book 5
Print ISBN 978-1-952447-07-5

Turkey's Fiery Demise - Book 6
Print ISBN 978-1-952447-48-8

Stolen Butterfly - Book 7
Print ISBN 978-1-952447-77-8

Churlish Badger - Book 8
Print ISBN 978-1-952447-96-9

Owl's Silent Strike - Book 9
Print ISBN 978-1-957638-19-5

While you're waiting for the next Hawke book, check out my Shandra Higheagle Mystery series or my Spotted Pony Casino Mystery series. Here is the QR code to my website:

About the Author

Paty Jager grew up in Wallowa County and has always been amazed by its beauty, history, and ruralness. After doing a ride-along with a Fish and Wildlife State Trooper in Wallowa County, she knew this was where she had to set the Gabriel Hawke series.

Paty is an award-winning author of 54 novels of murder mystery and western romance. All her work has Western or Native American elements in them along with hints of humor and engaging characters. She and her husband raise alfalfa hay in rural eastern Oregon. Riding horses and battling rattlesnakes, she not only writes the western lifestyle, she lives it.

You can find me at these places:
Website: http://www.patyjager.net
Blog: https://writingintothesunset.net/
FB Page: https://www.facebook.com/PatyJagerAuthor/
Pinterest: https://www.pinterest.com/patyjag/
Twitter: https://twitter.com/patyjag
Goodreads:
http://www.goodreads.com/author/show/1005334.Paty_Jager
Newsletter: Mystery: https://bit.ly/2IhmWcm
Bookbub: https://www.bookbub.com/authors/paty-jager

Windtree
Press

Thank you for purchasing this Windtree Press publication. For other books of the heart, please visit our website at www.windtreepress.com.

For questions or more information contact us at info@windtreepress.com.

Windtree Press
www.windtreepress.com
Hillsboro, OR

CPSIA information can be obtained
at www.ICGtesting.com
Printed in the USA
LVHW100532220223
740093LV00002B/17